I0555734

Escape From Bliss

Jacob Lucas Luciano

Rebel ePublishers
Detroit New York London

Rebel ePublishers
Detroit, Michigan 48223

Escape from Bliss
© 2017 by Jacob Lucas Luciano

ISBN-13: 978-1-944077-21-1
ISBN-10: 1-944077-21-9

Book and cover design by *Caryatid Design*

For she,
wherever she be,
on land or at sea,
for she's dear to me.

Sixth grade: the first time I saw him, I was new at the school. That was, Lord, sixty years ago. A little girl then, and not particularly tall, but the rest of me looked the part of the girl-next-door nobody wanted to talk to. Wearing a red dress that first day, sewn up along the right shoulder where my older sister's growing body had ripped its way out of the fabric, lugging a school bag too large for me, too heavy for a girl, or such was the thinking in those days.

I felt like an ugly mushroom growing in a beautiful garden. New kids always feel some emotion like that, but, especially shy, I sat in the front row away from the other children so they could only see the back of my head, and I hoped they wouldn't see when I blushed crimson when the teacher introduced me. "We have a new student today," he said, towering over us; not unkind, but neither warm. "Her name is Elizabeth."

I stood up and looked out at the faces looking back at me, my face hot, and imagined it the same color as my old dress, the one I would wear every day for the next few weeks, the only decent clothing I owned. My mother made me don it that day, and I wanted to curse her, but couldn't bring myself to do that.

"Hello," I said. My voice sounded like the distant scrape of a fork against a plate. Nobody responded for a moment, and that was the worst thing – the feeling of reaching out from turbulent waters, hoping someone on dry land would grasp my hand and pull me to safety. And someone did.

He sat in the middle of the class and wore a dopey grin. On first impression, he was the kind of boy my mother softly scolded about. One who paid little attention during lessons, whose handwriting looked as though he had done his homework with his toes rather than adept fingers. Blue eyes squinted in a friendly way, and one hand reached out. "Hello," he said, his voice warm and confident. I loved him in that instant.

I took his hand.

We spent our childhoods together. He broke my heart when he married another girl, eight years after I took his hand; we never lost our love, but we lost touch. We traveled together; we lived, and our souls died together, a thousand times. The fire always burned. As I write this, he has been committed to a fine place where they put old people like us. These places go by many names: retirement homes, old folks' homes, respite care, purgatory.

This wicker chair is too hard for my aching back as I write all this down because I want you to hear our story.

Our story of love. Because that is what we have: because he is still everything to me. Danny with the dopey grin. I'm getting old, and I fear I may not remember everything, that if I don't do it now, I won't do it tomorrow, and when I don't do it tomorrow, I'll never do it. I've learned how quickly a person's life slips through his or her fingers. You need to make a tight fist, or it will disappear.

The purgatory he lives in is called Bliss. I shall tell as much of this story as my old heart can take. And then I shall go and break him out of there.

One

That first day, we walked home together from school. The few automobiles on the road in those days kicked up clouds of dust as they passed. Danny walked between me and the road, and he did it in an unconscious way, a gentleman already. Pleased just to have someone to walk with, even though I was an intensely private person, I was also happy to answer his questions.

"So, where did you come from?"

I glanced over at him. A quick internal debate ensued – do I tell this strange boy anything about myself? On the one hand, I heard my mother and saw her gentle but disapproving scowl. On the other hand, Danny's face was right in front of mine, and though not looking at me, he was smiling. "Fort Wayne, Indiana," I said.

"I know where Fort Wayne is. Why did you come here?"

"My father took a job."

"Here?"

"Of course." I giggled. "That's why we came here."

Here was a small town called Hamilton in Michigan, in mid-September. The air was hot but not muggy. An easy breeze between my calves as we walked made my dress flutter ever so slightly. I lived mostly alone with my parents. Rosalinda, my sister, was in high school and, in those days, practically a non-presence in my life. She was gone most of the time, vanished to some unknown, disgruntled teenager place, breezing through our house once in a while, eating herself back to good health before disappearing again.

"Well," he said, "there isn't much to do around here. We go fishing. Do you know how to fish?"

I smiled. "I know how to fish."

"What's the biggest fish you ever caught?" he said, looking at me from the corner of his eye in a very sly way.

With my hands in front of me about two feet apart, I lied, "About this big." I had never caught a fish. The fishing hooks frightened me, and I would never touch a worm. "What's the biggest fish you ever caught?" My voice took on a mildly competitive tone.

He held his own hands in front of him. About two-feet-three-inches apart. "About like this," he said, smiling at me. "And it had teeth."

"Fish don't have teeth."

"They do so. Ask anybody in class. It tried to bite my finger off."

I laughed, terrified. I wanted him to ask me to go fishing with him and I definitely did not want to go. "Can I come, sometime?" My heart raced, and my stomach burned. Why had I said that?

But already he'd answered. "Why not?" His tone indicated it was highly irregular for a girl to go fishing with the boys, but that he would not mind. "Do you have any worms?"

I pretended to feel in my pockets and said, "Darn, I don't have any."

"It's all right," he said, "we can dig some up."

So I followed Danny to his house, which was near my own, and on our hands and knees we raked through the dirt in his garden with our hands. I anticipated with chagrin how my mother would kill me for the extra laundry. I watched Danny's fingers plow through the dirt, turn it aside, make it crumble. He worked efficiently, tossing clumps here and there as he saw fit, and when he located a worm, he dropped it into a glass jar between us like a man dropping a coin in a street performer's hat. "I can't seem to find any," I said. I had seen a few, just pink ribbons in the earth, and each time I located one, I gasped, but Danny didn't notice. Each time, I pretended not to see and arranged the dirt in such a way that the worm would be buried again. I don't know how many worms got a reprieve because I was afraid to touch them, but I imagined they thought of me as a divine goddess for letting them evade the hook and water.

After about ten minutes, Danny said, "I think that's enough. We should get going."

He had only one fishing pole, which leaned against the wall of his shed, a dusty, dark place, which smelled like a barn. I didn't mind the smell. I thought it was nice. Like old things that had fallen into misuse, but were still important to somebody. The fishing pole was the only item that looked well cared for. He let me carry it while he carried the jar full of worms. Secretly, I hoped he'd drop it along the way and that all the worms would escape. But Danny had sure hands. We didn't speak as we trudged along a narrow path toward the river about a half mile behind our houses. We walked side by side, bumping into each other occasionally.

The river was swift. It rushed over a protruding rock, half-wet, half-dry, near the shore. A small piece of refuse caught my eye as it drifted downstream; it looked like a baseball card. I looked over at Danny and saw that he, too, was watching the card go.

"Do you want to start?"

"I'll let you take the first cast," I said, emphasizing my knowledge of angling vocabulary.

"No problemo." That was the first time I heard him use this expression. I remember the lopsided grin on his face. "That's Spanish," he added. "It means no problem."

I rolled my eyes as dramatically as I could and then I watched him thread one of the worms onto his hook. He arranged a bobber so that it was a foot or so higher than the worm, and then with practiced fluidity, cast the rigging into the river and let it toss about for a few seconds until it found a calm area, where it simply floated.

"No luck yet, huh?"

He snorted. "You never catch a fish on the first cast. You have to try a few times."

I pondered that while he reeled in the worm and then handed me the rod. "Here. You do it."

Well, I tell you, I had never done that in my entire life. My eyes were closed tight when I sent that poor worm hurtling end over end into the river, and they only opened again when I slowly reeled him back toward us. Although I expected nothing, a sudden tugging on the line ran through to my elbows. "I think I got something!" I hollered.

Danny looked incredulous, but he changed his position to stand right behind me. A breathless moment later, he said, "Oh yeah. You got a catfish! Bring him in!"

Not knowing how to bring it in, I pulled on the rod and reeled in furiously. "You're doing it wrong!" Danny shouted from behind me. But he did not intervene. After a moment, he chuckled. "You're doing it all wrong, but you're going to get 'im."

It took the better part of a few minutes to bring the catfish onto the shore. That fish was an ugly sucker, with long tentacles, which Danny referred to as whiskers, prodding and feeling the land around the fish, like alien feelers. I suppose that was what it was like for that poor fish. And it looked old, almost dead; I wondered if that was because of the fight with the fishing line, or if it was just a tired old fish. Part of me believed, even then, that God had put that fish right there, right then, so that I would be able to smile at Danny and say, "And I got him on the first cast, too."

Danny was gentle when he removed the hook and cradled him back into the water. The fish seemed to hover there for a moment, almost as if to thank Danny before it glided away into the depths of the river. Hard for me to watch, it was somehow raw and barbaric, the way the metal tore through flesh and created a hole that would never heal, but at the same time, it was fascinating. "We should be getting home," Danny said.

The sky was turning gray, and a sudden thrill of dread ran down my innards. Dad would be home soon. "Yes. I need to hurry."

He helped me climb the short bank up to the trail, and we rushed home. I tried to pretend I was in no great hurry, but indeed I was. Perhaps this is the time in the story when I mention a few words about my father.

A hard man, my father, he was prone to drinking too much in the evening and then taking it out on my mother and me. We took it, and the neighbors kept quiet. In Fort Worth, at least in those days, that was how things operated. My father was not the only man who laid his hands on his woman. I was too young to understand it and, truth be told, I still don't understand it even today. Back then, I thought that it was normal and that all the men who went to work the next day could smile about it in a secret kind of code that the women were not privy to. Part of me forgives him and even justifies his behavior, difficult as that is for me to say.

So Danny and I arrived home. My house was half a block down, too far to hear or see anything. If I hurried, I hoped I might be able to arrive home before my father came back from work, in which case everything would be perfect. But if my dad arrived first, I knew there would be trouble ahead. Despite my fears, I stopped at Danny's shed and said, "Thanks for taking me. I really enjoyed myself."

"I didn't know what it would be like to take a girl fishing," he admitted, looking sheepish, "but it was pretty good fun. Can you come tomorrow?"

"I don't know," I said, edging away. I wanted to kiss him. The foreign thought made me feel like a wild cat. I felt hot, and he looked so cool. "I will try. But I really need to get home."

"I'll walk you there," he said. He exuded a sense of comfort and level-headedness. He must have sensed my trepidation because neither of us spoke as we approached my house. Lights burned in the kitchen and the living room, and shadows moved across the shades, distorted and monstrous. All seemed silent until I heard an explosive bang as if a baseball bat had whacked a cooking pot. I knew Father had arrived first.

His yelling came next. Muffled by the house and the sweet evening air, I couldn't understand the words, but the tone was unmistakable. Fury. He sounded like a primate, fighting against a much weaker enemy and enjoying it.

"Is everything all right?" Danny stuck his hand out and stopped my progress toward home.

"It's my dad," I said, casting my eyes toward the ground. "He's probably upset about something."

"No kidding," Danny said. I looked up to see him staring at me, utterly concerned. "I'm not letting you go up there."

Persisting, like the echoes of some tenacious ghost that refuses to leave its haunt, my father's screams were punctuated by occasional thumps and weak-sounding whimpers. "He's only going to get angrier," I told him. That was only a half-truth. He would indeed become angrier over the next hour or so, but would probably burn himself out and collapse on his bed into a dreamless world of snores.

"Then I'm going with you," he said. Even now he grinned. It seemed to me that he was always smiling.

"No. That will make things worse. Just ... just wait with me."

"Okay." He nodded once and we crept around to the backyard and sat against a tree.

We sat against that tree and listened to my father rant and throw things and hit my mother. Once, we heard the unmistakable sound of an open-handed slap. But my mother barely made a sound. Danny sat with his right shoulder pressed firmly against my left. I let my head rest against his chest and I had the impression that he smelled my hair. The evening wore into night and the stars came out above our heads, and we looked through the tree branches at them. Too afraid to comment about any of them – look how pretty that one is, for instance – I had the ridiculous idea that I could never communicate to Danny exactly which star I meant. There were simply too many of them.

The yelling died off and, sure enough, an hour later my father's snoring was audible even at the base of our tree. In and out. I realized it was a sound I hated, although Danny pretended not to notice. "I guess he's asleep now," I said.

It was well past the time – hours beyond – when I could walk inside my house and pretend I had simply been held up at school or at the fishing hole. And yet I felt my mother would understand. Sitting at the kitchen table, holding her forehead in her hands, maybe gently crying, she would know that I had simply been afraid to walk through the door. She would understand.

"Okay. I suppose I'll be going home, myself," he said. We stood.

"Thanks for staying with me."

"No problemo."

Then I kissed him. I leaned in and planted my lips on his. I kissed him right on the smile. He kissed me back, and when we were done, I looked at his face. He was still smiling. Then I fled inside.

The next day, my father said nothing about my late arrival the evening before. Likely, he had by then forgotten. My mother never said anything, either, but when I did enter the house, to find her sitting in the living room, listening to the radio playing so quietly I doubted she could hear it even from that distance, we shared a knowing look. I read an apology in her eyes, something like, 'I'm sorry, but we have to put up with him.'

Well, I already knew that. I considered telling her about Danny, something like, 'Mama, I met this really nice boy today. And we hid in the backyard until Dad went to sleep.' But I said nothing. I was not ready to share Danny with the world.

School dragged on the way it does for kids that age, and slowly the girls there accepted me into the fold. I was certain they'd taken me in because Danny had befriended me, and everybody liked Danny. Still, a girl needs girlfriends, just as a boy needs other boys to be his friend. And Jamie was my best friend.

Taller than the rest of us by a head, she was gorgeous in a country kind of way. I guessed her family had a little more money than most others, but she never made a big show out of that. She wore clean clothes, and I felt sure she was their first owner, which for me was an unimaginable luxury. Her teeth were white and straight, her eyes brown, and her skin dark, like an Egyptian's.

She had a problem with jealousy, though, and while most people would never have guessed that about her, she confided in me all the things she was too scared to tell anybody else. She told me about her father stealing chickens from one of the local farmers, for example. Her father's wealth only came at a later age; he had grown up scrappy and mean.

It sounds strange, talking about that today as though it's a big deal, but times were different then when acts such as theft meant indefinite excommunication from the community. She made no secret, at least to me, about her hatred for her father, a drunk, a philanderer, a thief and a sarcastic bastard. They could have been the richest family in town, and he still would have stolen things.

Our disdain for our fathers was the point at which we connected, even if the feelings I had for my father were not exactly hatred. Jamie sensed that inside me before I knew it existed, and so we sat beside each other at lunch, and during lessons, and she came over to my house a few times per week.

My mother loved Jamie. Each time she came to our house, my mother served pie. Jamie ate and savored every morsel, and made sure to compliment my mother's cooking. I didn't realize it then, but my mother was starved of appreciation; to get it from this stranger was nectar.

One Saturday in October, Jamie came to my room with me. I remember that because of a program on the radio every Saturday morning, about local happenings. Not exactly the news, mind you, but rather a kind of down-home rendition of all that had taken place in the community over the past week. Someone had lost his dog. There was a garage sale on Haley Street, all prices negotiable. Sheriff Townsend was looking for whoever smashed the back window of old Farmer Whalen's tractor.

Anyway, as we sat on the floor, out of nowhere, she asked me, "So, do you have a boyfriend?"

Unsure of how to answer, I paused for a moment. There was a boy who was a friend. Whom I had kissed. "Danny is a friend.

"I know he's your friend," Jamie said, with the slightest of sneers. "But is he your boyfriend?"

Jamie was my best friend, and I loved her. While I did not consider her a threat in any way, in the years that followed, I regretted not telling her that yes, he was my boyfriend and he was all mine.

What would I have lost by saying so? I suppose it was not the truth, not exactly – Danny would not have considered us boyfriend and girlfriend, not at that point in our relationship. I was a friend and he was a friend, and we loved each other as children love one another, free and innocent in that moment, before stepping off the precipice and into adolescence. "Ew," I said aloud. "He's just a friend. Why? Do you have a boyfriend?"

"No," Jamie said, sighing, "but I want one."

"Who?"

She looked me straight in the eyes. "Not Danny. I wasn't asking for me."

"Okay."

We sat in silence for a few more minutes. During those minutes, the first fingers of doubt massaged my heart. What would I do if Jamie did try to make Danny her boyfriend? Could I simply sit back and watch it happen and feign happiness for them both? They were both my friends, after all. But I shooed these thoughts away as quickly as they came; they were too adult for me. I was twelve years old, and so were they. And when you are twelve, you feel like you have eternity to set things right.

We spent the rest of that afternoon chatting and playing with toys we were becoming too old for. I tried to show Jamie a doll my mother had made me. Fashioned from cotton and wool, she had sewn it together when I was six. I loved the little thing – its expressionless face, its limp arms – and had named it Girly. Nobody but my mother knew that.

But when I showed it to Jamie, expecting an appreciative look, all she said was, "I don't play with dolls." She didn't even touch it. Nothing else Jamie could have done that day would have hurt me as much, although I was to learn, in the coming years, that Jamie possessed the power to cut me far deeper than that.

*W*e saw each other in places besides school and the fishing hole at the river. On Sundays, there was church, and on Wednesdays, we always met for ice cream at a little shop downtown. By 'us,' I mean Danny and I and then, as October wore on, Jamie, too. Her presence was a joy, at first, but by the time December came and it was cold, with the first thin layer of snow on the ground, I had grown impatient with her.

We went to a special class in the basement of the church while our parents sat up in the pews listening to the sermon.

We were at the age we could still get away with that, although that would change very soon; teenagers were expected to sit with the adults and understand exactly why they would go to hell. It was not enough to stay in a concrete room with small children and talk about the more awe-inspiring stories: Noah's Ark, Daniel and the Lion's Den, Job and his undying faith.

Those mornings were torture, my attention trapped between those Biblical stories and keeping my eye on Danny and Jamie. Stories of lust, of curiosity, and killing. Those stories were the background noise to their growing infatuation. Danny always sat between us in Bible class, and although we never spoke openly about it, both Jamie and I knew that that was the fairest arrangement. By then, I think she knew I pined for him as much or more than she did; perhaps that was why she was so interested in him.

Brotherly betrayal was the theme that day. Cain and Abel. The further our teacher, a stumpy old lady named Mrs. Kraft, got into the story, the more Jamie reminded me of the evil brother. Even as that thought entered my head, I tried to push it away. Comparing my heartache with that Old Testament story was blasphemous.

But each time Jamie moved, it seemed she ended up a half-inch closer to him.

Danny seemed not to notice any tension between us girls at that point. He sat in his chair, his hands on his thighs, his smile faraway and patient. He nodded at certain points in the story, but I could not tell if he was genuinely reacting to something Mrs. Kraft had said, or if he was in automatic mode.

During the break, we drank a cup of juice and nibbled some cookies. The kids ran around through the basement, but they were all disciplined enough to keep their voices to a low screech. The pause from class was only five minutes, and as we shuffled back into the classroom, neither Danny nor Jamie was there.

"Where are your friends?" Mrs. Kraft said to me.

"I don't know." I hoped I hadn't blushed enough to give away my heart.

"Do you want to go find them?" the teacher said.

In truth, I wasn't sure that I did want to find them. What if they were doing something like holding hands or kissing? I did not want my soul to be shattered that morning.

Begrudgingly, I agreed to search for them. At the very least, it allowed me to get out of class.

The basement of the church was a maze. Corridors led to other corridors. Rooms lined either side; some full of boxes, some with chairs, some with religious paraphernalia like crosses and Bibles. I knew my way through fairly well, but my heart raced. This felt wrong. I hoped – I even prayed – that I would find them sipping cups of juice, unaware they had overstayed the break, innocently talking of nothing. But God rarely answers prayers like that.

Soft whispers scratched softly from the next corridor down. It was dark there. Each bare bulb hanging from the ceiling cast a halo of sickly orange light. I moved quietly; I had abandoned the idea that my prayer would be answered. Slowly, quietly. A ninja, a thief of hearts. A failure, in that regard. I turned the corner.

They were holding hands, all right. They were also kissing each other.

I gasped, and they broke their embrace instantly. "Oh, it's just you," Jamie said, patting herself on her chest.

Danny's smile faltered. "Liz?" he said, looking at me.

"What are you two doing?" I hoped I could hide the fact that my soul felt like it had been ripped out of my ears.

"Everyone is looking for you."

"Don't tell," Jamie pleaded. "Please keep this a secret."

What could I do? Telling was not a viable option. I knew that even at my age. "Come on," I said. "Get back to the class before old lady Kraft sends out another search party."

Jamie walked past me, swift and arrogant. Danny remained, and I stared at him for a moment, his face hidden in the shadows. I realized how chilly it was in the basement of the church. "It just kind of happened," he told me. "We just walked away and then we were here."

"Okay."

"Hey," he said, as we walked back toward the classroom. "Do you want to go fishing later?"

"I can't go today," I said. And that was true. I would be too busy choking back my tears.

Two

don't want to give the impression that my life ended on that Sunday morning. But my eyes were opened, surely enough. They opened wide, but not wide enough to let the tears out; those, I kept burning inside for years to come.

Here I sit at my kitchen table, looking out of the window at the shafts of sunlight streaming down from the morning sky. I've always loved the morning and I've always loved the evening. My knees ache, and my sight is not what it once was. All this to say nothing of my hearing – when the doorbell rings, it may take me a couple of minutes to answer it, between hearing it and shuffling to the door. That is the price I must pay for having lived my life as fully as possible, I guess, and as prices go, I think it was worth it.

It rings now, and because the front door is close to the kitchen, it takes me only half a minute to answer. "Who could that be?" My voice is weak, my throat is dry. Spit, my bird, tweets from his cage in the living room. "Hold your horses," I say to Spit as much as to the person standing outside my front door. "I'm coming."

Standing on my porch is my postman. He is a young man, tall, and he wears sunglasses every day, rain or shine. There is something a bit unwholesome about that, but besides his glasses, he is a wonderful mail carrier. "Hi, Elizabeth," he says. "Here's your mail."

"Thanks, Bill," I say. He always tries to hand me my letters because he knows it is difficult for me to bend to pick them up. In return, I try to be sure to be near the front door when I know he is on his route, and I also give him a generous tip at Christmas. This is the way my little world works.

He continues on his route, his legs long and shimmering in the sun. It is spring, and summer is coming, and I will force open the windows in my house and let the fresh air blow through and sit and breathe it all in, for perhaps the last time. At my age, you realize that everything might be the last time.

I shamble over to the kitchen table and let the letters drop. My thoughts turn suddenly back to Danny and how he is living at Bliss. Do they open the windows for him there? I have a feeling that they do not; that the whole campus is probably air-conditioned and climate-controlled. That open windows would present a security risk, a danger, the menace of irritating allergies.

Gas bill, an advertisement for take-out Chinese food, a flyer for a local car wash. Do they know I've never held a driver's license? My mail depresses me: the sum total of my life, like a bad hand at poker. It has all been ordinary, at least as far as anybody looking in from the outside can tell. Of course, I know that is not the truth.

By the time we were sophomores in high school, Danny and Jamie were going steady. They built a new school that year, to accommodate all the growing families in Hamilton. Many evenings my father muttered because the school was paid for by what he called "our money." He was of the opinion that we did not need a new school; he had always thought school was, in general, a waste of time. He was nearing retirement by that year; he would end up dying with a bad liver just a few years later. But I would miss the funeral.

Our class schedules were designed so that we did not have all the same teachers, as in previous years. I went to Chemistry, Jamie found herself in English; Jamie changed for gym class, I was in Geography with Danny. And so on. We all three shared Mathematics, and we no longer had to sit with Danny between us. The only real rule was that Danny sat beside Jamie. And there was nothing unusual about that.

It would be wrong to give the impression that I was simply cast aside and forgotten. There were plenty of boys interested in me. Marcus, Roy, and Charlie were the main contenders. Marcus was a football player. He was the one who kicked the ball through the uprights. Roy was a poet and an artist and I liked him a great deal, even though he was not good looking. His hair was a bit too long and a lot too greasy, but he showed me his artwork, and he drew pictures for me, and you might be surprised at what little attentions like that can do to a girl.

It doesn't work that way anymore, I know, but I think it should.

Charlie was a fairly standard boy, in that he looked fine and took good care of himself and got decent enough grades and, looking at him, one could tell that he would be successful in life, if not wildly so. But he was also good friends with Danny, and that made him slightly more attractive than either Marcus or Roy. I started hanging around with Charlie more often that year, and as the first semester wore on, we sometimes went out on double dates.

Charlie would casually put his arm around me. Our relationship was fresh, and so that was as fresh as he got with me. But Danny and Jamie, having the oldest relationship in the school, could afford themselves more freedom in terms of their physical contact. They kissed, they snuggled. She pecked his cheek.

I watched his smile to see if it ever faltered. It never did. I pulled Charlie closer to me in an automatic response. Letting Charlie hold me, and looking at Danny, I could almost fool myself into believing that he was the right man with his arm around my shoulders.

Jamie, for her part, turned a bit strange during these high school years. I know now that there is nothing particularly unusual about that; in fact, it is a bit fashionable for kids these days to become weird. But she was sullen more often than happy, withdrawn, quiet, and there was a sadness in her eyes that nobody's smile seemed able to erase.

The four of us were in the park one afternoon. It was early spring, and still a bit cold. Danny draped his jacket around Jamie's shoulders and she shivered beneath the fabric. Charlie held me, but he did not put his own jacket around me; I was not especially cold. Jamie said, "Do any of you wonder what happens when you die?"

Nobody spoke for a moment. The thought had crossed my mind, once or twice, but I never gave it any serious consideration. Charlie said, "Heaven." And he looked at

Danny with a dopey grin and added, "Or hell."

"Do you really think so?" Jamie said.

"You know it's so," I told her. "If you hadn't skipped Bible study, you might not doubt it."

I meant it as a joke, but it failed to land that way. Jamie looked at me gravely, her gaze murderous. "You're just mad," she said, her voice pouty, "that you never skipped Bible study."

I didn't know if Danny understood the hidden meaning of our conversation but I was fairly certain that Charlie did not have a clue. He wasn't very bright, anyway. There was a question in my mind about whether Danny even remembered how I caught them in the church basement all those years before. He only sat there, his smile darkened just a shade, those lips of his wilted ever so slightly at the corners. I wanted to kiss those lips.

"It's all a little deep," Charlie said. His voice irritated me. "We don't have to worry about going off to war, or anything. If we did, then I'd be asking those questions. But we have our whole lives ahead of us."

"You never know," Jamie said.

I could not imagine a more striking juxtaposition between happiness and melancholy than Charlie sitting across from Jamie. And yet, here we were, and somehow Danny and I were pushed to the edges of the conversation. I caught his eye, and he returned a fleeting long-suffering gaze my way.

His look said everything I needed to know; everything I longed to hear. It told me that he loved me and was scared for Jamie. That this conversation was evidence of what he felt.

"Let's try to enjoy ourselves," Danny said, breaking our exchange. Already I wasn't sure it ever existed. "It's a beautiful day. So let's have some fun."

Jamie pouted for the rest of the day. She remained quiet and sullen, and the better angel in me worried for her. We walked through the park, which gave way to the Catholic cemetery in town. The grass around the graves was short and most of the markers had flowers on them. Atop one of them lay heaped a handful of loose change; another supported an empty liquor bottle.

Jamie took her time, reading each gravestone. I imagined what was going through her head. I could picture her, making up stories to go along with the graves. The liquor bottle was there because the deceased was a drunk driver and his sobbing girlfriend, enraged and heartbroken, left it there as an eternal proclamation: This fool killed himself. Or the spare change, left on top of the gravestone like a tiara because the girl lying beneath the grass was once a beautiful princess.

In my mind, I saw her lingering on this last story. Wondering what it was like, down there, beneath all the dirt: it must be silent. It must be dark, so very dark. The darkest dark you can think of. It must always be cold.

The cemetery was fairly large and, in walking the paths, I somehow ended up alone with Danny.

"I'm worried about her," he said.

"Why?" Although I too was worried.

"She seems depressed lately."

"Do you know why?"

Danny shook his head. I was terribly sad to see that his smile was gone. "She's always liked to be alone. I mean, it goes in shifts. Some days she wants to stay all by herself. Other days she practically begs me to take her out and see people."

"She's a mysterious girl," I said, because I wanted to

say too many other things. I wanted to tell him I loved him; I wanted to tell him I'd always loved him, from that first moment he said hello.

"I'm just a bit scared, that's all," Danny said. He was the only boy I knew who would admit such a thing. Charlie would never have said anything approaching that; he would have done anything to avoid it.

"You are both my friends. If I can help you, please let me help you."

But Danny shook his head. "I don't think so. Maybe it's just a phase. She'll come out of it."

"Let's hope so."

We reconvened by a big gravestone with the name RAWLINGS, and beneath that, 1877-1941. And, down further still, in small script: A FAITHFUL WIFE MAKES FOR A HAPPY FAMILY AND GOD.

Jamie looked a little better; she even smirked. Danny smiled. Charlie put his arm around my shoulders and the four of us walked out of the graveyard. We would be back, soon enough.

I have two sons, but they rarely visit. They, too, have children, and it hurts that I see so little of them, but I know to expect that. Nicholas lives in California, where he works with computers. His wife is a tiny Asian girl named Min, and she is sweet enough. Timothy is divorced and living alone in Washington D.C., where he works for a non-profit organization, which has some kind of business with the government. His children and ex-wife live here in Michigan, but I see them perhaps five times a year.

Danny's kids decided to put him in a home when his

health started to go south. He has three children, by two different women. By then, he was living far away and alone, and I can't argue that it was a bad decision to put him there, but it broke the last hanging thread of my heart when they put him away at Bliss

His children all live nearby, his daughter right here in Hamilton. I can imagine them sitting in a dank garage, late one evening, discussing where they would put their father, how they would arrange it, how they would break the news to him, whether they would allow him to have a say in his own future.

Hamilton probably seemed the most logical option, because it is home, after all, even if he did move to some unnamed corner of the country, even if it would be a logistical nightmare to bring him back. But, as I have thought a thousand times in my life, all roads for him and for me lead to Hamilton.

Danny is diabetic, has failing kidneys, and a mild case of Alzheimer's disease. That last one scares me the most and is probably the reason I have not been over to see him yet. The fear that he will not remember me.

It was his daughter, Christine, who called me to tell me that he was in a home. "It's just the best thing for him," she said. "We can't take care of him – we didn't know what to do."

"I know, honey," I told her then. I wanted to say other things. But I did not. All my life, I did not.

"I think he would want you to visit," she said.

My heart fluttered at that. "Oh, I don't know," I said, assuming a sigh. "It's been so long."

"I know he would want to see you."

"Perhaps," I told her, and we broke the connection. That was two weeks ago. I stood in my kitchen after hanging up the receiver, staying on my feet for longer than accustomed, just thinking of poor Danny and his smile. How I wanted so desperately to see him. But I still have not been to Bliss.

Asleep one warm spring evening not long after our walk in the cemetery, it had been a quiet night. My father had had a few beers and collapsed, as usual, but without the yelling and bullying that evenings with him usually entailed. I had a math test the next morning, but I was unworried. I was a good student. I allowed myself a snigger when I thought of how Charlie would fare; he barely knew the multiplication tables. But that was unfair: he excelled at other things.

Something hit my window and roused me from my slumber. I lay there, staring at the ceiling, sure that I had imagined it. But it happened again, so I slid out from under the covers and crept to the window. In the moonlight, Danny stood below, with a pinecone in his hand, preparing to throw it.

"Hey," I whispered into the night.

"Good, you're awake," he said.

"What are you doing?" I breathed, so as to not wake my mother and father.

"Come down here. Please."

He could have told me to run barefoot through broken glass and I would have done it, especially if he was waiting for me at the end.

"Give me a minute." I was in a nightgown but I slipped my feet into a pair of moccasins and skulked downstairs, careful of the step that creaked, and met him in the backyard. He was not smiling. "What's wrong?"

"I'm in trouble.

"What trouble?" I hugged myself against the imagined cold coming from the night. "What's happened?"

"Me and some of the guys," he said, gesturing wildly behind him. I looked over his shoulder, but there was nobody there. "We had a few too many to drink. We did it. It was all that fool Wilson's idea. He got us into this."

"Slow down," I said. I took his arm and I led him to our tree, the same tree we had sat against on that first day, waiting for my father to fall asleep. "Start from the beginning," I told him.

He took a few deep breaths. The grass smelled fresh and prickled against my bare calves. Danny seemed unaware of how I was dressed, and I was actually relieved by that. "The train," he said.

I shook my head in confusion. "What about the train?"

"We knocked it off the tracks."

"What?"

He took a few more breaths and then told the story: he and five other boys from the school had drunk a few beers. He had not particularly wanted to, he said, but they were there and the night was young and he was feeling stupid. Okay. They drove a pickup truck outside of town and threw a bunch of bags of grain onto the train tracks where they intersected Mill Road.

They drove a half mile away, and because the land was flat, they could see the train coming from a ways off. It was a short one and, thank God, not a passenger train, but one of those freight trains. It locked its brakes ... the screech was terrible, but it was far too late, and the train slipped off the tracks just like a batter striking out. Those were Danny's words. The whole shebang was incredibly loud, and the sound delay because of the distance was what most haunted Danny.

In those silent seconds it seemed as though it was happening, but it was not real.

"We floored it all the way back to town," Danny said. And then, softly, "I think we killed somebody."

Unable to say anything for a few moments – I didn't know what to say to him – I put my arm around his shoulders and squeezed him closer to me. His heart throbbed beneath his chest, against mine; he struggled with breathing and for a moment, I thought he would cry, and prepared myself for his tears. None came. Finally, I asked him, "So, what next?"

"I can't go back there," he said almost instantly, as if I had proposed he should. "I don't want to see it."

My mind spun and my heart ached. Scores of scenarios played out in varying degrees of detail in my head: Danny hunted by the police, Danny in prison, Danny going fugitive. None of them were good. "You can stay the night here," I said.

"Oh. I couldn't," he said. His head was on my shoulder, and while I couldn't see his face, I felt his warm breath against my collarbone. "I don't want to get you in trouble."

"What trouble? It's not trouble." What I meant but didn't have the courage to say was, "It's worth it."

"I don't think the others will talk," he said. "They aren't that stupid."

"Where are they?"

"I don't know."

He looked into my eyes from his prone position. The moonlight filtered somehow through the tree, caught his face, and he looked both angelic and scared. I leaned my own head down and my lips met his. Our lips simply touched for a few moments, and then that moment morphed into a passionate kiss. Our breathing intensified.

He was so warm and vulnerable. His left hand found my right thigh and rested there against the silky nightgown. I wanted that hand to move, to rub, to search more deeply, and I was scared, too.

Already, I had gone far beyond the limits of acceptability for that time. I was breaking even my own moral code. And I did not care. When it came to the struggle between my heart and ethics, my heart would always win.

We broke our kiss after a few moments and leaned back against the trunk of the tree. "Don't tell Jamie," he said, some time later. "Never tell Jamie."

I didn't know whether he meant the kiss or the train. But I agreed on both counts. "Never," I said.

The next morning, snug in my bed, for a few fleeting minutes, I wondered if the previous night had been a dream. A dream: if it were a dream, it would be both a great relief and at the same time a sore disappointment. I did not want anybody to die, and I did not want tons of twisted steel strewn in some corner of some farmland, but if it were a dream, then that magical kiss never existed. Feeling my nightgown, nothing seemed out of the ordinary. No grass stains.

Climbing down the stairs, I tried to remember everything about the previous evening. My mother and father sat at the kitchen table, worried expressions on their faces, and I knew something was wrong. "What is it?" I said, entering the kitchen.

My father held up his hand; they were listening to the

radio. "Witnesses report seeing a truck speed away from the scene of last night's derailing. The conductor of the train said he had no chance of reacting to the bags left on the tracks until it was far too late. The investigation continues at this hour ..."

My father turned off the radio. "Damn kids," he said. I felt I hated him.

"Probably drunk," my mother added, standing from the table and moving over to the kitchen sink. "How are you this morning, Elizabeth?" She used a brighter, fresher tone.

Distracted that my parents had made so much headway in their own judgments about the guilty party already, I said, "Was anybody hurt last night?" Between them, they knew they were kids, and they knew they were drunk.

My father stared through me, then he shook his head. "Damn lucky," he said. "It was a small train, didn't have nobody on it. Farmer was saying a cow got crushed." He chuckled, although I failed to see the humor. "I could go for hamburgers tonight, honey."

My mom nodded, noncommittal as ever. "Are you ready for your math test?" she said, giving the impression that she wanted only to change the subject.

Was it possible that she knew? She was quiet because society dictated that she be, but she was smart. Perhaps she knew much more than she was letting on. Perhaps she knew I loved Danny; perhaps she knew Danny was sitting with me the previous night, his cheek resting snugly against the soft part of my neck.

"I am ready," I said, feeling anything but ready to think of dividing fractions.

I sat and drank a tall glass of orange juice. It tasted

bitter but I drank it, anyway. A strange silence had engulfed our breakfast. Or was I imagining it? I heard birds chirping outside the window, and I saw the tree under which we'd sat the night before, looking the same as it always did. Keeping its secrets.

Walking past Danny's house slowly that morning, I hoped he would come out and we could walk to school together. Doing my best not to look at his windows, his front door, as I always did when I walked to school – pretending I was on legitimate business when, in fact, all I wanted was to see him. I would have failed every math test in my future to see him that morning, but his house was silent. Either he had already left for school or he was still getting prepared. Either way, I continued.

The school was abuzz with the news of the train. Nobody looked twice at me, and I took that as a good sign. It meant that nobody knew Danny was involved. If they knew, then surely they would come to me to find out more, because I was his friend.

I saw Jamie by her locker, surrounded by a small gaggle of students, and then a new realization struck me: they would go to her, not me, if they wanted information. She was his girlfriend. She was the one who would know.

I moved over to their group as discreetly as possible. Jamie was in the middle of them, and I strained to hear what she said. I heard snatches of her monolog: "...barking all night long, I could hardly sleep ...parents will kill me, literally kill me, if I flunk this test ..." She noticed me at some point during her speech and said hello. "Are you ready for the math test?"

"I'm ready," I told her, watching her eyes.

Someone else joining the group caught my attention: Wilson, the boy Danny claimed had come up with the idea to derail the train the previous evening. His eyes were red and his cheeks looked sunken. He was tall but walked with a slump in his shoulders. Jamie's conversation continued unabated until class was about to begin, and she ceased her prattling. Wilson lingered, touching my sleeve.

"What is it?" I had had little contact with him up until that point, and for some reason I could not pin down, I did not particularly like him.

"Have you seen Danny?"

"Why don't you ask Jamie?" I said.

"Because it's you he loves," Wilson said.

He said those words in such an offhand way, but they destroyed my world and created it again, all in an instant.

"What?"

"Have you seen him?" Wilson insisted. "I need to talk to him."

I couldn't even think straight, not after what Wilson had just said to me, but I found the mental reserves to say, "I know what happened. Just don't talk to anybody about it."

"They know it was me," Wilson said. He snorted and shook his head at the same time. "We were so goddamn stupid."

"What do you mean?" Although late for math, suddenly I did not care. "What do you mean they know it was you?"

"We used the grain bags from my old man's farm," he said, his voice distant, his eyes lost. "Can you believe that? We used my own grain bags!"

Not a master criminal myself, I didn't know what to say to him, and I knew that if the police asked me whether I knew anything about the previous evening, I would have difficulty in keeping Danny's secret. The very idea of it terrified me: I tended to crumble in the face of authority.

"Just don't say anything," I told him, thinking it was best for everyone. "Just keep your mouth shut."

"They know," he said, his face ashen. The few pimples on his forehead had turned an angrier shade of red. "We're the only ones who use that grain on our farm. They're going to come by." His voice was soft and far away. "They're going to show the bag to my old man, and then he's going to say someone took them – he probably called the police this morning to tell them someone took some bags from the barn. Oh, Jesus," he keened. "He probably called the police. They don't even have to put the puzzle together!"

"Just stay calm," I told him, but it was obvious that he was cracking.

"It was so stupid," he said. "Why did we do it?"

"I need you to keep this a secret," I told him. I grabbed his arm and pulled him close. He came without resistance. "You can't tell that Danny was there. Please."

He nodded, staring over my head, and then I slapped him. I had never done anything like that before. My palm stung from the connection and the smack was wet and loud. The halls were almost deserted, but I didn't care if anybody heard or saw what I had done. It echoed down the corridor.

My finger marks livid on his cheek, he brushed at them absently and looked down at me, momentarily refocused. "Okay," he said, nodding.

"I mean it. You can't help yourself by hurting Danny. If you're in trouble, you're in trouble. Bringing someone down with you won't help. So promise me, Wilson. Can you do that?"

"I promise."

"You promise what?"

"I won't say anything about Danny. If the police come. But maybe they won't come, huh? That's possible, too."

"Sure," I crooned. "That's possible."

We parted ways and I scuttled off to math class, not feeling particularly encouraged by Wilson's attitude. But I had to pray it would be enough to keep Danny clear of trouble.

I sat through my math test, and I knew I'd failed even as I gave it to the teacher for grading. But, I did not care. There were things much more important in the world than fractions: how to add them, how to divide them, how to multiply and subtract them. It all seemed a bit ridiculous to me when there was heartache and tragedy going on all around us.

By the time Biology class came around, a class I shared with Wilson, the school knew he was guilty. Any hope of keeping the secret under the lid was shot; I knew enough of small towns and high school and human nature to know that.

As it turned out, nobody had to be the first to talk. Mr. Dickerson was preparing for the class to dissect cows' hearts – he had been going on about it for weeks – when there was a knock at the door.

Nobody ever knocked at the door in our school. Mr. Dickerson stared at it in anticipation before finding words.

"Uh, yes?"

The door swung in and Sheriff Townsend entered. The sheriff was a tall, burly man, but he spoke *sotto voce*, unlike most police with whom I'd had contact at that point in my life.

"Hi, Ben," he said to Mr. Dickerson. With a note of apology in his voice, he added, "I'm here to see Wilson."

A long sigh came from the back of the room, and I knew Wilson would not be able to keep himself from admitting his crime for long. I only hoped he would keep Danny out of it.

"I don't want to go," Wilson moaned.

"Come on, son," Townsend said. "Let's go take care of this business you and I have together."

And, just like that, Wilson lifted himself from his chair and walked out of the room. I never saw him again. Danny and the other friends he was with that night were never connected to the train crash. Rumors abounded: Wilson would go to prison for ten years, Wilson would be fined a million dollars, Wilson was moving to France to begin a new life as a street mime.

Nobody, as far as I know, actually knew the truth.

We went back to our cow hearts, and I thought about the cow crushed by Wilson's train, and this life seemed more a waste to me than ever before. Maybe Jamie was right about a few things, I thought.

As we cut into them, I imagined the heart was mine; I imagined the scalpel was in her hand.

Three

Dredging up the past is an exercise in self-harm. Most of my life has been happy. Why, then, is it so easy for me to focus on the painful parts of it? It must be some kind of disease in me, eating my happiness from the inside, out. For that's where happiness lives, I've learned: inside you.

It can't be gotten or bought, only found. I've learned too many things. There's another lesson this world is too good at teaching, and that is how we hurt each other. Every person hurts at least one other person. But probably many more than just one.

I never thought much about Wilson, after he'd gone. But it is now, in my final years, that I think of Wilson again. I am eternally grateful that he did not give Danny's name away. How history would have changed! It would have been his sweet name I wondered about – and Danny would not have survived in prison.

Oh, those words stab at my heart. Because he is in prison, now, and not because he did anything wrong. Only because he got sick and old.

As I mentioned, I have spent these past few months in

indecision after speaking with Danny's daughter, Christine. Due partly to not wanting, I think, to stir up all those old memories lying dormant within me. I have not seen Danny for so many years, but I have kept tabs on him, and I have followed his movements, occasionally wondering if he did the same for me.

But now, I have made a decision. "Spit," I tell my bird, "I'm going on a little trip."

He cocks his head as if he is trying to understand; perhaps he understands the words perfectly well but cannot understand what would drive me to such madness. Although I love that bird, I decide I do not care. I carefully check his water and food supply to be sure that he has enough for my absence. Then I take a wad of cash from my kitchen drawer, without counting it, and my purse.

After I step outside, it feels as though I have not felt the sun on my skin in ages. That is not true, however, because I do get out. I take walks around the block, and I pick up sticks in my backyard, on good days. Today is a better day, and I take a deep breath before I set out in any specific direction. Then I think of downtown, where I might be able to catch a taxicab, and I turn that way.

Although ginger at first, my legs find a rhythm and they obey my wish for them to move: I am walking. Each step brings a little more youth into my soul, although I know the sensation is temporary, and that I will be sore for a long time once I have finished this walk and rested for a while. At my age, there is little alternative to accepting the pain that life hands you; perhaps that is true at any age. Perhaps it is simply easier to accept when you have reached my age.

I think about him as I walk, and that is as natural as anything else; I muse that I was unable to tell even the bare beginnings of the story of my love for him before I set out to see him again. But he always had that unnamable power over me.

The sidewalks are wide here, and level, and smooth. Perfect for little girls and little boys to ride their bicycles on, and perfect for old ladies like me to shamble onward toward whatever awaits them in the near, but unforeseeable, future. Cars are driven by responsible drivers in this neighborhood, most of whom obey the speed limit. I have never had a driving permit, and I have never understood the first thing about cars. While I know a nice one when I see one, I base that decision on gut intuition rather than any experience or actual knowledge.

A big one stops at the curb beside me and the passenger window rolls down automatically. "Elizabeth?" I hear.

Tricia Longwell, from church, is behind the wheel. She is one of those mothers who has several children; one in this elementary school, another in the middle school, one or two in college already. She wears a gigantic diamond wedding ring which glints in the sunlight as she rests her hands upon her lap.

"Why, hello," I say to her, moving with care over the narrow strip of grass separating the street and the sidewalk.

"How are you?" Tricia gives the impression that she is genuinely interested.

"Never better," I say, although more accurate would be to tell her that I am rarely better anymore. I am excited and anxious. But nobody wants a response quite that long.

"Are you going somewhere?"

"Yes, I am." As a child, people stopped what they were doing and chatted about anything. It had not even crossed my mind that Tricia might take me where I wanted to go, but now it is clear that she will. I am relieved, but that makes me sad, too, although I cannot explain why that would be so. "I'm going to Bliss. The retirement home."

"Oh, uh-huh," she nods. "Vern just went there."

It takes me a moment to understand that she is speaking of one of our congregation who has not been to church in about a month. His health had been failing, but I was unaware until just now that he had taken that big ride to Bliss, too.

"Are you heading out to visit him?"

"Yes," I say, unsure of why I am lying. But telling this fib sends a small, pleasant shiver down my spine.

"Get in," she says, motioning toward the passenger seat. "I'll give you a lift."

I open the door and slide in. The seat is high, and it takes me a moment to find where to buckle the seatbelt.

*D*anny got his first car during our senior year. I mentioned how little I know about cars, and I suppose I knew even less back then, but I still remember it was a white, 1957 Mercury. From behind, it looked more like a boat than an automobile, but it ran well, and Danny was openly modest about it, although I knew he was swelling with pride in his heart. There were patches of rust he could not fix and a rattle that came from somewhere underneath the thing that he did not have the money to repair, but none of that mattered. I was the first person he took for a ride in it, and we listened to a young singer named Elvis on the radio, his honeyed voice cutting through the static. Danny grinned, staring through the windshield, driving well below the speed limit. There were no separate seats, it was just a bench in the front, and it was beautiful. I had never seen anything so beautiful in my life.

He picked me up and I sat in that front seat with him, where I did not belong. "Where's Jamie?"

"She doesn't like riding around," Danny said. I thought I saw a shadow flit across his face as he said this, but I probably imagined it. "She thinks it's a waste of time."

I did not respond straight away, but I could not fathom anybody thinking that cruising with Danny in this beautiful machine was a waste of time. "It's really nice."

"Thanks," he said absently. Riding through town, we stopped at the traffic light, the only one in our little community, and reverently listened to the animal growl of the engine beneath the hood. "It's not new, or anything."

"I love it anyway," I said, touching the dashboard. It was padded and soft beneath my fingers. Telling him I loved his car was the closest I had come to telling Danny that I loved him.

"I need to talk to you," he said, heading out of town. "It's about Jamie."

While unprepared for a serious conversation, the wind blew through my hair, the radio cut in and out, and it was a beautiful day, so I was ready for anything. This might be the moment, I hoped, when we would have it all out in the open: how he felt about me, how I felt about him, how Jamie fit into all of that. I wanted to have it in the air, between us, so that we could make some kind of a move, around it, or through it, or over it – but it was none of those things.

"She's in trouble," he said, in response to my silence. "She took a bunch of pills last night."

It took a moment to comprehend what he was saying,

and then it smacked me like a hammer. "You mean she tried to kill herself?"

We exited town and Danny pushed the accelerator a bit. The car ate up the highway like a hog.

"I went to her house last night. Nobody was going to be home."

Danny did not look at me as he spoke, and I thought that was from shame and embarrassment, but I will probably never know. What I do know is that those words sent a pang of jealousy and sadness through my very core that I will never forget. Danny went to her house, to see her, alone. It was beyond serious, then.

It was the end of my fantasies, at least for that moment: I suppose that, somewhere in my mind, I harbored thoughts of him running away from Jamie and confessing his love for me. It was true, and I knew it and he knew it, so what stopped us from speaking of it in his new car that day? I felt no shame for not worrying over Jamie. Besides, if she were dead, Danny would have led with that information.

"She was lying on the kitchen floor but her eyes were closed," he said, his voice grim. "She was breathing and lying on her side with one hand stretched out above her head, like this."

He demonstrated just how her hand splayed out above her, as if reaching for something unattainable. But what did it need to attain? She had him, already, and so she had the world.

"I tried to shake her awake. I yelled, 'Jamie, Jamie, wake up.' She moaned and opened her eyes into little slits. I don't think she even saw me."

"My God," I said, mostly to break the silence from my half of the automobile.

"I slapped her, not too hard, and I splashed cold water on her face, sure she was going to die. But she started to wake up. I kept asking her, 'What did you do, what did you do?' And she just kind of smiled at me, but not like anything was funny. More like she couldn't be bothered with my questions. I was freaking out."

"And then what?"

We drove down what seemed to me aimless side roads, some of them gravel. The Mercury kicked up a long plume of dust which settled in the air behind us like the trail of a Soviet rocket. Danny drove us up to an abandoned gravel pit now filled with water. Local legend held that it was some ninety feet deep, cold as ice, and hid a terrific undertow that could drown the strongest of Olympic swimmers. He parked the car at the side of the road and killed the engine. We listened to the clicking sounding from beneath the hood.

"I called the doctor," he said. "He told me to stay with her, and that he would send somebody right away. I waited. I held her hand. It seemed cold, to me, but I was probably just imagining that. I thought she was slipping away. Then a doctor came – a young guy, probably only twenty or so, at least that's how he looked – and he made her stand and walked with her to the bathroom and made her puke into the toilet. She didn't get it all into the toilet."

That detail seemed too intimate for me, but he'd said it, and I imagined her whitish vomit, sitting on the bathroom floor, growing cold and slick. "And then she was better?"

"A little better. Let's go for a walk."

Opening my door without argument, I stepped into a patch of soft knee-high grass and slammed his car door. He sat on the hood of the car and stared out toward the gravel pit. It was at the bottom of a steep, sandy cliff, and from our vantage point, we could see the entire lake. The water was as blue as anything I had ever seen; it was the definition of blue.

I approached him and, after a moment's hesitation, I sat close to him on the hood of his Mercury, his body beside mine, relaxed and electric at the same time. Our elbows touched, reminding me of the time we sat beneath the tree in my backyard. I thought I would bring it up, but he spoke first.

"I guess this isn't much of a walk, huh?" he said, smiling. But, even in the sunshine, with the cool wind blowing against our faces, sadness tinged his smile.

"It's enough for me," I said, feeling stupid.

He took a deep breath and sighed. "I used to come here to think." He gazed out at the lake below. "I used to ride my bike all the way out here. It took me an hour. And then I would just sit here, staring out at the pit down there, thinking."

"About what?"

"Lots of things," he said without hesitating. "I thought a lot about you."

I wanted those words to hang in the air forever, but they seemed to be blown away by the swift breeze. Perhaps in an attempt to grab them back, I said, "I think about you all the time."

"I know," he said.

He looked over at me.

"I know," he repeated, and said, "I know it and I love you so much." His right hand found my left hand and grasped it.

His skin was soft and his fingers warm. He rubbed his thumb against my palm in slow, delicate circles, seemingly unconscious of doing so.

"It's just so hard. I can't leave Jamie. Not like this."

"I know." I wasn't adding much to the conversation, and wondered if he felt just as foolish as I did. It was not like this, in books, in films. The characters always knew what to say and nobody feared rejection. Nobody tiptoed in the world of fiction. But this was on the hood of his car, at the pit, and the words we said could not be taken back or edited out.

They were all permanent, whether they were blown away by the wind or stuck like ice picks in our hearts.

"You are special to me, Danny. You're the one I want."

He nodded. He looked down at his knees. His thumb stopped massaging my palm, and he leaned over and we kissed. It was different this time; it was hard to believe it had been so many years since our lips had met! This time it was slower, an invitation from the angels to peek at heaven for a moment. His lips were soft and pliant, and his kiss was giving. Charlie kissed like a newborn calf searching for its mother's udder.

He grabbed my shoulder and we lay back on the hood of his car. Somehow it was more comfortable than I would ever have imagined. We broke our kiss – I experienced an absurd moment when I wondered how we had managed to kiss as we lay back – and we stared at each other for a few moments, without speaking.

He whispered, "You are a goddess."

How can a girl in love respond to that? I ran my fingers through his hair. It was thick, dark, soft, warm. He closed his eyes as I did it, as if my fingers there brought him great pleasure. I trailed my right hand down his side. I felt his ribcage, hard, beneath his t-shirt. His belly, his hip. I let my hand fall to his crotch, and I brushed the bulge there with the backs of my fingers. His eyes did not close this time, and somehow that made me trust him even more.

"Do you want to do this?" he asked me. "Are you sure?"

I struggled to unbutton his pants. As I did, he cupped my breasts, first one and then the other. My nipples hardened into little pebbles, and I savored the chill his touch sent down my nerves.

Once his trousers were unbuttoned, he took over: he sat up and yanked them off with his underwear, and then, in one quick, fluid movement, he ripped off his shirt. Well-built, but not yet tanned, he lay on his back and stared up at the sun. I kissed his chin and continued kissing until I was biting one of his nipples. His hand was on the back of my head, but he led me nowhere. I was free to choose where my mouth went.

And so I kissed further down; down his hardened abdomen, which trembled when I grazed it with my lips, with my hair hanging down. I slowed my descent as I neared his penis. I kissed his pubic area. It smelled musky, not unpleasant.

My chin ran into his erection. I pulled my head back for an instant to get a better view. It was throbbing into the air at the angle of military artillery. His pubic hair was dark and wild. I ran my fingertip from the base of his dick, up to the head, back down, and then I massaged his scrotum for a few moments. It shrank in a very minuscule way when I did that.

I stood from the car and pulled off my clothes as quickly as I could. I tossed my dress into the knee-high grass, where it caught like a kite stuck in a tree. I felt like a raging fire, my belly full of molten lead. I needed him inside me.

I lay beside him, and he rolled over on top of me. There

was no more need for words. I stared down between my legs at his member as it searched out the softest part of me. It looked like a hungry animal. I grabbed it with my right hand. It was hot and hard, and his balls swung against my knuckles and rested there. I led him inside me.

I did not cry out, I did not even make an unpleasant face when he broke me. I gritted my teeth and suffered that moment of pain so that I could reach higher levels of ecstasy.

Danny went slowly, and he looked into my face with every cautious thrust. He did not ask me if I was okay, but I could read the concern, mixed with his own animal lust, sketched across his features. I grabbed his back, his shoulders, and I held on, feeling myself moving on the hood of the car. Soon the sweat trickling down my back acted as an adhesive, and I stuck in one place as we found a rhythm: the tempo of life, of love, desire, at last fulfilling a long sought-after dream.

Though the pleasure was intense, I don't know whether I had an orgasm, but whatever I did have, it was the best thing up until that moment of my life. He left me satiated and breathing deeply; in bliss, you might say. He rolled off me and we lay on his hood in the sun, naked and saturated with harmony.

I was the first to sit up and peel myself from his car. My back felt stained by my own sweat and the miscellaneous grime from the metal of the Mercury. I felt free. There was a streak of blood on the top of Danny's hood. He sat up and I tried not to stare at the place where his legs met, sitting on display in the sun. He slid off the car and stood in front of the grill of the Mercury. His cock was hard again, jutting up at a lively angle from his body. He stared at me.

"I love you so much," he said.

I nodded. "I love you more," I said, sure it was true. Because it had to be true: my love for him was infinite.

"Let's go swimming," he said. His smile was broad and warm, like the sun on my shoulder blades.

I grabbed my dress and followed him down a trail which led to the lake below. I walked a few feet behind him and watched his perfectly sculpted butt as he negotiated the varying terrain, from stones to sand, over roots and around little holes in the ground. I wanted to squeeze him there for the rest of my life. His butt was so symmetrical, and the muscles seemed to work in such perfect, beautiful unison as he walked. I did not think anybody would find us there. It seemed the entire world was ours, to frolic naked and be joyful.

We arrived at the shore and I dipped my toe in. The water was cold, and it sent a pleasant jolt up my leg.

"Are you sure?" I said.

He stuck his own toe in the water and smiled at me. His penis was a stiff beam, and it cast a shadow against his left thigh as it bounced and jiggled with his movements.

"I have you to keep me warm," he said, and then he took my hand and I followed him in.

It was like sinking into perfect debauchery. It felt wrong, because it was wrong, on many different levels. There was society, and Jamie and Charlie, neither of them aware or even suspecting, as far as I knew. But I did not care. It felt wrong and it was wrong, but I wanted it too much.

He wrapped his arms around my waist and pressed himself into my back. I felt his hard, throbbing dick jut against the small of my back, and we remained perfectly still for a moment, the water up just above my knees. Then he started rubbing on my back, up and down, his penis against my spine. I felt his testicles contact my upper buttocks, and I craned my neck back in pleasure. With each thrust, we moved a few inches deeper into the pit. Before long, I was nearly up to my waist.

He nuzzled me beneath my ear. His breath was hot and alive. This was not even sex, and yet this time, passion's flame was burning even hotter in my loins. Each time he rubbed against me, something tightened and then snapped loose inside my lower belly, my womanhood. It felt looser there, and as though it was heating up.

The water was cold but I no longer noticed. I was too hot. I pushed his hands against me; I wanted to melt into him, to become a single, writhing entity with his warm body. His breath quickened, and he bit my shoulder. He latched on there with his perfect teeth and he tasted my salty flesh. He turned me around to face him, his penis engorged, pointing up and out from the sweetness that was him.

He grabbed my buttocks and pulled me against him. He rubbed himself against me, his penis sliding up and down, the head searching out some hidden place, the balls slapping against my vagina. He increased the rhythm of his thrusts. Both of us stared down at his cock, and when the semen exploded out from it in a spray of white glory, I gasped and said, "Oh!"

He gave a few deep, passionate thrusts as his orgasm continued. His cum erupted from his penis and splattered my stomach, my pubic hair; a few ropes of it jumped into the water, where it seemed to float for a moment before diving under like some exotic sea creature searching for colder, darker waters.

Afterward, we held each other tightly, his dick

softening, flaccid against my belly. I held onto his butt and never wanted to let go of it. I breathed in his breath; I let him kiss my eyelids, each individually. I closed both eyes, both times. His lips there felt like the best-kept secret I could imagine. He rested his head against my shoulder, and I stroked his hair. Neither of us spoke.

After some time, we left the cold water. I dressed quickly. I felt no shame. He watched me, still naked, and then we climbed the trail to his car, where he quickly tugged on his pants and shirt, tied his shoes, and then sat behind the steering wheel. We took deep breaths. I listened to his breathing as it synchronized with my own. We stared out through the windshield. Because of the hood and the angle of the car, we could not see the lake; only the blue sky.

"That was something," he said, glancing over at me. He was not smiling anymore, not because he was unhappy, but because we spoke about something too serious for smiles.

"I'll never regret it," I told him then, and that has always been true.

"Me, neither," he said, rubbing my knee. He left his hand cupped over my leg for a moment. "But we can't tell Jamie. Or anybody."

"Of course."

And this is the first anyone has ever heard of it.

Four

Charlie and I met the evening of the next day, when we went to get ice cream at a shop at the edge of town. The sky was a bruised violet color, the moon a thin sliver of silver rising over the tops of the trees: Now the world was different. It had accepted me as a woman. Somebody entitled to her own secrets, her own life, her own secret world. With this new understanding of the ways of the world and of womanhood came a tinge of sadness at having lost my innocence.

Images of Jamie, recovering at home in bed, flashed through my mind. Danny beside her, caring for her. Or at least pretending to care. I told my mother about Jaime. She had spent the last day in a sad kind of haze, herself, mourning Jamie and what she had done.

"You're worried about your friend," Charlie said. He licked at his ice cream. Turning to look in his eyes, a dull sort of kindness shone, a joy at eating something cold and sweet on a warm spring night.

"Yes." But it was mostly untrue. I worried about her, yes, in a cursory way. But there were bigger things weighing on my mind.

"She'll be all right. Danny told me," he said, trying to comfort me, and yet his words had the opposite effect. Danny was mine, to think about myself, not to be spoken of by others.

"I think so," I said. I tried to cross my arms across my chest, but it proved awkward while holding an ice cream cone in one hand. I settled for a small sigh which I hoped would encourage our conversation to go in a different direction.

We licked our ice creams. He had just taken a job at a local supermarket, and was proud of his responsibility, stocking shelves, bagging groceries. Unfailingly polite to older customers, he worked mostly with his head down, not easily distracted, one of his traits which I found most appealing. Sometimes he asked me some random question, and my mind wandered, and I wouldn't reply for far too long, the time stretching out like a void, like outer space; but when I finally did answer him, he was always just the same, still waiting for my response.

"Liz," he said, his voice faltering. "There's something I want to talk to you about."

Although I had no idea what was coming, a small part of me hoped he knew about Danny and me, and that he wanted to broach the subject. Then we could have it in the open, and he would likely not want to see me anymore. "What is it?" I said, pretending my heart was not beating fast, that my nerves were cool.

"Well, we're seniors this year."

"I know that," I said, chuckling.

"That means we're leaving high school."

He had such a simple way of putting things! Sometimes I wondered if he was piecing together his own elementary logic when he spoke like this. "So it does."

"Well, I want to talk about what we're going to do next year."

It was the first time I had even thought about *we* and the *future*. High school was a limbo, a safe holding place, a welcome mat, an invitation to a larger, waiting world. But now, it truly was ending, and I realized, for perhaps the first time, that we would be scattered, unless we decided to do something about it. And on top of Charlie opening this subject up before us, I could only think of Danny: where would he be, come August, September? College? I knew Charlie would not be planning to attend a university. It simply was not in him. But Danny had a brain, and I was nervous about how he might decide to educate it further.

"What do you mean?" Suddenly I was unwilling to have this conversation.

"Well," he said, then stopped. A long ribbon of ice cream had melted down the side of his cone and leaked over the backs of his fingers. A moment after I watched with distaste, Charlie noticed too, and changed the cone to his left hand and licked the back of his right hand clean. "I guess what I mean is – I mean, do you want to get married?"

I gaped at him. A man-child whom I had professed to love but whom I did not love, not with my secret heart, had just asked for my hand in marriage.

He stared back at me, expectantly. He looked like a coiled snake and an oversized plush toy at the same time. "I don't know what to say," I said at length. "I don't think I'm ready to marry."

"Oh," he said. The disappointment flushed out of him. At that moment, his ice cream fell from his cone and made a sickening plopping noise as it fell on the concrete between his feet. We stood for a moment of silence, and then I exploded with laughter, and, after another moment, Charlie joined me.

"I guess I won't finish that," he said, and even then there was a note of disappointment in his voice. It amused me to think that he was more disappointed about the ice cream than my non-answer to his proposal.

"Charlie," I said, taking his hand – I chose the right because it was cleaner, less sticky, than his left. "Let's not rush. Maybe in a little while."

He nodded, giving my fingers a squeeze. "I know. I don't want to hurry too much. It's just that Danny and Jamie, you know."

I squeezed his hand, an involuntary reaction, and his eyes bulged in surprise. "What about them?" I snapped. Anybody else would have seen what was passing through my head, but not Charlie.

"Oh, you haven't heard?"

"Heard what?"

"They're getting married." He shared the news with a smile on his face, genuine happiness for his friend, I am sure, but those same happy words shocked me as fiercely as a sudden fall through thin ice. When you felt like you were alone, maybe that was all it took for you to give up and die.

"No way. That can't be."

But he nodded. "They are too. I talked to Danny earlier. He asked her today. She's not feeling so hot, ever since, you know ... but she said yes. She wants to marry him. So they're getting married this summer."

So soon! I could not believe that time, which just yesterday seemed endless, was in reality so short. "Okay," I said. "That's good. We will have to go."

"Well, yeah," he said, as if it was as obvious as washing your hands before cooking a meal. "Danny's asked me to be his best man. And I'm sure Jamie will want you there. You are like her sister."

"Where are they going to live?" It was not appropriate to pump poor Charlie for information, but my knowing was more important than keeping up the appearance that I was pure and wholesome.

Charlie just shrugged, infuriating me with his apathy in response to my urgency. "They will figure all that out. They like to take things as they come. They don't want to have a plan."

That was true; Danny was not the type of man to stick rigorously to a set plan. But Charlie said these things so casually. "Well, we will have to wish them luck," I said, trying my hardest not to rip out my hair.

We threw our cones in the nearest trash bin and walked home. Charlie could barely keep up with my pace. That seemed to epitomize our relationship.

With each step, I imagined I was walking back in time, bringing me closer to the moment when I could head things off; change them for the way the future was supposed to play out. But my steps brought me no closer to that moment. All I did was arrive home, ignore my aging father's racket, and go to bed. Where I did not sleep at all that night.

ricia Longwell is a surprisingly aggressive driver. I had always assumed she was a quiet wife and mother, the kind who let her husband dictate the family schedule, who always cooked dinner, packed the kids' lunches, and did not concern herself with paying bills, talking to telemarketers, or making simple household repairs.

But now my opinion has changed. Stop signs are given barely a cursory glance left and right before we accelerate through the intersections. I want to ask her why she is driving this way, but I hold my tongue. Something about taking a free ride means you do not have the right to question the route. Her driving makes me wonder if this is how she releases her aggression. The pent-up anger and pain that are results of years of a marriage she is not truly happy in; years of watching her own beauty fade, watching this happen on her husband's face, in the way he kisses and caresses her. Watching her kids grow further apart from her, finding their own interests and needs as they go.

"Vern used to make a chili for the potluck. You know,

the church potluck. To raise money. He called it a *six-alarmer*."

"I remember that," I say, although I do not. "I couldn't eat more than a little bite."

"That's what they all said." Tricia laughs heartily. "My husband always thought he was tougher than any pepper. But old Vern's chili taught him a lesson."

"I'm sure they don't serve that kind of thing where he is now," I say, perhaps too bitterly.

Tricia looks over with a pitying glance. "He's on a special diet, Elizabeth."

Keeping my face stoic, inwardly I roll my eyes, resisting the urge to tell her that once you have reached that point, where they put you on a special diet, your life is over. That point when you cannot eat solid foods, or go to the bathroom without somebody helping you and then watching you.

And not somebody kind, who cares about you, but more likely some kid barely out of high school, rushing through his duties so that he can make it home to smoke pot. Some kid who makes it clear you are nothing more than a burden. But, that is what you have become.

Ours were simpler times – we graduated, we had photos taken, we had a class party – which is not to say that we never got into any trouble, but it is to say that we did not have the confusion that kids have nowadays. It was enough for us to shed the responsibility of high school, to look forward to what was coming.

Charlie planned to move to Detroit so that he could take a job working in the automobile industry. Danny and Jamie intended to do the same, but they were moving to a city an hour's drive north of Detroit, called Flint. Exactly what their jobs would entail, I did not know, nor did I care.

Ever since our frolicking good time at the abandoned pit, I had found it difficult to get time alone with Danny. Jamie and her recovery preoccupied him and after that, preparing for their wedding and their move to Flint.

At our graduation party, in the school gym, I watched him from afar. Seeing him from a distance was both warming and chilling, watching him laugh and smile, imagining that he was pretending I was not there so that he could keep up appearances. Jamie stayed glued to Danny's side throughout the party, laughing at the appropriate times, looking somehow too thin.

Charlie was in fine form, and despite his lack of intelligence, or perhaps because of it, he was remarkably well-liked by our classmates. They congratulated him on graduating, throwing in quips about how they thought he would never make it; he laughed in response. Danny watched me, just as I watched him, but I never caught him doing it.

We existed for each other during the entire soirée, but it was such a deep secret that I almost fooled myself into believing it was not so, that he was a stranger.

Nobody spiked the lemonade and punch we drank, the music played through large speakers, and we danced. Charlie held me close and I allowed him, but I peered around his arm to watch Danny's dance. Jamie kept her head resting on his chest, and they moved slowly to The Platters, The Miracles, Elvis. The melodies echoed throughout the gymnasium and floated up to the rafters where I imagined them being caught, somewhere between here and Heaven.

The graduates drifted in and out, most of them going to the back of the school for quick five-minute smokes, something which was officially unlawful but which, by tradition, the school administration allowed us as mini-adults, almost as a conciliatory prize for having lasted through their educational system. They went in varying groups, and I finally found an opportunity when Charlie and Jamie had snuck out, but Danny had remained.

Edging over to where he stood, near the punch bowls, a sad smile playing on his face, as he watched the couples dance on the hardwood floor.

If I closed my eyes, I'd hear the song playing as I approached him: 'You Send Me' by Sam Cooke. That man's voice melted the very fabric of existence, and for perhaps the first time, I felt nervous looking at Danny.

He smiled at me. "Hey, there."

We had spoken several times since our romantic encounter, but always supervised, seen, observed, held accountable.

"Hi." I wanted to touch him, but I did not dare.

"Do you want to dance?" He took my hand and I did not even answer. I just let him lead me away from the tables and to a quiet section of the dance floor. We swayed to the music for a few beats. "I've been thinking of you," he said, his lips close to my ear so that only I could hear him.

"I've been thinking of you."

"I know."

For a few more bars, we danced. It was a slow, lilting song, happy and dreamlike, and yet ever since it has held sad connotations for me. "I can't believe you're getting married," I said. I felt, rather than saw, his head nodding.

"August."

We had, of course, spoken already about this, but now I sensed we could speak freely. It was like a chess game between two wily opponents who had abruptly decided to tell each other their unedited strategies for gaining checkmate.

"You'll come?"

"Oh, Danny." I felt my feet miss a step, but we recovered as if nothing had occurred. "I don't think I can. I don't think I should."

"Why not?" He pulled his face away and looked down at me for a moment. He was not smiling. He looked concerned.

"You know why. Because I love you. Because I always will, and do you really think I can watch you marry another girl and be happy about it?"

He looked down at our feet. I knew he was pondering, and deliberating saying something, but to anyone observing, he was perhaps only worried about his dancing skills. "For Jamie," he said. "She still loves you."

"Do you?" It was too forward. It was not ladylike, my attitude and my brazenness, here in the school gymnasium. But I did not care.

"Of course I do. So so much. More than you could ever know."

"Then, why?"

But he just nodded. "It's complicated. Jamie ... she is hurting. She was always hurting. She's not okay. She needs me."

"I need you."

"And I need you."

The whole thing seemed like an intricate web of need, a maze from which there was no escape. "She won't make you happy," I told him. "We could be happy. Together."

"What about Charlie?" He pulled his face away yet again and looked into my eyes. "Are you telling me that you feel nothing for him?"

I sighed, inaudible over the music. "Well, I do. I love him, too. But it can't be compared. I love him because he's there, but I'd love you no matter where you were."

"We are going to move to Flint," he said.

Of course, I knew this; I thought often of it and looked at roadmaps and traced the highways that would take me there, letting my finger linger on the spot on the map which demarcated the city. "Will I see you?"

Now that so much had been lost, this last piece was so important. Now that I could not have him, I felt I needed the reassurance that I would still be able to see him, to prove to myself that he was okay and still smiling.

"Of course," he said. "No matter where you are, I'll come running to you, if you ever need me to."

"I will need you."

Sam Cooke's song faded away and there was a moment of static over the speakers, but we continued dancing for a few more precious seconds. They would be the last seconds we would dance together for many years.

The next song, 'In the Still of the Night' by The Five Satins, was even better to dance to. But we did not dance. We each sat on metal chairs lined against the wall. We half-faced each other. I saw him looking over my shoulder, and when I turned, I saw Jamie, Charlie, and a few others coming in through the big double doors leading outside.

"Promise you won't forget me," he said.

"Never." I did not need to clarify that I would never forget him, not that I would never promise such a thing. He knew, of course.

Jamie seemed to know exactly where we were, and she came directly over. She sat on the other side of Danny, and Charlie sat beside me so that we were four: two true lovers surrounded by satellites. I watched Danny and Jamie hold hands, and heard them exchange a few words.

The saddest thing was watching Danny surrender some integral part when he composed himself to be around Jamie, as though he was on guard, careful not to upset her in any way. I also felt bad because I largely ignored Charlie, but he never seemed to notice, or if he did, seemed not to care.

We left the party an hour later. A few of them were going on somewhere for drinks, to toast their collective futures, but I begged off. Charlie looked hurt, but he recovered quickly and laughed soon enough. They piled into their cars.

Danny and I exchanged a long glance as some of the guys started their motors. It was years before I saw him again.

Six

Charlie and I married at the end of August. We did it in a church and invited only our families. Charlie's parents sat beaming in the front pew; my mother shared a melancholy ghost of a grin. My father, drunk, looked on with bleary eyes. We wrote our own vows and probably no one remembers what we said. They were unexceptional, I do remember that. The rings slid easily onto our fingers, my future settled.

Danny was not there. Jamie was not there. I entertained the idea of him crashing through the back doors, holding his hands up, and yelling for everything to stop.

The look of bewilderment on Charlie's face, the hushed gasp as everyone in the church turned to see who was so brazen, such a victim to the whims of his heart. He would be smiling, because he knew, of course; he knew I would rip off the ring, newly placed around my finger, mutter some half-hearted apology to Charlie, and run to Danny.

My father would stumble out of his stupor long enough to be interested in something again, and my mother, worry sketched across her face, would look on as I fled my vows.

But that didn't happen. Danny was already married.

We didn't go to their wedding because I could not subject myself to it. Charlie didn't understand, and I never expected him to. I told him I was tired from making our own plans: plans to wed, plans to move, plans to buy a house and settle. Settle in more ways than just down, that was – to settle for someone whom I loved but for whom I did not feel any passion.

So they married without us, and the day passed like any other, except that even the brightest blue sky seemed to me a gray shadow.

Charlie was upset because I had caused him to miss his best friend's wedding, but he had told me, "I'm yours now. So, if you won't go, I won't go."

His dumb words made me feel guilty, but I was prepared to accept the guilt and forget it, to avoid seeing my lover claimed by another.

Their wedding was mid-month, and ours late-month. By the time we moved to Detroit, Danny and Jamie had already gone. The hollowness of life, after they departed, was almost too much to bear. I'd lost Jamie, but I had lost her many years before, and that wound had healed. But, losing Danny ripped away some essential piece of my guts.

We moved to a suburb of Detroit not far from where Charlie had found work. Two-storey brick, the house sat back from a wide residential street where kids rode their bikes and people took their dogs for walks. The windows were clean and the door was a calm, creamy color. I helped to move our things, but I did it in a haze. Some of Charlie's friends helped, too, guys from the football team. Whenever they mentioned Danny and Jamie, always the two together, I pretended to do something else, such as study the fabric of the couch we had purchased. But I listened.

Not that they said anything of great interest. Through

them, I learned that Danny was doing well at his new job and that he and Jamie had bought a house much like the one I was moving into with Charlie. They were a mirror of us. Or, perhaps, we were the mirror.

The first few weeks allowed me some distraction. The newness of Detroit, the finality of having married and bought a house, was so heavy, it afforded me something to take my mind off the lover I missed so dearly. Charlie went to work and I always had dinner waiting when he arrived home, always at the same time each evening. Sometimes he came home with smudges of oil and grease on his neck, and he always took a clean towel from the kitchen to wipe them away.

He had to pass the bathroom on his way to the kitchen to do that.

He told me about his days over supper, and I pretended his stories interested me, although they were most often about his supervisor, whom Charlie described as a dictator, or his co-worker whom everyone called Stalin. "He's a communist," Charlie told me, winking.

"Really?" I said, nibbling at my food. "What makes you say that?"

Charlie shrugged. I doubted if he even knew what a communist was. "Everyone says so. He drinks tomato juice, too."

I raised my eyebrows.

My days were monotonous and it did not take long for regret to settle in. I waited for the mail in the kitchen – I would still be doing that as an old lady – and one day, in December, I received a letter which was not a bill. I recognized the handwriting instantly. It was from him.

I tell you, I sat with that letter for an age before my heart calmed enough to open it. I half-expected some magic dust to puff out, or a genie to grant me three wishes. But it was just a single sheet of paper, the writing neat and efficient.

I have kept all his letters. I have memorized them.

Dear Liz,

My heart aches for you every day. Some nights I lie awake, next to Jamie, and I wonder where you are and what you are doing. We have made a terrible mistake. How did we let our paths separate? How could we have? Love is too precious in this world to be so careless with it, and I am afraid we will pay for our foolishness for the rest of our lives. Well – who am I kidding? The mistake was mine. I should have taken your hand years ago and I should never have let it go. I hope you are happy with Charlie, and I hope you are not happy, because I want you. Isn't that horrible? That I hope for your sadness? Know that I am a thousand times more than sad. Every day I die again because you are not next to me, except that secret part that only we know about. That part of you that knows that part of me, that makes us special. Our destinies are not written yet. I want to see you. Know that I struggled writing this, and finally dropping it in the post took all the courage I could muster up. I understand if you do not want to see me. The pain is great, but it can be solved. Can't it?

Danny

I sat for such a long time after reading through his letter. It was dense, and it tugged at something horribly close to my soul. The dangling question at the end of his letter left me feeling empty and more alone than I ever imagined was possible.

I wanted to go to him that instant. To leave my house, my husband, and my drab little life, unfolding before my eyes. To catch a bus or hitchhike. I had stared at the road atlas enough times to know the route. But I did not go.

What a pitiful feeling: to want to do something so badly but to lack the courage. I felt the way a young man must feel when he is pushed through the corridors of life by men bigger and stronger than he is. Like a piece of dust, blown hither and yon, swept up by years and work and life at large.

I called my sister, Rosalinda. I had not spoken to her since my wedding when she sat in the front row next to my parents and stared stolidly at the proceedings. She was a bachelorette, and really the only reason I sought her advice was because I did not have anybody else.

She lived alone in an apartment in Toledo, Ohio, and she worked in a bottle factory. I knew her life was hard. But I knew her from such a distance that it was difficult to claim her as having my blood. I remembered snippets of conversations, which I only began to understand once I was a junior in high school. Talk about her not liking men, for example.

Things like that would not be acceptable for a few more years, and my father was unappreciative of independent thinking on matters such as sexual orientation. For my part, I had never asked her, but I did come to accept that she wouldn't make me an aunt anytime soon.

The phone rang three times that afternoon before she picked up, her voice thick. "Hi, Rosalina," I said. "It's me. Liz."

I heard her sigh. I didn't know what to make of that long breath, so I waited for her to speak.

"So how's married life?" she said at last.

"It's a good life," I said, telling the truth. Because it was a good life. I knew I had no room to complain. "But I need your advice."

"*My* advice?" She laughed. "You must be desperate. The only things you ever took from me were my old dresses."

I remembered the hand-me-down clothes, saved for ten years by our mother because of the gap in our ages. "I hope your advice is more attractive than they were," I said, trying to sound smug in a friendly way, probably failing. "It's about marriage, actually."

She laughed again. "I'm probably not the right person to ask about marriage."

"Why do you say so?"

"Haven't you noticed?"

Was Rosalina about to broach the unmentionable subject that had haunted the corners and crevices of our relationship for such a very long time? We had never spoken of it. I waited for her to go on, but she said nothing more. So I prodded, "Noticed what?"

She sighed again. I imagined her rolling her eyes, on her end. "Marriage isn't for me," she said. "I'll never marry. I'm satisfied with that."

"Don't you like men?" I plunged forward with the question.

And her response, given in matter-of-fact tones, was, "Not particularly."

I let that sit between us for a moment before pressing on. We were getting into a new territory. This was a conversation I could not have imagined having with anybody a few bare months ago, but now I felt very adult; this was the kind of thing adults spoke about in hushed tones so that others could not hear them.

"Why not?"

She laughed yet again. I could not remember her ever being in such good humor. "I like women. The way they smell, the way they talk, the way they look and the way they let you get close to them without hurting you."

"You have ..." I paused before saying, my tone softer, " ... you have, like, a girlfriend?"

"Sure," she said.

"Who?"

"Her name is Wendy. It's not important. I don't think you'll meet her."

"Why not?" I said, offended. "You've met Charlie."

"Yes, but I've never met Danny."

Now I could not think of anything to say. How did she know about Danny? And if Rosalinda, who lived in another state and with whom I shared so little over the years, knew, then who else must know about my secret passion for him?

"Don't be surprised," she said. "I've been keeping an eye on you for the past few years."

"How?"

"It isn't important."

Despite wanting to know how she knew so much about me, even more than that, guilt overwhelmed me. Here, I had given so little thought to Rosalinda and her own problems, and yet she had kept an active interest in my life and the direction I was headed.

"That's what I called you about," I admitted. "About Danny."

"You still love him." This, as if she had been expecting it for a long time.

"More than anything or anyone on this planet." It felt good to say it, to finally confess to somebody. And it was terrifying.

"So what's the problem, then?"

It felt as if she were playing Devil's Advocate, trying to provoke me to give what she thought was the correct answer.

"The problem is that I'm married."

Rosalinda hummed a short note: *hmm*. That sound signified that my answer had not been sufficient; partial credit, at best. But I didn't know anything better to say. As far as I could tell, my situation was intractable. I had made my choice, and it was not a particularly bad one, in terms of social standing, financial comfort, the possibility for progress. But my heart knew better. And so did my sister.

"What do you suggest I do? I've only been married for a few months. I can't leave Charlie. That's impossible."

"Is it?"

"Yes, it is. Besides, it would ruin Danny's marriage, too. So I would ruin two marriages, just because I love somebody else. You can't do that. I can't do that. It's unfair."

"Let me tell you something."

Her tone indicated she would no longer try to tug me along, that she was prepared to lay her cards on the table so that I could read her hand.

"True love is such a rare thing. You may never find it. Maybe one person in a million does. That's what I believe, anyway. And that one person who finds it is either the luckiest or the unluckiest son of a bitch on the planet."

She cursed like a mill worker with his finger caught in the machinery when she wanted. She could talk like a man – harder than any man I had ever known.

"Unlucky? How?"

"The way you are unlucky. The way the world stops you from expressing your love. Do you understand what I'm telling you?"

"Yes," I said, although I was half-lying.

"The point is, if you really love somebody, and I mean it is the real thing, not some puppy dog love, not just wanting to take somebody to bed, not just wanting to feel comfortable and safe with someone ... if you really love someone, then you should take all the risks in the world to be with that person. To make that person's heart beat with yours. No matter the price."

"No matter the price," I echoed.

"Yes, goddamn it, that's right. Look at me."

"What about you?"

"What do you think people say about a woman who loves women? Do you think they say it's okay? That she should follow her heart and love her?"

I had given homosexuality precious little thought. Even then, at that moment, I did not fully understand that my sister was a lesbian. She was, in my mind anyway, simply less sexually magnetized.

"They say it isn't okay."

"Of course they say it isn't okay. They say that about boys who love boys and girls who love girls. They say that about women who love married men and want to leave their husbands. People say bad things about every kind of people in the world. So you just say to hell with them, and you do your own thing. Because your happiness is what counts. Not Charlie's and not Jamie's. They will hate you. That is part of the price you pay for love. But if you are sure, and I think you are sure, then you pay that price. You pay any price."

"So you think I should leave Charlie."

"I'm not telling you what to do." Her voice softened, indicating that our discussion was drawing to a close. "I'm not the best person to ask, as I said. I'll never be married. But I do know, that if I found that one soul in the world I loved more dearly than anything else, I'd give anything for that love. I promise you that, sister."

I nodded for a few moments, then I thanked her and we broke the connection.

She'd made me feel better about Danny, but just as powerless as before. I still wanted to run to him and I still knew it was impossible. Ultimately, my fear won out.

My sister was right, but in my universe, it didn't matter. There was right for me, and there was right for the world. I was too little focused on me, too worried about the world. Oh, the agony of the decision was too great. I had loved him since the first second, and I would always love him. The truth was that I was terrified, and back then, scared, I froze, incapable of making a movement.

But I could still write the truth. I picked up a pen and scribbled:

Danny,

I love you more now than ever before. Your absence is a daily wound for which there is no cure. No cure except you.

I need some time. I need to develop a plan so that I can get to you and so that we can be together forever, the way it was always meant to be. Please be patient. Until then, I will continue to think of you every day, dream of you every night. I will not pray to God without asking for your happiness and your health. You asked in your correspondence if we can fix this problem. No problemo. We can. And we will. I promise.

Liz

I posted the letter the following day, while Charlie was working. I spent a few days imagining its transit, its arrival in their postbox, Charlie reading it with shaky fingers, unsteady hands, a quickening pulse. I waited for a response but did not receive one for some time. But I knew that everything would be okay.

Seven

We stop at an elementary school. The building is busy with cars pulling to the curb, collecting children, and zooming off to whatever activities the families have diligently planned. Tricia Longwell pulls up to the curb and looks at me apologetically. "We need to pick up the kids. Then I'll drop you right off."

"That's great," I say. I love being around small children. They are the only blameless souls in the world, and every time I interact with one, I feel a breath or two younger than before. Tricia's are beautiful, a boy and girl, about three years apart in age, the girl older. They are blonde and smiling when they slide into the backseat.

"Say hi to Ms. Beamer," Tricia says.

My maiden name is Beamer and I have used it for several years, even if my mail is addressed to Elizabeth Toll. I really don't even know who Elizabeth Toll is. The kids say hello and I turn with some difficulty and salute them with the biggest smile I can manage, considering the pain in my hip. They give me a moment's attention before turning back to their mother and asking if they can play on the computer later. I turn my attention back to the front, with a sigh.

I did not go to see Danny when I wanted to. To tell the truth, I was afraid ... afraid of meeting Jamie's cold stare at the front door. I didn't know if she knew about Danny and me, and perhaps simply because I lived with the thought of him, my love for him, every moment of every day, I assumed it was a universally understood thing.

Perhaps it never occurred to me that I could go to Flint, and even if I met with Jamie at the door, I could simply pretend I was visiting as a friend. A regretful friend, which in truth I was, at least to some degree.

So the months slipped by and turned into years. Danny's letters were infrequent and all of them hit the same notes as his first letter, in which he proclaimed his undying love for me. They were all approximately a page long; some of them were written with penmanship which made me think he had been drinking or even crying. As time went on, his letters were stained with darker notes. He talked about Jamie sometimes. How she cried, how he never knew the reason why.

Too many were the long nights I spent, wondering why he didn't come to me. His letters betrayed his feelings in the most transparent way. Also betrayed by his written words was the responsibility he felt for Jamie and the fear he felt sometimes when he was around her. He should have abandoned all of that. He should have listened to his own hungry heart, which, if it were like mine, growled with desire for its counterpart in the wide universe.

Before too many years, I received the news that Jamie was pregnant. One of Charlie's old football friends from high school rang us, and he could not contain the news. I no longer remember the caller's name, but I attribute that to old age.

"Is Charlie there?" he asked; I remember his breathless voice perfectly, and can even picture his face. But there, my memory runs dry.

"He's still working." My own tone was perhaps a bit too sharp. I had never had good telephone manners. "Can I take a message?"

"Oh yeah!" the caller said. "Danny and Jamie are expecting a kid!"

And, just like that, with those simple, plastic words, my heart broke again.

I could not speak for a few moments because the news was just too large to process. A year or so later, I would see Kennedy shot, my reaction similar. A few moments of sheer awe and fear, followed by a period during which I could move and speak and function as normal but during which I felt, at best, half-alive. Finally, I found a word, "What?"

"Yep," the voice on the phone said. "I just heard myself. Jamie is preggy. Can you believe it?" The caller took on a suddenly suspicious tone. "Hey, this *is* Liz I'm talking to, ain't it?"

"Yes, I'm Liz." It was the first time I had heard a term like preggy. I never wanted to hear it again, and at the same time, I hoped that maybe I had misunderstood, and the term referred to some disease unknown to me. Somehow, I formulated a coherent conversation in my state of shock. "How far along is she?"

"A couple of months," the man said. "I was over there a week ago, and I couldn't tell nothing. She's still a skinny one."

"Good for her." I groped for more to say, but nothing came to me.

"Well, give Charlie the good news, will ya?" he said. Promising him I would, we broke the connection. I slumped at the kitchen table for a few minutes, imagining what their baby would look like, how it would smile, what its name might be. I tried to push those thoughts into some darker recess of my mind, because I did not want to dwell on them anymore and because I wanted to prepare myself to seem happy when I told Charlie the news.

He was late home that night, and I knew immediately he had stopped off for a drink at the tavern on his way after work. His breath carried with it the fruity odor of alcohol, and his eyes were just slightly watery.

He was not yet an alcoholic – that would come years later – but that was the day I realized he was too much like my father for me to ever be completely comfortable with him. Even further buried in my mind was the voice which told me that was the reason I married him.

A misguided part of me found him sexually attractive when he was buzzed or even drunk. I liked the smell of him, I liked the way he stumbled when he walked around the kitchen table; I liked the way he smiled more. Maybe I liked it because I could assign a reason for his lack of intelligence.

He kissed me at the door and I breathed him in. I led him to the kitchen, where I already had dinner made, and I fixed him a plate with potatoes, green beans, and ham. He loved ham, and he beamed when I served it.

"You must love me extra, today."

"I love you every day," I told him, even though each time I said this to him, it felt like a more brazen lie. "I have news."

"Oh?" he said, raising his eyebrows, already chomping on the meat dangling from his fork.

"Jamie is pregnant. They're going to have a baby."

He paused his chewing for a moment, and then grinned around a mouthful of ham. "That's great!" he said, his enunciation poor because of his overfull mouth. "That's just really great!"

I sat across from him and picked at my own food. I never ate much, and today I felt like eating even less, but I wanted to appear happy, and happy people are not afraid to eat. So I ate and listened to the sounds of Charlie chomping on his own food.

Between bites, I wondered about our own plans to have children. We had discussed it before, the conversation always couched in terms such as "When we're ready," and "Soon."

Charlie finished quickly and headed for the telephone after he took a beer from the refrigerator. I had not considered that he would call Danny to congratulate him. I hadn't seen them talk, not even on the phone, since we'd moved to Detroit.

A sudden nervous fear struck me. "What are you doing?"

"I need to call Danny," Charlie said, already holding the receiver in his hand. "You know, it's been forever since I've talked to him. How about you?"

The question was stupid in its innocence. "I haven't spoken to him."

"What about Jamie?"

I just shook my head.

He dialed the number, his finger scraping over the rotary wheel, somehow finding the correct digits. He looked at me as he held the receiver to his ear and he winked.

"It's ringing." His eyes popped open after a few more

moments. "Jamie?" I watched him nod his head for a moment. "This is Charlie. How are you? I just heard the news! Congratulations!"

He nodded his head vigorously for another couple of moments, and I felt like screaming at him that she could not see him doing that through the phone lines. He laughed and he waved me over. I shook my head. I did not want to talk to anybody.

Charlie let his hand drop and he said, "Hey, lemme talk to Danny. How's the old boy doing?"

This was the moment I feared most. I would be able to hear his voice, tiny and far away, from my spot at the table, interrupted by Charlie's guffaws and the sounds of him occasionally sipping from his beer can, which he held close to his belly. Charlie waited for a moment, looking over at me with what I thought was contentment and even love, and then another, even bigger smile broke open on his face. "Congratulations, old boy!" he yelled into the receiver.

And then I heard it, as though it was a million miles away; Danny's voice sounded so weak and inconsequential. I wondered if he was thinking of me, if he imagined exactly where I was in the house as he spoke with my husband. That maybe my ear was up to the receiver, too, so that I could hear their conversation, and if so, why wasn't I saying anything? Charlie waved me over again, and this time I stood automatically and walked over to the phone. "Tell Danny congratulations," he whispered, covering the mouthpiece with one meaty hand. "Danny, here's Liz," he said as he thrust the receiver at me.

And, just like that, I had him in my hand. I put the phone up to my ear and I heard his steady breathing. I tried once to speak, but nothing came out. The one person in the world with whom it was easiest for me to speak; yet I could find nothing to say. I had to start simple.

At last, I found the courage and the strength, and I said his name. "Danny?"

"It's me, Liz." I didn't hear a smile in his voice. I imagined that Jamie was nearby, on his end, and of course, Charlie was still standing near me. I suddenly hated him, not with any particular passion, but in the way we hate things which stand in the way of our dreams. For a moment, I just wanted him to disappear.

"How are you?" I knew he would detect the flutter in my voice. I knew he heard me tremble, and I knew that he understood exactly what it meant.

"I'm doing well," he said, evenly. "How are you?"

"Me, too." This was not right. This was not how our first conversation in all these months was supposed to go. I wanted to be in his arms, safe and tight and warm. "Congratulations," I managed to say.

"Thanks. It's all kind of a shock. To think I'm going to be a father." He chuckled, but to me, his laughter did not sound authentic. "We've missed you," he added.

I heard the truth in his words; he meant, "I've missed you." He had said it in a way which would fly under Jamie's radar, including her, by using 'we,' and using 'you' in the plural sense, as in "We have missed you both." But we both knew the truth.

"We feel the same way. It's been too long."

"Why don't you come and visit us?"

"Yes," I said straight away. "I mean," I added, recovering, "we'll find a good day to come."

"Here's Jamie," he said. I imagined only I detected the note of sadness that stained his voice when he said her name. "We'll talk more."

And with that, he was gone. There were a few moments while he transferred the phone, and then I heard a different cadence in the breathing coming from the other end of the telephone.

"Hello?" I said into the mouthpiece.

"Hi, Liz. How are you?"

"Congratulations, Jamie. I'm happy for you."

"Thank you." Her words clipped, her tone melancholic, I thought there were many things we didn't say to each other which impeded our discussion.

Things about Danny, about weddings, about how friends grow cold and apart and how neither of them knows how to fix the relationship. But I have learned that you cannot open a discussion with those things.

Women especially cannot do it. They are delicate and they must be danced around. I would have occasion, in the following months, to wish that I had been more forthcoming with her.

"Are you going to visit us?"

Here, when she used the word *us*, she certainly meant herself and Danny, together. I felt all the rage that I had so carefully bottled bubbling toward the surface, but I pushed it back down to the dark place where I usually kept it hiding.

"Definitely," I said. "In the next couple weeks, we're coming up. I can't wait to see you." I tried to sound as chipper as possible. I probably failed.

"We're looking forward to it," she said.

We did not discuss much else. It was a long-distance call, and I cited our bill as a convenient reason to break off the conversation. We would visit during the coming weekend. Charlie would drive, and I would sit shotgun, my heart beating faster each mile closer to Flint.

I was literally sick the morning we were supposed to leave for Flint. I vomited three times, and by my last trip to the toilet, all I could do was wretch pathetic dry heaves that hurt my diaphragm. Charlie did not have a clue. His miserable face, as he waited for me to feel better, told me just how clueless he was. I felt bad for him.

"Maybe we should cancel," he said. "We can always go next weekend."

"No." If we did that, I would simply be sick the next weekend, as well. I would be sick until it was done.

"Are you sure?"

I nodded, and so we left for Flint. We took the expressway, and on the way, I had the chance to see the vitality that was Detroit, growing. The houses were big and inviting. The lawns were well manicured. Nobody could have anticipated the desolation that place would see in the coming years.

It was snowing lightly and the flakes rushed past us as we joined the interstate. The pale gray of the concrete and the gray world zoomed by outside the truck. Charlie and I spoke little. He probably supposed that I was too sick to devote myself to conversation, and I was, but of course, it was so much more than that.

It only took us about an hour to reach Flint. It was another thriving city which would, in coming years, become a kind of hell on earth. When people opened their taps, brown water came out. But that would come later. For now it would be a personal hell for me, a place which was full of more devious problems than just blight and crime and sin and danger. It held connotations that were too close to the bone.

We spent a half hour searching for the house. This was

well before the days of technology that could give you precise directions to your destination. All we had was a road map that did not give the necessary detail to accurately guide us to their home. Charlie, a breathing stereotype, refused to ask for directions, and so we kind of stumbled across Danny's street, and from there we counted down to his address.

Their house was similar to ours, and we parked on the street. "Finally," Charlie said as though assigning blame for our inability to find the place to some unknown factor. "Are you ready?"

"Of course," I said, smiling.

Charlie had already unbuckled his seatbelt and opened his door. I was still buckled in. He paused, as though he had only just noticed me. "Are you coming?"

I took a few deep breaths. "I just feel so bad about skipping their wedding."

"It's history," Charlie said, still hanging out through his half-open door.

A cold wind blew in on me. "I know, but it still feels like it was yesterday. And it was my fault. It wasn't hers."

"She forgives you," Charlie said in his stupid, ignorant way.

He knew nothing. He knew nothing about why I was still sitting in the truck, and even if what I was saying was the truth, he was still too ignorant of the ways of women to know that she would never forgive so easily.

And what if she knew the whole truth? My inner mind spoke up, as it often did at the least opportune moments. "I don't know if I can go in."

"We came all the way here," Charlie said. "You're going."

"I can't," I whined. I hated to whine and I hated to

complain. But I was doing just that.

"Get your ass out of the truck," Charlie said.

His voice had changed. It had taken on a menacing note that I had not heard before, not even when he was at his drunkest. I was not afraid, but I was reminded again that I could never love him.

My understanding of what defined love had changed. No longer did Charlie's everyman antics serve. Love was more than comfort and pleasure now. Love was a skewering, a crucifixion, a burst into the warm sunlight.

There were times I honestly wondered if I felt love even for Danny, if I was capable of feeling that for anybody except myself. And, ultimately, that thing I called love for myself was really only fear for myself. Fear of being judged, mostly. And if that is not a sad story, I don't know what is.

I unbuckled my seatbelt and stepped out of the truck. The cold wind snapped against my face, froze the ghosts of the tears threatening to flow. I walked around the truck and with my husband, approached the big house where Danny and Jamie lived.

The front door opened as we drew near. I saw Danny first, smiling broadly, displaying his even teeth and looking directly at me, his eyes squinting in the cold. I grinned despite myself.

"Hello!" Charlie bellowed. I drew an inch away from him.

"Hi, you two," Danny said, opening his arms in a welcoming gesture.

I imagined myself running into them. But Jamie snuggled closer against him, and as a kind of automatic reaction, he put his arm around her shoulders.

Charlie and I climbed the front steps and I hugged

Jamie as Danny and Charlie shook hands. In Jamie's arms, all I could imagine were Danny's arms. Everybody was smiling. They were asking us how the drive had been, Charlie telling them that I had been feeling ill that morning, but the drive was pleasant and quick. Did we have any trouble finding the place? No, no trouble at all.

It was a messier house than ours. Magazines and newspapers littered the kitchen table, and dirty dishes waited in the sink. I wondered if those things could be attributed to pregnancy. We proceeded through the kitchen and to the living room, where we sat on the sofa. Jamie started coffee brewing and the smell was bitter and strong as it filled the house.

"So, congratulations," Charlie said, pulling a bottle of wine from a bag for them.

"Thanks," Danny said, perfunctorily taking the bottle and placing it on the coffee table.

Charlie watched the bottle and I hated him again. I knew that he wanted to drink from it already.

"How have you two been?" Charlie asked.

Jamie joined us, gave each of us a cup of steaming coffee. Mine had cream and sugar; Charlie's was black. I had no idea how she knew that was how he took his coffee, and I did not care.

"We've been great," Charlie said. "I've been working. Same as Danny."

"It's a shame you haven't visited before," Jamie said brightly.

As soon as she had uttered the sentence, she became silent and withdrawn again. She seemed like a shadow, and although she appeared happy, I knew her too well. I had known her since sixth grade, and I had been privy to so many of her private thoughts, that I could read her as well as anybody. Perhaps better than she could read herself. She was a woman drowning. I could not understand it.

"We're sorry about that," Charlie said. "But that's going to change."

"Now that we know how to find the place," I added, trying for a joke. Charlie shot me a sharp glance.

We made small talk. We drank our coffees, and Jamie refilled our cups. I spent the whole visit hoping for a chance to get Danny alone. I did not even need to talk to him by myself. I just needed to see him look at me the way he did before, with his eyes full of innocent love and my heart full of adoring, unashamed need for him. He was an expert at hiding his love while our spouses were in the room with us. As was I.

But first, I was alone with Jamie. The boys went to the garage, where Danny was working on his '57 Mercury. As an everyday vehicle, they had changed over to a Ford Galaxie, parked in the driveway. Their absence created a void of noise and life in the room. The house seemed a few degrees colder and a few shades darker without the men.

"So," Jamie said, sipping at her coffee, sliding a cigarette out of a fresh pack. "Want to smoke?"

"No, thanks." I had never smoked.

She lit up and blew toward the ceiling. It smelled awful.

"It's been so long," she said. "You remember how things were with us."

It was a statement, not a question. I sat on the sofa and waited for her to continue. She took another drag and exhaled from the corner of her mouth. It was a ritual that seemed unwomanly to me at the time.

"I'm in a bad way," she finally confessed.

"What do you mean?"

She shook her head. "I'm just not happy. Not the way I thought I would be. You remember, how we always thought we would end up happy and living near each other."

Again, it was not a question.

"I thought getting pregnant would make me feel ... make me feel something. But I don't."

"Why not?" It struck me a moment later as a ridiculous question.

"I don't know," she said. "I just don't feel anything. And sometimes it scares me. And other times, it feels like it's right. I can't explain it."

"Do you talk to Danny?"

"Of course." She took another hit from her cigarette. "But he doesn't understand. Nobody does. Not even you."

And it was true. I knew her as well as anybody, but I could not fathom having Danny and not being in a perpetual state of bliss. If he had not been in the world, then perhaps I could have better understood and better helped her, but the way things were, it was impossible, and the consequences would be terrible.

The boys came back from the garage shaking off the cold. Jamie and I held our stare for a moment longer, and I saw a desperation in her eyes that I would never forget. I felt a tremendous pity for her, even if she had the man I loved. I knew she was strong, but I knew that she was not strong enough for whatever inner turmoil she was facing.

She looked at me, the truth buried deep in her eyes: she knew I still loved Danny. And, even deeper than that truth: she knew that Danny still loved me. How, then, could she truly love either of us?

Danny and Charlie entered the living room and Danny

said, "How about you, Liz? Do you want to see the car?"

"Yes," I answered, forgetting Jamie and her problems instantly.

Aware of her watching us as I raised myself from the sofa, I followed Danny out of the living room. Charlie sat beside Jamie and said something; I couldn't hear what it was, nor did I especially care.

We went through the kitchen, my heart pounding already. The refrigerator started humming just as I passed it, and it gave me a start, as though it was accusing us of something. Danny opened the door leading to the garage and motioned me through.

In the dimly lit garage, I watched my breath waft against the bare bulb hanging from the ceiling. Tools and dirty rags lined the walls; a pile of newspapers lay in the corner. In the middle sat his Mercury, silent and beautiful. Beneath the exhaust pipe lay an assortment of metal parts, strewn haphazardly against the floor.

"There she is," Danny said from behind me.

"I've missed it." I walked once around it, reminding myself that I did not even like cars – except for this car. Danny followed me, but a few paces behind, so that there was always some big piece of automobile between us. I counted his steps and I listened to his breaths. I saw his reflection in the windshield. I sat on the hood and he sat beside me. I did not, I could not look at him for a few moments. The last time we were on this hood together, we were naked and free. Finding the fortitude to glance at him, he was staring at me intently and grinning.

"Just like I remember it," I said.

He slowly ran his hand along the contours of the metal. His hand was smooth and clean, even if it worked every day with machines and oil.

"I'm just doing a few things to it. I'm hoping that it will be ready to go, soon."

"How soon?" I said.

"As soon as possible."

His hand caressed the hood, now up, now down. I heard his flesh sliding against the metal. It made my lips dry.

"God, I've missed you so much," I whispered.

"I know," he said. Now up – his hand paused near my thigh. "If it's half as much as I've missed you, it's been hell."

Shaking my head and staring down at his knuckles, I wanted to kiss each one of them, like solid little pieces of candy I could never eat. I moved just a hair closer to him in the cold garage. My butt was getting numb but I did not mind. The smell of oil was strong on the air.

"I think about you so much."

As I turned to see what effect my words had had on him, his lips met mine halfway. He was so warm; like a bonfire on a chilly night, like curling up in the sheets on a cold morning and refusing to get out of bed. Caught by surprise, I moved my lips to say something, but I did not know what. To protest? Surely not. Surely never.

I kissed him back.

His lips were softer even than I remembered them being. I grabbed the back of his head and pulled his face into mine, to make the connection between us as tight as possible. We stayed locked like that for a few delicious, terrifying moments, not caring if anybody came through the door and saw us. I half-expected the Mercury's engine to rev up below us, our touch was so hot.

He pulled away from me, still smiling. He kept his eyes closed for a moment before opening them, and his gaze met mine.

"Seems like every time we do this, it's on this car."

I laughed. "Never sell it."

"What do you think our better halves are doing?"

"Who cares?"

I kissed his warm neck beneath the jaw. The skin there, rough with stubble, scratched against my lips. I reveled in the sensation of it. He smelled like soap. His hair smelled sweet and somehow damp. He petted my hair, ran it gently through his fingers. He rubbed me all down my spine, left his palm against my lower back. I kissed my way to his Adam's apple, up his chin, on his lips, on the tip of his cold nose.

"It's just Jamie." He put his hands on my shoulders and pushed me away. "I can't do this to her."

I closed my eyes, sad our moment of fantasy had to end so soon. But I knew that he was right.

"I know. She's ... she's in a bad way."

"You noticed that?"

"She told me. She needs you to take care of her."

"It's you I want to take care of."

The fiery first seconds of touch over, we leaned against the car, some inches away from each other's flames. I wanted to run my fingernails up his leg, search out the throbbing piston of his penis, encircle it with my hand, tug, my breath hot in his ear, bite his earlobe, jerk him off until he spewed semen all over his trousers and the hood of his car.

"I can't live like this," I said. "Just seeing you, like this. Unable to touch you. Unable to be with you. It's like my heart is being ripped away from me."

"Me, too," he said. "Some dreams are impossible. Like being a millionaire. Or becoming king. But my dream is you. And you are right here. It's not impossible. But it is."

We let those words hang in the stale air of the garage for a few moments.

"I'll leave him," I offered. "We can go away. The world is a big place."

He nodded for a long time, staring into some distance space.

"Don't think I haven't thought about it. I thought of going to another state. Even another country." His smile slowly dimmed until he spoke in a monotone voice, almost as if reciting a poem, or as though he was sleepwalking. "I thought of Mexico. Ha. Like a couple of criminals."

"We could rob banks all the way there. Nobody would catch us. We would take this car." I patted the hood beneath us.

"We would rob from the rich and give to the poor along the way."

"And keep a big bag of cash for ourselves, to buy a house on the beach."

"We would sneak across the border. Swim across the river. We would have to eat rice and beans for a long time."

"We would lie on the beach and get so dark that nobody would recognize us anymore."

"And we would have a little dog named Pogo."

We sat for a few moments in silence, each of us dreaming our dreams. It amazed me what beautiful thoughts could emerge from such ugly places and desperate situations. He kissed me once more, just a peck, on the forehead. I knew it was the last time we would touch that way, and so I let the feeling of his lips linger on my skin. It stayed well after he had pulled his lips away and slid off the hood.

"They are going to wonder about us," he said, making for the door. "We better get back."

"Yeah," I agreed and jumped down off the car. "No problemo." How quickly my bliss turned to wretchedness! Danny cast me a sad, longing look before opening the door and herding me inside.

The kitchen was warm in and the smell of coffee hit me first. Charlie's and Jamie's voices came from the next room, filling me with bitterness, both because they existed and were so close, and because the tone of the voices made it clear we had been in no immediate danger of being interrupted.

But, now that we had entered the house, we could never go back, we could certainly not steal another kiss. I walked slowly in front of Danny toward our realities, and suddenly, silently, he cupped my butt with his hand and squeezed. He kept it there, groping, for a few sumptuous seconds.

My entire body felt shocked and gushed warmth, suddenly and amazingly hot, in a way I had never been hot before. I wanted to turn around and tackle him to the linoleum floor, rip off his clothes with my teeth, all while he grinned up at the ceiling, tickled by my tongue in new places.

I let out a staggering breath which had caught in my throat, accompanied by an almost inaudible yelp. But we kept moving toward the living room. By the time we were visible to our spouses, he was a respectful few feet away from me, still grinning, but there was mischief beneath that smile. I hoped the lighting was too poor for anybody to see the ardor which surely colored my cheeks.

I truly think that day was the last time Danny was

really happy. I felt his happiness emanating from him like a sickness. He hid his sadness from everyone but me; he hid his joy from everyone but me. I knew his heart because it belonged to me as much as my own did.

We left a few minutes later and the ride home was a quiet one. The sound of the tires eating up the highway almost lulled me to sleep, but my heart was still too much on fire for me to rest.

Charlie made small talk. He mentioned Danny's car and I felt like screaming. He talked of Jamie, too: how she seemed healthy, and happy to be bringing a child into the world. That time, I felt like laughing. Are you really so blind? I wanted to ask him. She's a mess.

At home, I put my things on the sofa and wrapped my arms around Charlie. He felt so different from Danny! His smell was different; Danny smelled sweet, and Charlie just smelled like the soap he showered with, which was not in itself unpleasant, but certainly nothing special. His body was different from Danny's too. Charlie was taller, more muscular. His shoulders were harder and broader than Danny's, and when I pressed myself against his abdomen, it was harder than Danny's, more like a coiled spring.

"I want a baby, too," I said to him.

He laughed. I found his laugh distasteful. "Really?" he said.

"Come on."

He put his arms around me and kissed my lips. His kiss was different from Danny's.

"Right now?"

"Right now," I answered, unbuckling his belt, pulling his pants down with his underwear in a sweep. His penis had already sprung into action, itself a coiled spring. I grabbed him and squeezed gently.

"Ah," he said, becoming even harder in my hand.

"You like that, don't you?" I said.

He breathed hard, above me, looking over the top of my head. I worked his dick until it was as hard as a cobra, preparing to strike. He pulled me close by the shoulders and it poked and prodded my abdomen through my dress.

I took a couple of deep breaths and then shed my clothes as quickly as possible. Charlie stood back a few steps, as if afraid I might hit him in my undressing. He looked ridiculous, standing there with his erection still saluting me, eager.

"You're pretty," he said after I was completely naked.

I laughed. I let a few short barks, and then found myself in hysterics. I tried to choke them back, but I simply could not do it. They bubbled out of me in a mixture of pure amusement and self-hatred. I punctuated my cackles with the words, "Come on. Let's do it."

He did not seem perturbed by my laughing; if anything, his penis reached higher and harder upwards than it had before.

"Okay," he obeyed, taking me in his arms. I could no longer track where his cock was. He lifted, turned and threw me to the couch, and he stretched out above me before I had the time to exhale. "I love you," he said.

"Let's do it."

I led him inside me. It was not our first time, of course. Other times had been clinical, efficient. Most weekdays, he was too tired to engage me much after we turned out the lights. Weekends were another story, but even then we went through the motions rather than making love. This time, he slid into me, rough, and pounded away immediately. The pleasure caught up a moment later, and

I scratched at his broad back.

"Yes, yes, like that," I said. I trapped him with my legs, making us a bouncing, jouncing machine.

The couch protested but nobody listened. It was growing dark, and it was snowing harder outside, making it more difficult to read his face. I imagined pleasure sketched there, and perhaps dumb confusion, wonderment at his own luck: the face of a man who has just found twenty dollars lying on the street and does not know where to spend his unexpected fortune.

He pulled out of me and I thought he was done. But I knew it could not be, not so quickly.

"Get up," he said.

"Huh?"

Now he laughed. After a moment, I joined in his laughter.

"I said, 'get up'." I stood from the sofa and he walked behind me, his dick trailing against my side as he went. He stood behind me, placed his hands on my shoulders, and said, "Let's try something new."

And he bent me over. I felt filthy and sexy at the same time. I wondered if he was going to ram himself up my ass. The thought petrified me and excited me. I wondered if I would be able to walk straight for a few days following.

I concentrated on his movements, but I was blind to what he was doing behind me. I could see only his grainy shadow, falling on the couch. Then I felt his penis, dragging against my buttocks. I felt him slap my thighs with it. It was warm and I felt the contours of it as he played it against my flesh. I never knew I was sensitive enough back there to be able to feel anything like that. Then, with one of his hands on the small of my back, he slowly jammed himself into my vagina from behind.

This was certainly a new sensation. He touched new parts of me this way, and after he started properly fucking me, I began moaning. This was the best we had ever had by miles, by light years. His thrusts picked up in intensity and he increased his rhythm. His hardened abdomen and pubic area slapped against my butt and made a wet smack each time.

I screamed, then grabbed a pillow from the sofa and buried my face in it to muffle my shriek. Both of his hands were on my hips, and he was pulling me into him, ramming back at me, reaching so deep inside me that I thought I would simply rupture.

He exploded inside me. His penis swelled to a magical size and then came his cum. He hissed as he did so; he'd never made that noise before when he had an orgasm. He stayed inside me even after he became flaccid, and I stayed in my prone position for as long as he wanted, until he pulled himself out. I stood up to my full height, and he pressed himself against my back. He grabbed my breasts and squeezed them hard, ran his hands over them, toyed with my hardened nipples. His penis, no longer bone-hard, but not floppy, either, I knew that with some minimal work, we could do it again, and soon.

But instead, I went to the bathroom to clean myself up. I made short work of it and done, I looked at myself in the mirror.

A girl I found hard to love stared back at me, satiated and hiding a very dark secret. Feelings passed like shadows over her face. One moment, her eyes were wide, scared; her lips trembled. In the next moment, she was smiling. It was then that her reflection was happy, but her soul was sad. She found it hard to look at herself for more than a few seconds at a time.

This woman was a lot like Jamie, I understood. But Jamie would take it further than I ever dreamed she could.

Eight

We arrive at Bliss. Tricia Longwell's kids only make a slight protest when their mother does not take them directly home. They are hungry and tired from their day at school. I never would have dreamt of complaining so openly when I was a child. I walked. Besides, my father would never have suffered it.

"Thanks for the lift," I say as I open the door. "I'll see you kids at church," I say to the back seat. My words are met with hasty goodbyes and an apologetic look from Tricia.

"Tell Vern I said hi, and that I hope he feels better."

So locked into this moment, being so close to seeing Danny again, I am confused for a moment. I catch myself before I ask Tricia to whom she is referring. "I will. See you."

I stand at the curb as they drive away. I feel younger than I have in so many years that I am almost scared. '*See you?*' Had that been me? Those were not my words. Those were the words of a younger person.

After the big SUV is out of sight, I turn back to the behemoth building that is the retirement home. It is made of brick and the tinted windows reflect the sunlight in a black fashion that feels ominous. The front lawn is excellently manicured; in fact, there are three young men cutting the hedges which line the front of the building like sentries.

It strikes me that all these types of places look alike. They are designed to look professional, not home-like. They are places to die: I think I can smell it from where I stand, at the street.

Moving determinedly up the walkway, I feel I am walking on air, a dangerous feeling for someone my age. I wonder if one of the landscapers would help me if my heart gave out now and I collapsed.

My reflection in the front doors as I approach gives me a start; that must be someone else, coming from within the building. That is a woman who knows exactly what she wants and exactly where she is going. I envy her for a second, before I realize she is me. That is the woman I wanted to be, my whole life. And now that I am her, it is too late to do much about it. As they say, youth is wasted on the young.

The doors whoosh open as I near them, startling me. I move through the foyer and I truly smell this place. Antiseptic. Plastic. The smell of slippers scraping against hard floors, food carts wheeled through the corridors, an out-of-tune piano rarely played, magazines with yesterday's pop news, hard pillows, boiled silverware, coffee served in little plastic cups.

The smell of age and hopelessness. The smell of people watching their loved ones waste away. Now, I am one of those people.

It only takes me a moment to conclude I hate this place. A family sits on one of the couches in the main room. The children are perhaps twelve and ten years old. I wonder what this place looks like to them. Big and incomprehensible, probably. The urge to tell them the truth devours me. To use their years – to fill each unforgiving minute with sixty seconds of distance run. It is worth the out-of-breath feeling; it is worth the pain.

A receptionist sits at a desk. She looks frazzled, pulled in nine directions at once. Her desk is cluttered with clipboards and pens, little medication cups and a case for her glasses. She must sense me watching her, and looks up.

"Can I help you?" she says, smiling.

I cannot find my voice for a moment. She misinterprets this and a flash of concern jets across her face. But I find my voice before she can apologize. "I'm here to see Danny," I tell her. "Room 302."

She looks down at some papers and holds up a finger while she consults her records. I am struck by a terrifying thought: he's dead. He waited for so long, his heart resisted all that time, and now I have finally found the courage to come here and face him, he is dead.

Sometimes the most horrible thoughts strike me as the most plausible, even if they are unlikely; this is one such moment, and my own heart skips and burns like a meteorite streaking across the pale sky. I am also flooded with anger. Why does time bring me these thoughts?

Younger, I never assumed someone had died when I wondered where they were; I assumed they were coming back. But, at this ancient age of mine, I am forced to consider that the people in my life are going, and they aren't coming back.

Not that it should have been a surprise to me. I have outlived almost everybody. Some people I have known have taken pride in that. They are the kinds of people who skip to the obituary section of the paper so that they can gloat, at least privately.

The first such shock came just a few months after our visit to Danny and Jamie's house. I had not spoken to him since then, but I had, of course, spent nearly all my waking moments dreaming of him and envying Jamie. My heart would not let me feel close to Charlie because my heart was elsewhere. Even the passion I'd shared with Charlie had slowly ebbed since that wild encounter after we visited Danny and Jamie, and could not keep me faithful to him in my heart.

The phone rang. It was spring, late afternoon, Saturday, and Charlie was outside, cutting the grass. It was a chore he seemed to enjoy, and he worked up large pools of sweat under his arms and down his back as he walked back and forth. I stared out of the window at him, contemplating how I would tell him about my symptoms. Wondering if I would use the word preggy.

We had been trying, and although I had heard that a woman always knew, I had no idea when he had impregnated me. Was it that first day after our visit? Or sometime in the following week, when he tossed me on the bed and slithered above me, tired and wrecked from his day at work but still full of enough sexual energy to ravish me?

The frequency of our sexual dalliances dropped off after that week, but we still did it regularly. More than our neighbors, I was fairly certain. And now I had the proof. I wondered how he would react, although certain the news would be met with pride and happiness. And then he would call Danny and Jamie. They would be first, in fact.

But, as things turned out, we did not need to call them. Broken from my trance, I answered the phone.

"Liz," Danny said, breathless. "Oh, Jesus Christ."

"Danny?" I said, instantly petrified. Something horrible had happened.

There is a quality in someone's voice which relates this, and it reminds me of a sick wild animal which would normally run away from humans but, because of its poor health, only lays down, tucked into itself, appearing almost docile.

"Liz," he said, his voice gravelly, as if from crying. "She's dead."

"Who's dead?"

But I already knew, in my heart.

"She killed herself. I found her this morning."

"What?"

"She was in bed. Gray. And cold." His voice trailed off and I thought he might weep. But when he spoke again, he sounded strong and somehow distant.

"I went over to her and shook her. I knew she was dead. I was scared and thought I was going to vomit. My baby was inside her."

"Oh, Danny." I did not know what to say.

Some may doubt whether I was shaken up by the news of Jamie's suicide. But truly, I was. She was a friend, and that she had what I did not have was not enough to totally ruin my love for her.

"I'm so, so sorry."

He took a long time to respond, and with each passing moment, I worried more. Finally, like old, cracked leather: "So am I."

"What can I do?" I imagined him, sitting by the telephone, slouched, defeated. My heart breaking for him. I wanted to comfort him; to caress him, to whisper that I would always love him, to kiss his frown. I wanted to wipe his tears away. But he was not crying.

"I called an ambulance. They took her to the hospital, even though she was dead. Ha," he scoffed. "I don't understand that. Why did they take her to the hospital? Why would they do that? If she was already dead?"

"I don't know."

I shook my head in unseen condolence.

"I can't understand it," he said, his voice fading.

It sounded like a bad connection, but I knew it was something else. It was difficult to understand whether he was talking about the ambulance or what Jamie had done.

"Neither do I."

In either case, that was the truth. I would never understand why she had taken her own life. She was always unhappy, and she would have been unhappy regardless of the circumstances in which she found herself. She was married to a beautiful man, having a baby by him, but it was not enough. She should have been content. More than just content, she should have been exuberant. But her unhappiness was like a big shadow cast by a cloud rolling over the sun.

"Did she ... did she ever say anything to you? I mean, like she was unhappy? Like she wanted to do something like this?"

I took a few deep breaths, considering how I wanted to answer. I would not lie. I would never lie to Danny. But at the same time, I did not want to tell the truth and, by so doing, give him a wrong impression. Because that would be the same as lying, at least in my mind. A lie is not just in the words we tell, but also in how they are perceived.

"I knew she had times when she felt bad. When we visited, she said—"

"Yes? She said what?"

"She said she didn't feel anything. She said she thought expecting a baby would make her feel something, but it didn't."

Danny sighed a long, sweet breath into the nothingness between us.

"Danny, I'm so sorry."

"Please ... I need somebody. I need you."

"I'll come."

I did not think of the logistics; I did not think of Charlie. I did not even think of Danny in a lustful way. All I thought of was his broken heart, and how I might help to mend it.

"I need to go now," he said. "I still haven't told her mother."

A small sound escaped my lips, but I could not find any words to say. At last I found them.

"I love you, Danny."

"Okay," he said weakly and then broke our connection. I stood for some time with the telephone receiver in my hand, staring into space. Already I knew that my entire life had changed. Jamie's decision would have a rippling effect and it would touch us all, from Danny all the way down to our high school teachers back home.

Charlie came in from cutting the grass some indeterminate amount of time later, sweaty. He stopped in the doorway, staring at me.

"What's wrong?"

Standing there with the telephone in my hand, I looked up at him, certain my face betrayed my emotions. In what seemed an infinitesimal eternity, I replaced the telephone in its cradle, and then I sobbed twice, hard and fast, before they faded into dryness.

"It's Jamie. She's dead."

"What?" he said, rushing over to me, wrapping his arms around me. It all seemed too dramatic, almost rehearsed. "What do you mean, she's dead?"

"She killed herself."

"Oh, Lord," he said.

"I know."

"She seemed fine when I saw her."

He smelled bad from his sweat, mixed with the shards of grass stuck to his flesh. But I found comfort there, anyway. He kissed me on the top of my head.

"I'm going to miss her so much," I said.

"I know you will," Charlie said.

Nine

We buried her. Funerals have always been difficult for me, and hers was the first I'd ever attended, with the exception of my grandfather's, when I was four years old, and which I barely remembered, even then.

She looked youthful and nearly alive in her coffin, her hands crossed over her pregnant belly. That image burned itself into my mind with a ferocity that, to this day, I can summon it with such intensity that it blisters. Her hands, as if protecting the little baby inside. The baby she killed, herself.

Danny sat motionless through the proceedings. A priest said a few words. I stared at the man I loved throughout the entire service, and my greatest pain came from not being able to comfort him in the way I wanted. His parents sat by him, and he rested his head on his mother's shoulder. She patted his temple to comfort him.

My parents were there, too. My father looked sober, and I gave him a begrudging nod for that. My mother, devastated, cried the most during the funeral. I knew she was recollecting those times when she baked special pies for her daughter's best friend when she came over after school.

We put her in the ground and that was the end of it. It felt like an ending and at the same time, I knew her ghost would always follow me. I was still young, early twenties, and I legitimately wondered if the people who died might not become omniscient, might not be able to view all our misdeeds and dirty thoughts and mischief from wherever their souls were transported.

Even during her funeral, all I did was stare at her husband. If it was true that she could see me, she must have been furious.

But I convinced myself that, even during life, she'd known about my feelings for Danny. She must have. I had felt that way ever since we were little girls, and although I could hide from most people, I could not hide my true self from her. I regretted that we never talked about it on this earth, but I had to let that chapter close and I did my best to forget about it.

Danny's house seemed empty even though it was full of people. My mother made soup and sandwiches and put out coffee for everybody, but hardly anyone ate anything. Danny moved among us like a shadow, and I watched people, many of whom I did not even know, take his hands in theirs and whisper nice things to him. He nodded and moved on to the next person. His shoulders stooped, his gait slow and shambling, his eyes lost. His smile gone.

Charlie hugged him and patted him on the back three loud times: *bump, bump, bump*. I hugged him, and when I held him in my arms, it was like holding onto a dream after you have already woken in the morning. Even in your hand, you feel it slipping away. So it was with Danny. I wanted never to let him go.

"I'm so sorry," I told him in a voice which other people could hear.

"Thank you, Liz," he said, also audible to everyone in the living room.

But we had a secret conversation which only we were privy to. It lacked words: it consisted of the way I moved my fingers along the fabric of his suit, lightly down his back. Only an inch, but an inch which represented a million miles; in the way he breathed down the collar of my dress as we held each other for just a second, only a second, but a second which represented a million years.

We broke our embrace. We held each other's gaze for a moment longer. That was a moment full of apologies and regret. And then he turned away, to face his own world of pain and loneliness.

Charlie and I were the last to leave, except for Danny's parents. I would not have gone if they had not been there.

Despondent, Danny took an excruciatingly long time to answer even the simplest questions. I wanted to run to him and to leave Charlie there. But we went home, and the ride was silent. What was there to discuss? Hers was not a normal kind of death; anytime someone kills him- or herself, there is a lifetime of silence which follows for those who remain. Even if they talk about it, they avoid certain things. And it was still so fresh a wound, and she had a baby inside her.

The next couple of months went by slowly, but my life returned to normal. I tried to call Danny several times, but the phone just rang and rang, on his end, until I gave up and hung up.

The first few times that happened I worried. What if something terrible had happened to Danny, too? But I would feel it in my heart if anything did happen to him, and I felt nothing there, and so I trained myself to accept it when he did not answer my calls. He was readjusting to his post-Jamie life, naturally.

The weather turned hot and I grew bigger.

I told Charlie one morning as he sipped his coffee in preparation for work, "We need to make that bedroom upstairs look good."

He raised his eyebrows. "Oh? Why is that? Are your parents coming for a visit?"

I put my hands on my growing belly. I was not huge, not yet, but I had noticed myself bloating for several weeks. Charlie only stared back at me dumbly. I decided to help him out with a less subtle clue.

"Our family is getting bigger."

He stared at me for a few moments and I swore to myself that if he did not understand my meaning even after all that, I would divorce him. But his eyes started to bulge and I felt just a kiss of relief.

"You ... you are pregnant?"

I nodded and suddenly felt like weeping. Charlie jumped up from the table. He spilled some coffee on his hand as he put his cup down and, distracted, wiped his fingers away on his shirt. He put the same hand on my belly, very gently.

"Oh my God."

"I know. It's amazing."

He bent down and lifted my shirt. The gesture annoyed me; it made me feel just a little too much like property.

He kissed my stomach. "Our baby," he murmured. "Does anyone else know?"

I shook my head, although I thought even the mailman might have noticed my expanding belly and supposed I was expecting. But I could imagine how hurt Charlie would be if I told him that, and so I just kept shaking my head, and then I pulled his face close to my stomach and felt the warmth of his flesh there against me.

It was a tender moment, but I felt little while it transpired.

I ran my fingers through his hair. "Do you want a boy or a girl?"

He looked up at me. "A boy," he said with finality.

"I figured."

"But a girl is good, too," he added. "I love you two so much."

"We love you."

He left for work giddy and lighthearted. He'd tell all the guys, he said, and they would smoke cigars and have a celebratory drink after their shift ended. Charlie drank when he was sad, and he drank when he was happy; he drank when he was emotional and when he was bored.

After he'd gone, I thought about who I should officially tell next. I picked up the phone, and the only face flashing through my mind was Danny's. I imagined how he would take the news. Would he be happy for me? Would he become depressed, thinking of what he had lost?

Even though I was thinking of Danny, I called my mother.

"Hello?" she answered on the second ring.

"Hi, mom."

"Elizabeth. How are you?"

"I'm pregnant."

Just like that. No build up, no suspense. I heard her breathing through the telephone, and I considered simply hanging up the receiver. But I waited for her words,

"Oh, my baby. I'm so happy for you."

"Tell Dad, all right?"

"Why don't you tell him?"

I heard a voice in the background, low and groggy.

"No, no," I said. "I can't talk long."

But she'd already passed over the phone, and so I waited through the clunks and rattles.

"Hello?" a gruff voice said.

It was my father, drinking. I already knew what the scene was, over there.

"Liz?"

"Hi, Dad," I said.

"What's your news?"

"I'm having a baby," I said.

"Sweet Jesus," he said, his voice trailing off in a mixture of despair and confusion. "What do you mean, you're having a kid?"

I didn't know how to answer his question. I had not expected this reaction from him.

"I mean I am pregnant. Charlie is the father."

I hated myself for adding that last sentence, and I would have given anything I owned to take it back. But he hardly seemed to notice.

"How is that?" He sounded irritated. "I thought you liked girls."

I inhaled sharply and held my breath for a few seconds. What had he said?

"I don't understand."

"You know what I'm talking about," he said, and only then did I realize just how slurred his words were. "You ain't never having kids. You like tits."

So he was confusing me with my sister, Rosalinda. But I would not give him the little victory of telling him that.

"Go to bed," I said to him.

I heard my mother's voice in the background, and I

could tell that she was asking for the phone.

"Go choke on your own vomit."

He laughed, a rattling, wheezing sound. "You. Having a baby. Not in my life."

Mom got the phone back from him somehow, and her voice came through much more clearly than his. "I'm sorry, Liz. He's ... he's not feeling well."

"He never feels well," I said, unable to disguise my scorn. "It's fine, though."

She sighed. "How is Danny?"

I wondered again, as I had so many times over the years, how much she knew or suspected about Danny and me. I thought it must be impossible for her not to at least have an inkling of the way I felt for him. "He's hurting," I said, although I was not entirely sure. "Truthfully, I haven't talked to him for a long time."

"He needs friends," my mother said. "He needs to feel loved. He's always been that way."

I didn't know where she got that impression, although it was true enough.

"He knows he is loved," I said.

My mother took a deep breath. If she knew something, this was the moment to say it.

But all she said was, "Well, I hope he does."

Our conversation ended cordially enough, without either of us speaking of Father again. We had ignored his brutish behavior for so long that it seemed more natural than addressing it.

Now that the truth was officially out, I felt a strange sense of relief. I could not explain it, not even to myself, but it was real enough. It helped me to see that I had been worried about how Charlie would react to the news of our baby. Perhaps I had thought that he would respond negatively to another mouth to feed, even if we did live quite comfortably.

About two weeks later, I spoke with Danny on the phone. He called me; I had given up on trying to contact him. Those were dark months after Jamie's death and I felt I was floating in outer space, entirely cut off from love and humanity. That was often what I imagined: being caught on some distant moon, staring up at the blackness of the universe, wondering where everybody was.

By then, I was quite large, and I suspected that anybody who saw me would know I was pregnant. I did not often leave the house, both because I was a bit self-conscious and because Charlie wanted me to stay protected inside.

"Hello?" I answered after the phone rang three times.

I heard breathing and knew they were his breaths. The depth of them; the rhythm.

"Liz."

"Oh, Danny," I said, my voice catching in my throat. "How are you?"

"Very good," he said, though his voice betrayed him.

He sounded bright, and anybody else might have been fooled. But he was my heart.

"I'm getting married," he added, almost as an afterthought.

I did not answer for some time. It was only a few months since we'd buried Jamie. An image of her, rotting in the ground, sprang to mind. Instead of feeling sorry for her, though, I felt sorry for Danny. I knew he was not acting rationally.

"What?"

"Yes," he said, dropping his voice a few degrees. "I met her at the grocery store. She helped me pick out a melon."

I thought this must have been a joke; she helped him pick out a melon? I pictured some faceless woman knocking on cantaloupes, nodding at one and handing it to Danny. Them, enjoying it together.

"It's so soon," I said. "Are you sure?"

"I'm sure," he said. I only paused. I knew he had more to say, and I wanted him to come with it on his own terms, in his own time. He did.

He dropped his voice to a near-whisper. "I just can't face being alone, Liz."

"You're not alone."

"Yes, I am."

"You'll always have me."

"You're married."

I almost said 'I'll leave right now. I'll run away with you. We can go to Spain. We can live in a villa. We will love each other until the very end of the world. Come on.' But I remembered the baby growing inside me, and I knew I could not do any of those things. I was trapped, and Danny was trapped, too.

"I'm having a baby."

"I heard," Danny responded, his voice flat and emotionless. "I'm happy for you and Charlie."

We exchanged ragged, emotion-laden breaths over the line.

He spoke first. "Does it ever seem like a joke to you?"

"What do you mean?"

"How things work out?" he explained. "How we should have been together. How I kissed the wrong girl in the church." Danny laughed once, without humor. "How maybe, just maybe, just now, we could have made a run for it together. But you have a baby coming. You can't run anywhere. Even if you were fool enough to want to come with me …"

I felt he was on the verge of proposing something drastic. I wanted him to propose something drastic.

"Danny," I said, but stopped with a sharp inhalation.

"I wouldn't let you do it," he said. "Did I ever tell you? My dad isn't my real dad."

"What?" This was new information to me.

"He married my mother when I was just a little guy. Just two years old." He laughed again, but the sound this time carried at least a little mirth with it. "I never knew my real dad. And through all these years, my dad, I mean the one who raised me, he was great. I love him. Always will. But it doesn't stop you from wondering, you know? And I couldn't let you do that to your baby. Not in a million years. Not for all the hearts in the world."

"Oh, Danny," I said again. "I'm so sorry. For everything."

"I know," he said.

I visualized him nodding his head, with a sad smile.

"It's okay." Now he whispered again. "I'll always love you. I'll always come back to you. In my dreams."

"I'll be waiting for you there."

And I did wait for him there; I dreamed of him every night, even as I grew bigger and bigger with Charlie's baby. And, as many times as I saw him in the world of dreams, and as many times as he saw me in his own dreams, I still felt I had lost him forever.

Ten

The receptionist looks back up at me from her records and gives me a pale smile. "He has a note here that says he doesn't want any visitors."

I have always been respectful toward authority; anytime anybody has asked something of me, if they were wearing a uniform or a vest or a nametag, I complied. An usher at a movie theater, even if he were only sixteen years old, could easily send me to another seat at his whim, and I would never question his ability to do so. Bus drivers could kick me off their bus, even if I had a valid ticket, simply because I would do as I was told. Age has not changed much in me, but this is Danny.

"He would want to see me," I say, already feeling myself start to tremble.

I do not like conflict, and this is already shaping into one.

"I'm sorry," she says. "I have to respect his wishes. It's a privacy issue."

"Please."

I will not beg, I tell myself, but I know I will if it comes to it. I will do absolutely anything to see him again.

But she just shrugs her shoulders and gives me an apologetic look. As if we are co-conspirators.

"I'm sorry," she adds again.

I turn away and head toward the front doors. I cannot believe I have been stopped so easily, and for what? If he only knew – would he want to see me? Or had he given up on life so much that he would refuse even me?

The front door slides open in its efficient way. The heat from outside rushes over me but I barely notice. I still feel cold. I inhale deeply outside and look down the front of the building. The bushes go all the way to the corner, where it looks as though they bend around the side of the building. For no particular reason, I walk in that direction. I do not even know if his room is this way; I just feel I need to see.

The ground is flat enough, but it is still tough going for me. I am too old for this sort of thing. I remind myself that I am doing this just to see him again; that after that, I can die and I will be happy. But I cannot die without at least speaking to him one last time.

I reach the corner and I smell smoke and hear several voices in hushed discourse. I do not peek around the corner. I simply step around.

It is a private area, blocked off from view of the main grounds, and there are three young men taking a break there. They do not see me at first, and I see they are passing a joint amongst themselves. One takes a hit and then gives it to the next person. They do not cough after hitting it. They seem like old hands, just by the way they hold it, gingerly between the thumb and forefinger.

One of them sees me. "Oh, shit!" he says, throwing the joint to the ground. "Who are you?"

"Ah, shit," another one adds.

The third's eyes are wide as egg yolks, and I think he is about to pee his pants.

"I'm Liz," I say, smiling. "And you?"

"Nobody," the first one says.

Wearing white uniforms, they pull the food carts through the corridors here; they push the brooms, change the bed sheets, lift the less able elders onto the toilets and watch them so they do not fall off, onto the bathroom floor.

"Oh, you're somebody," I say, delighting just a little too much in the trap this boy is in. "You're going to help me with something."

"What's that?" the kid asks, stepping forward.

His friends look positively mortified. But their leader, this one, seems perhaps just slick enough to be able to help me.

"I need to see somebody inside."

The kid squints at me. "Oh yeah?" he says, smirking.

He seems like a good kid, this one like he's ready to play ball.

"And he has a no visitors order," I explain like a patient teacher of dull students. "So I need you to get me in."

"I don't know," he says, casting a glance at his friends. "I could get in a lot of trouble doing something like that."

"You could get in more trouble if you don't help me. But nobody here wants that to happen. You look like three nice young men. I could forget everything I saw back here." I pause for dramatic effect.

My nerves have settled down; this is the most fun I have had in years. I like watching him and his friends squirm. "Or I could go back in and discuss things with that pretty receptionist at the desk. She looked like she could call a manager fast, what with that new-fangled telephone system she has. What should I do?"

Talking so much at a time dries my throat out awfully, but I enjoy the pain.

The kid holds his hands out in a defensive gesture. "No, let's not do that. I'll get you inside. No problem. But you might have to wait a little while."

"Robbie," one of the kids says. "What are you doing?"

"Shut up," Robbie snaps. "You want to get fired? Or arrested?"

Robbie's friend shuts up. Robbie turns back to me. "We'll get you in through the back door. Only kitchen people go through there. Nobody's going to check you. It's not like this is a prison or something."

"Well, be sure it works out," I say. "Or you might see what prison is really like."

The boys are silent for a few moments, and it is clear I have won.

Now they have agreed to do as I require, there is an awkward pause between us. Our business has terminated, but we are still standing in a semi-circle. They are staring at their feet.

"Okay," Robbie says at last. "Meet me at the back door in an hour."

I remind him I do not know where the back door is. He sighs, but he is smiling. He leads me around the building again, and here the hedge ends. There is a small, oil-stained parking lot, and a small, brown, heavy door.

"Here it is," Robbie says. "One hour."

"I won't be late."

The boys disappear inside, and I wonder briefly if they will show up. I suspect they will. They are not smart enough to realize they could disappear and I would not know how to identify them, except for Robbie. Nor would I care enough to tell their boss about their secret smoke breaks.

Now I am alone, again. This is exciting, and I realize I am loving this bit of mischief. It reminds me of the trouble I got into with Danny in that magical summer before I gave birth.

I was big with the baby and he was engaged to a girl named Paula. Paula, of the melons. They had not set a wedding date, and they were not particularly serious, at least as far as I could tell from the brief conversations I had enjoyed with Danny over the telephone. We called each other much more often, even if we kept the discussions short. Our relationship was melting into a deep friendship, and although it wasn't everything I wanted, it was better than spending every minute wondering about his soul.

Charlie was going to his parents' house in northern Michigan. They needed his help laying a pipe, or some such work; when he told me he was leaving for the weekend, I put up a nominal fight.

"They need my help, baby. You understand. Besides, I know you can take care of yourself around here."

A couple of months shy of giving birth, I was surprised that Charlie was willing to leave me alone in that big house. Who knew what kinds of trouble I might have gotten into? But he only smiled at me and my dull protests.

"I'll be back on Sunday evening," he said, thinking to comfort me.

I pouted, but it was fake. He didn't seem to notice. He smiled and hugged me tight. I lost the sour look on my face, my head buried in his chest, and when we broke our embrace, I tried to look moderately appeased.

"I'll miss you."

"I'll miss you, too," he said.

That was Friday night. He left very early on Saturday morning, and as soon as I was awake, I called Danny.

"I've got the house to myself," I told him. "What are you doing, today?"

I had not expected much. Perhaps for him to say that he was going to spend the afternoon walking in the park with Paula. But he didn't say that.

"I haven't got any plans."

I heard the smile in his voice.

"Do you want to come see me?"

I would have gone to him, but I didn't have a car and, even if I had, no way to drive one.

"I'll be there in an hour."

So I spent an hour tidying the house in small ways that I knew wouldn't matter. I didn't know what to expect. Would he love me? Would he want to make love to me? Even if I was seven months pregnant? I knew he wouldn't. And yet, I hoped.

I watched out the front window for his Ford Galaxie to pull up. But it wasn't the Galaxie that pulled to the curb. It was that beautiful machine, that gorgeous dream of a car, the '57 Mercury. I heard it coming up the street and I recognized the engine's roar, and my heart skipped. Danny parked smoothly and stepped out of the vehicle. He seemed to check the address to be sure; I realized he had never been to this house. He strode up the walkway, his smile beaming.

He knocked at the door. I took a deep breath and answered it. We stared at each other for a few moments before he said, "You look beautiful, Liz."

"Thanks," I said, rubbing my stomach.

I waved him in and shut the door behind us. He touched my belly and we felt the baby inside me kick. Even if the child was not his, his hand there felt so perfect, so right.

"You look good, too."

He mocked himself by rubbing his cheek. "I need a shave. Where's your husband?"

"Building a house or something up north," I said. "It doesn't matter. What do you want to do?"

"Let's go for a ride."

My loins were reminded immediately of the last time we took a ride in that Mercury, all those years ago. Fire flared deeply between my legs, and I wondered if it was normal to get so excited when you were pregnant. I assumed it was not.

I hurried to lock up the house and followed him to the car, moving as well as I ever had, even if I was almost thirty pounds heavier than usual. None of those pounds mattered because I walked on clouds, and the way Danny looked at me was the greatest affirmation of my beauty that I could ask for. Charlie did the same; he always kissed me, even passionately, but somehow just a glance from Danny meant so much more.

I sat in the passenger spot. It felt like returning home after a long absence. Danny started the engine and I felt the purr of it beneath my butt. "Where do you want to go?"

He smiled and turned to me. "It doesn't matter. I just want to go."

I nodded; he shifted into first gear and we pulled away from the curb. The neighborhood looked different to me now. Day to day, it seemed like a quaint, peaceful place where it would be a joy to raise a family.

Now, it seemed dull and quietly menacing. It just felt

right, leaving it.

We did not talk until we were on the expressway, and I thought that was because we wanted to create some psychological distance between the house I shared with Charlie and ourselves. The freeway was almost empty, and Danny eased onto it, heading west.

"So how are things?"

He stared through the windshield as he spoke. "I'm okay," he said. "I had a rough patch. You know."

"Yes."

I always felt that Danny and I could talk about anything, but that sensation grew when we were alone in his car. This was the first place we opened our hearts to each other, and even pregnant, and him engaged, a sense of déjà vu greeted me.

"You know I've never been to her grave."

"Neither have I," I confessed.

She was buried in Flint, and it was perhaps not too unusual for me to not have visited her tombstone, but by telling him this, I wanted him to feel I was complicit in his abstinence from laying flowers at her grave.

"Yeah," he said, trailing off. "She must hate me."

"Oh, Danny. She didn't hate you."

Somewhere in my mind, I noted that I had used the past tense and that he had used the present.

"She hated herself. She had a lot of problems."

"I know that."

Although he still smiled, it was difficult for me to see whether he was only using that as a shield against his true emotions.

"I always knew that. You know," he uttered a short, smug laugh, "we started seeing each other, Jamie and me, back in middle school. We were just kids. It started as a ... I don't know, a novelty, or something. She was a girl and she liked me. It was just easy to go with her, you know?"

"Sure," I said.

"And the whole time, all I thought about was that you were the one I really wanted. And it hurt me so much. All I wanted to do was run away from her and go to you. You were the one, Liz. You had my heart from the first day in sixth grade, when you were new in school and Mr. Wendell introduced you. And then we went fishing, and we sat under the tree, and you helped me with the train. The whole time, I just loved you so much."

"I know."

"Jamie did, too."

I sighed, close to tears. "You don't think she did what she did because of me, do you?"

It was a hard question to utter because the answer might have pierced my heart.

"I think it might have been part of it," Danny said.

"We can't change that, now."

"There's a lot of things we can't change now."

I nodded my head and kept my silence. The truest conversations were always the hardest ones to have.

"Then let's not worry about them."

"I never told her," Danny said. "About what we did. About making love to you. I've never told anybody."

"Neither have I."

"Do you think she knows now? I mean, wherever she is, looking down from heaven or whatever. Do you think she can see all the truth that we hid from her all those years?"

"I don't care if she can," I said, trying not to sound spiteful and surely failing. "We don't have anything to be ashamed of, Danny. I loved you. I still do. More than anybody else on the planet. I always will. I'm married and

I'm going to have a baby with one of your best friends, who is my husband, and I don't care about him even a fraction of what I care for you. If that's a bad thing, then I'm guilty. Throw me in prison, paint a big letter A on my forehead. I don't care."

I realized my heart was beating fast. There was a pressure behind my eyes that should not have been there, and I took a few deep breaths to try to calm myself down. Danny still smiled, and he appeared as calm as he ever had.

"I feel the same," he said. "But I care too much about you to put you through that. Do you think I love Paula even half as much as I love you? Do you think I even love her? I can't love anybody when I love you."

"Then don't marry her." I stared out the windshield at the highway ahead. We went under an overpass and when we came out the other side, a cloud had passed over the sun and everything was a shade darker.

"But we can't be together," he said. "You know that and I know that. We really messed this up."

"Yes, we did."

"I should have just picked you up in my arms at that graduation dance," he said. "You remember the Sam Cooke song. I should never have stopped dancing with you."

"We were fools. But we can't go back."

"We could have done it even sooner."

The tone of his voice indicated reflective reminiscence.

"When I knocked that train off the tracks with those asses I was friends with. I could have run away from the law with you by my side. Maybe Jamie would be alive, married to Charlie or something. And everyone would be happy."

"We shouldn't talk about it," I said.

"You're right. It just makes it hurt more."

We rode for a few minutes in silence. Danny took an exit onto another expressway, and we spoke little until he found a side road and took us onto it. I realized then where we were going: back to Hamilton.

Everything was quieter here than in Detroit, and I realized how much my new home had changed me. I had grown accustomed to having neighbors right beside me, and the air smelling like car exhaust and hot asphalt. We had been driving for an hour by then and I needed to go to the bathroom.

I had no qualms about telling Danny, "I have to pee."

He grinned. "Pregnant women pee a lot."

"You are a tactful guy."

He pulled off the road and I went behind a tree. It was a strange thing, urinating outside, squatting with the wind caressing me, but it wasn't entirely unpleasant.

Danny had his hands in his pockets as he leaned against the hood of his car when I rounded the tree, patting down my huge dress. That familiar heat returned to my loins. I leaned up beside him and he put his arms around my shoulders and hugged me close.

"You know," he said, "Jamie knew all about us. She accepted it and learned to live with it. Until she couldn't live with it anymore – or live with herself – oh, whatever it was."

He spat the final words out, as though he had been going over them for so long that they had lost all meaning for him.

"But Charlie? He doesn't have a clue. It's almost embarrassing."

I nodded. We stayed like that for a few moments, and I shuttered away the recurring thoughts of him throwing me onto my back on the hood and lifting my dress like a rutting animal. I wanted him on top of me again, I wanted his hands all over my flesh, I wanted his hot breath on my lips, on my breasts. But he made no move.

"We better get going," he said, with finality. "We don't have forever."

His words rang all too true, and we took our seats again.

Driving down the road, we were isolated and it was easy, if just for a few minutes, to imagine that humankind consisted only of us.

Twenty minutes later, we were in Hamilton. It had not changed since our leaving it: the ice cream shop where we spent our limitless youth; the park where we so often took long walks, even if we were with Charlie and Jamie; the river where we fished.

We stopped first at his parents' house. His mother came out the front door when we pulled into the driveway, smiling broadly.

"Should I come?" I asked, suddenly a bit nervous.

"Why not?" he said, his face searching mine.

"Well ... okay."

I stepped out of the car and followed him to his mother.

The visit went perfectly normally. Neither his mother nor his father questioned why I was there with Danny: a pregnant woman, married to one of his best friends, spending the day traveling with him. It was a taboo then, and, once I was over my initial anxiety, I found I did not care who saw us and what they thought of me.

After his old house, we had to visit my parents. "We should have just kept driving," I said as I slid into the front seat. "All the way to Chicago."

"We can still go," he said, winking at me. The afternoon turned to gray, evening approaching.

"No, I haven't been back since I moved away," talking

to myself as much as to Danny. "I need to see them."

Danny shrugged and put the Mercury into gear. "No problemo," he added, and then we drove to my old house. It was a short hop from his; I had forgotten how close he lived to me, once upon a time. It was comforting in a strange way. We waited outside my house for a few minutes, and nobody appeared at the front door. "Maybe nobody's home," Danny said, putting his hand on my left knee.

But I knew better. "My dad will be home, at least." Although I suspected they would both be home.

"Should I come?"

Danny's hand still clutched my knee, gently squeezing every few seconds. It warmed my entire leg.

"Why not?" I asked, repeating his own words.

So we walked up the drive and climbed the steps to the front porch and I knocked on the door. I heard movement from the other side, and I waited to see who would appear. To my surprise, it was my father. The door swung inward and there he was, a few feet away from me, sizing me up.

"Elizabeth," he said, as if convincing himself I was really there.

Then, his eyes shockingly gentle, he looked over at Danny. "Come in."

We stepped inside as he yelled out for my mother to come. She shambled her way to the foyer where we stood, and she rushed over and embraced me. She touched Danny's cheek and ushered us further inside, to the kitchen table, where we sat.

"What are you doing here? How are you doing? Where is Charlie? Is everything all right?"

"Everything is perfect," I said, sitting down gingerly. "Charlie is working with his parents up north for the weekend. We're just driving."

My mother studied us for a second too long, and I knew that she knew, too. I wondered if she blamed us for Jamie's suicide, and then I pushed those thoughts away with as much force as I could.

"It's a long way for a drive," she said.

Danny shrugged, still smiling. "I just got the Mercury working again," he explained, although I knew he was at least partially lying. "I wanted to open it up and see how it ran."

"And how's it running?" My father's voice betrayed a hint of suspicion.

"Runs great," Danny answered. He sat beside me, my parents on the other side of the table. Stealthily, his right hand found my left knee again, brushed it, and then caressed it. I jumped in surprise, and my parents glanced at me, but neither said anything.

I quickly changed the subject. "And how is everything here?"

"I've quit drinking," my father said.

He was sitting so that the gray afternoon light caught him from the side, and I observed, for the first time, that he was clean-shaven and his thin hair combed. He was less sweaty than I remembered, and his posture was fairly straight. I wasn't sure if they were illusions or fragments of reality, some reality, but they seemed like positive signs to me.

"That's good," I said, not ready to forgive all his years of abuse: abusing the bottle, abusing his family afterward.

"I'm supposed to make amends," he continued after taking a deep breath.

"Amends?" I said.

"It means to apologize," my mother said. Her voice was

urging me to accept these new changes with a smile, as hard as I might find it. "To the people he has done wrong to, over the years."

"There are a lot of them," he said, nodding gravely. "You're at the top of the list."

Danny squeezed my knee harder and made my leg warmer.

"And then what happens?" I asked.

"I hope you forgive me," my father said.

Danny moved his hand, slowly, up my left leg toward where my legs met.

"I forgave him already," my mother said. "Because I love him. I know, it isn't easy to do."

Danny's hand cupped my upper thigh and then did a little dance there, comfortable like a domesticated animal seeking out a warm place in the house in which to bed down.

"I forgive you."

I became hot.

"Thank you," he said, sighing with relief. "I know I don't deserve it. But thank you, anyway. I love you so much."

I thought of all the thrown pots and pans, all the broken lamps and curse words, yelled for all the neighbors to hear. All the nights when he collapsed into his bed, drunk and exhausted from his anger.

Danny's hand retreated toward my knee. I was sorry for that, but there was nothing I could do to stop it.

"Have you called Rosalinda?" I looked directly at my father.

"No," he said, shaking his head slowly. "Why do you ask?"

"If you are making amends with me, then you should

do the same with her. Don't you think so?"

He sighed. My mother shifted uneasily in her chair, opened her mouth as if to say something, and then shut it again with an audible click.

"That is difficult," he said, finally.

"Why?"

"I don't agree with what she's doing." He spoke with the air of a man who weighs all his words with great care.

I nodded my head. "She misses you. She thinks you don't love her."

"Of course I love her," my father said. "She's just living a sin."

"Just like you."

He snarled, but his face shifted back to its former genteelness quickly thereafter. One could almost have been fooled into believing his face had not transformed at all.

"I'm trying to fix that. That's why I'm asking your forgiveness."

"And all I'm telling you is that you should ask hers too."

I remembered wishing that this man would fall asleep and choke to death on his own vomit. I went from loving him to seeing how easily I felt that way in a matter of seconds.

"Maybe you're right," he said with apparent difficulty. "I'll call her."

My mother watched us like a boxing referee looking closely for low blows. I tried to gauge how Danny felt, but he betrayed nothing of his thoughts, motionless beside me. The silence between us seemed to drag on for ages, and it was my father who broke it.

"Do you expect me to do it now?"

I shrugged. I felt like an insolent child, but I knew I was right.

"There's no time like the present. *Carpe diem.*"

To my shock, he stood from the table and walked to the telephone mounted on the wall. He stared at it for a moment before he lifted the receiver and dialed my sister's number. He seemed to know it by heart.

We three sat watching him with clinical curiosity. My father stood still as a stone, holding the phone to his ear, his knuckles turning white before he said "Hello" into the mouthpiece.

We waited to hear his end of the conversation.

"Yes. It's me."

A few deep, listening breaths.

"Listen," he said, "there's nothing wrong. Well, something is wrong. The way I've treated you."

More pregnant silence. This was more painful than I had either expected or desired, not knowing what I did expect, in fact. My mother stared at me with something like accusation in her eyes. I just glanced at her; my interest was with my father, this time. Even Danny watched with close scrutiny.

"I'm sorry," my father said. "It's your life. And I love you. And I was a terrible father. And a terrible person. Yes, I was. I was, Rosalinda. Forgive me."

He hung up the phone a few moments later. He looked truly defeated, his shoulders slumped, his head bowed.

"She said she forgave me. But I don't think I believe her."

I felt sorry for him. God damn me, I did. All the bad things he created in my world, and I felt sorry for him then. "I'm sure she does," I piped up. "I talked to her not too long ago. Trust me. She forgives you. She forgives everyone who ever did anything bad to her."

My father nodded. "Sometimes it's easier to forgive

strangers than it is to forgive the people you love."

Danny and I did not stay much longer, but my father's words haunted me even after we left. I promised I would visit more often, but I was not certain I would; in fact, I was fairly sure I would not. And I never saw my father alive again.

The last image I had of him was completely different from the man I had known my entire life. He was broken, sad and old, somehow cleaner than he had ever been before. It was a relief but also hard to look at him that way. He was not the same man.

We drove away from my parents' house and after a few blocks Danny said, "Are you feeling all right?"

"Of course."

He nodded, shifted, slowed to a stop, checked for traffic and then continued through an empty intersection.

"They change, too," he said. "Our parents, I mean. They accept that we have changed. We have to do the same for them."

"I know," I said.

"That was a good change," he continued. "I mean ... I don't know ... I can't pretend to know what you're thinking. But he seems like a better man than he was."

I nodded. We drove away from the city on roads I did not recognize.

"Where are we going?" I asked.

"I haven't been out this way since I was in tenth grade," Danny said. "You remember that problem I was involved with?"

"The train?"

He nodded, still smiling, but it was a pained smile now.

"I was so stupid. And you helped me out of that."

"I would have done anything to help you. I still would."

"You helped me stay out of trouble," he said, "but only I can repair it with myself."

We drove down dirt roads. We left a long trail of dust in the air behind us like the exhaust from a jet. The fields here were desolate, choked with corn. It was an empty part of the world and I was at least a little scared. There were very few houses out this way, and my mind traveled along less-traveled roads: what if one of those houses were home to a homicidal maniac? What if one of them were haunted, or if a monster lived in one of the vast barns standing bleak behind the houses?

We approached the train tracks and Danny stopped the car and killed the engine.

"What if someone sees us?" I said.

"Don't worry. They'll think we're just teenagers trying to get some time alone." He winked at me. "But we have another spot for that, don't we?"

"This spot would work," I said, despite myself.

"No," he said. "I can't do it."

He looked over at me for a few seconds.

"Not now. Not with Charlie behind you. Not with a baby coming."

I noticed that he mentioned nothing of his fiancée, Paula. Perhaps she meant nothing to him, after all.

"There is an old farmer who lives here." His voice changed to one of conducting business.

"Okay," I said, to lead his thoughts onward, so I could understand why we had stopped here.

"When the train went flying off the tracks, one of this farmer's cows got crushed beneath it. I saw it happen."

"Oh, Danny."

"Yeah," he said, looking down the tracks.

They were empty. Ghost tracks.

"There was all this noise. It sounded like being in the middle of a storm cloud when the thunder goes. And all this metal scraping, sparks flying, wood just shattering. I saw trees snap like toothpicks. And I saw this poor cow, trying to move out of the way, but way too late. And way too slow. It got crushed, smeared along the ground for a ways. The other guys laughed."

Here, Danny shook his head.

"They laughed. Can you believe that? We killed this poor animal, and we had no idea if maybe we killed a person, too, and they were laughing. All I said was, 'We need to get out of here!' And that's what we did."

"Do you know anything about Wilson?" I asked. "What happened to him?"

"He went away," Danny said cryptically. "I never saw him again."

"Good."

"Not good," Danny said. "We all should have gone away. He sacrificed himself."

"It was his idea."

"So what?"

It was a rhetorical question which was good, because the only argument I had for the reason Danny should not have gone to jail was that I loved him. But, for me, it was reason enough.

"Anyway," Danny went on, opening his door, pulling an envelope out of his back pocket, "the farmer should be repaid."

He walked around the car and stuffed the envelope into the mailbox at the side of the road. He lingered for only a moment before rejoining me in the car. "You paid him for the cow?" I said.

He nodded his head. "I have the cash now," he said,

"and once I'm married, I don't want to have to explain to Paula where the money is going." He ran his fingers through his hair. "It's been bothering me for a few years. Ever since I did it, actually. Now, I feel like I can put it behind me."

I nodded. "Did Jamie know? About the train?"

He stared through the windshield a long time before answering.

"No. I never told her. Only you and the guys I did it with know."

We drove away from that place, and I was happy to leave it behind. It was a haunted place, and it represented a different time in our lives, the moment when we jumped off the safe cliff of innocence and into the pit of guilt and adulthood.

The drive home was quiet and pleasantly long. I felt I was dreaming, but I dared not sleep. I didn't know when I would see Danny again, and I needed to savor every second with him.

Eleven

I am at the designated back door of Bliss. Nobody comes for a long time. A car circles around the parking lot and I am momentarily nervous: what if this person stops and demands identification? What am I doing here? What will I say? But being an old lady has certain advantages, and one of them is that nobody thinks you are a terrorist or a thief. Probably just lost. Or, perhaps, an escapee.

A warm wind blows across my face and puts me in a sentimental mood. I cannot place the exact memory it stirs inside me. It is like hearing a familiar song from childhood and getting that soft feeling, associating the music with something pleasant.

This is something connected with Danny, of course; all my best memories are.

A piece of machinery kicks in with a rattle and a hum and I jump an inch before settling back down. They will come for me. I just need to be patient.

I am a little surprised at myself for being here at this moment, so far from home. So far: in universal terms, I am not far away, only a mile or two.

But distances like this become much more daunting with age. I could have traveled the world and yet, in my state, with my soul, this excursion would feel like a trek into outer space.

And there is more than just that: I am going to see him. I have not seen him in years, nor have I written to him or heard from him in all that time. I can trace back through history to the point where we stopped seeing each other, but that is an exercise in self-loathing.

A few minutes later, the back door unlatches. My breath catches in my throat. It must be a manager coming. Someone has seen me on a closed-circuit camera and is wondering what I am doing here; perhaps someone thinks I have wandered away from my room and is afraid of a lawsuit.

Even that thought fills me with the hidden idea that I could pretend to have escaped, that they would lead me back in, try to find my room; I realize it would not work.

But it is Robbie, the kid with the joint. He looks at me conspiratorially.

"I was hoping you wouldn't be here."

"But I am," I say, controlling my voice the best I can.

"Well, come on," he says, hushed but not rude.

He holds the door for me as I shuffle inside. It is dark and it takes my eyes a few moments to adjust to the lighting. Everything is beige-colored in the corridor, with dim fluorescent lights on the ceiling. One of them, about halfway down the hallway, is flickering in an annoying *zap-zap-zap*.

"Where are we?"

He raises his finger to his lips.

"The kitchen is down here. And the—"

"The what?"

I want to know.

"The special room."

"What special room?"

"Where they take residents who die," he says, simply.

He seems to have regretted telling me this, although I do not see why.

"You think I'm afraid of death? Or that I don't want to think about it? Or talk about it? At my age, you think about it a lot."

"So do I," Robbie says. "Working in a place like this."

We are moving down the corridor, which, as far as I can tell, is empty.

"Think of it as a blessing," I say.

"How's that?"

We turn down another corridor. We pass several unmarked doors. My mind, for the first time, flies down one of its own dark corridors; this kid could be leading me to any place, any of these rooms, to rape or kill me. But my mind has always explored these dark places, and they have never happened. Not, at least, in the way I have so dreaded.

Reality was always bad enough.

"Maybe you'll enjoy what you have more."

It sounds weak. The truth is, at Robbie's age, nobody should have to worry about death.

"Maybe," he says, grim-faced.

We stop at an elevator and he calls it. I hear its *whoosh* from behind the metal doors.

"Listen," he says. "We're going up to his floor. I'm going to take you to his room and push you in. And then I'll disappear."

He is sheepish as he says this, as if he is embarrassed about leaving me like that. Perhaps he does not know that his vision of how things will transpire is exactly the way I want things to go. It is comforting, in a way, having Robbie here with me now, but I do not want his presence interfering with that special moment I am anticipating. Seeing Danny again.

"It's fine," I say, touching his arm.

He does not draw away from me, and I take pitiful comfort in that. It reaffirms my own humanity that he is willing to accept my old woman's touch.

"You've worked a miracle today already."

He nods and the elevator doors open. He allows me to step through first, and then he punches the button: 3. A moment later, the doors glide shut and we float upwards. I have not been on an elevator in what seems like ages; most of the lifts I have ridden have been in hospitals, and that bare fact is suddenly depressing. But I do not linger on it. Bigger things are coming.

We are on the third floor before I am ready. The doors slide open and we step out. Nurses, orderlies, old people like me, all walk around or sit on chairs. I experience a moment of fear. Surely someone will know I am invading and do not belong here. They will call the police. I walk beside Robbie. Nobody even looks twice at me.

We round a corner. A drinking fountain, mounted to the wall, has brown stain beneath it. It looks like rust.

We stop outside room 302.

"Well," he says. "Here we are."

I touch his arm again, and this time I leave my hand there. Again, he does not pull even a smidge away.

"Thank you so much. You don't know how you've changed my life."

"Take care," he says, and then disappears down the hallway.

And just like that, he is out of my life, having played his little role. Now, I pause. The moment is too huge for me. I rest my forehead against the wood of the door. I inhale deeply. I exhale slowly. I grab the doorknob.

We truly started to drift apart after that road trip we took; it was time. Nicholas was born early the following autumn. He was a fat, beautiful baby with a little tuft of blonde hair atop his soft head. I lay in bed and Charlie and some of his friends, not including Danny, puffed on some gigantic, stinky cigars. The smoke wafted up toward the ceiling and then out the window and into the blackness of night.

It was three in the morning and we were all wide awake after the birth. Things work differently in hospitals today, but back then, my firstborn was exposed to second-hand smoke in the first few hours of his life.

I spent the next few weeks recovering at home and sleeping when I could. Nicholas was a good baby, quiet, and he slept soundly. He always ate and he always pooped on time. He was so easy to take care of. Even Charlie, with his big, fumbling hands, looked like an expert when he changed a diaper or poked a little spoonful of food between Nicholas's lips.

Danny was married around that time. I, of course, missed the wedding, excused by having a newborn to watch out for. We called Danny to congratulate him, the same as he did for us after our son was born, but the conversation was stilted and polite. I realized that anytime I spoke with him when Charlie was around, our discussion would be moderated by that same impersonal tone and cold distance.

It was safe, that way, and that safety was, in its own sad way, a comfort. There was no sense that I might do anything, say anything, ask Danny to do something for me or to me; I could not allow those thoughts to enter my consciousness.

My father never saw Nicholas. About a month after the birth, I received a phone call. I was alone in the kitchen; Nick was asleep on the living room floor, surrounded by a pile of toys and stuffed animals, pacifiers, and bulky formula bottles.

"Hello?" I said into the receiver.

"Hi, Elizabeth," my mother said.

I knew something was wrong by the timbre of her voice, and I asked what the matter was.

My mother took a deep breath. "He's dead."

"Who?" I asked, although I already knew.

"The doctors gave him a few months to live. His liver, Elizabeth, his liver."

So my father was dead. I stood with the phone in my hand, listening to the quiet house, the barely audible breaths of my son coming from the next room, a car engine starting somewhere down the block. Everything was in slow motion and at the same moment; it was as if time no longer existed.

But this was not a surprise, was it? He was sick, and I knew he could not last much longer. is sickness was self-inflicted, and I did not forgive him for it.

So why was I emotional? It felt worse than when I learned that Jamie had killed herself. My thoughts returned to that man, a sad shambles, the man I shamed into calling his daughter to beg her forgiveness.

"Are you okay?" I asked my mother.

"Yes, yes. I'm okay. I'll be okay."

I knew she would not.

"Mom ..."

I truly did not know what to say.

I settled on, "I'm so sorry."

"It's okay," she said, her voice unchanged. "I knew this day was coming."

"I know."

So my mother was alone, and that would be hard. Their house was once full of life: my father, my sister, me, my mother; now only my mother was left, and what had her life amounted to? What would be the remnants of it, once she was gone? A half-consumed bag of cat food, a lawn left to grow too long, perfectly folded yet unused towels, an unopened bottle of nice wine, saved for a special guest? I began to cry, but it was for my mother, not for my father.

We buried him and my mother came to live with us in Detroit. She was home all the time, and old now, in a way I never expected her to become old. Her hair was thin and gray, and she'd lost weight.

She looked sad most of the time, and oftentimes I caught her peering out of the window wistfully. I wanted to talk to her, but I knew she wouldn't talk to me. Her generation was one which rarely spoke, and even more rarely about personal things. She was a private, quiet person, and she had seen too much heartache in her years.

Jamie broke her heart by killing herself; Rosalinda broke her heart by rebelling against society and the sexual mores of the day; I broke her heart by not marrying Danny; my father broke her heart by being the cruel, cold man that he was. I realized, in her final years, that life had been unfair to her, and that she had weathered every storm destiny had thrown at her without complaining.

Reaching an age at which I could understand my mother as a person, as an equal, almost, was at the same time scary and enlightening. It made me want to weep.

She helped me to take care of Nick and took great pleasure in feeding the baby. Nick ate for anybody, but he was especially calm with his grandmother. My mother's presence made communication with Danny almost impossible, and in the deepest part of my heart, the dark place where I loved Danny unconditionally, I was miserable.

My mother took ill about a year after my father died. Even then, she tried to hide the severity of her coughing fits, choking them back instead of hacking the way anybody else would have done. She did an excellent job hiding it from me, and by the time I realized it was serious, it was too late to do anything medically about it.

She was resigned to staying in bed, and for a short time I had to take care of both her and Nick, who, when grandma coughed, looked at her with big, brown, wondering eyes. Whenever she finished with a particularly rough coughing spell, she wanted to hold Nick, as if by taking him in her arms, she reminded herself was it was like to be young and healthy, to have the world ahead of her rather than behind her.

I always saw love on her face at those times, but it was moderated by a tinge of regret.

The day she died, she called me into her room to talk to her. Nick was asleep, as he always was in the late afternoons.

"Sit down," she croaked, motioning to the bed. She seemed so frail, so light; it was almost as if time had whittled her away to nothing.

"Are you feeling okay, Mama?"

"I feel great."

I saw the truth in her eyes. I knew, in that instant, that the end was near, and I suddenly wanted desperately for it not to come.

"Do you want anything? Water?"

"No," she said with a dismissive wave of her skinny hand. "I want to talk to you."

"Okay,"

"I'm going to die."

"No," I said, turning away from her.

Why did I look away? I could not meet her gaze. There was too much truth in the way she looked at me.

"Yes," she said.

I felt her hand take mine. There was next to no strength in the way she held my hand, and yet I could not have broken her grip under any circumstances.

"I don't have much longer."

"It's not fair."

"Ha," she said, and I did look at her, and she was smiling. "What's not fair about it? Everyone dies. Seems the fairest thing in the world. A lot more fair than most things."

I looked away again. "I don't want to lose you."

"I know. And I don't want to lose you. But here we are. So you need to be strong."

"I will be."

There was a long pause, her breathing steady but bubbly, foamy. I was afraid she would die right then.

"Let me tell you something," she said, her voice strong. Strong enough.

"Okay."

"I've lived a long time and I've had a long time to think about my life. That's what you do when you're old. You look back. You don't have so much reason to look forward anymore. And then it all depends on whether you made good choices and took good risks. If you did, you will smile when you look back. If you made too many mistakes, or if you refused to take any risks, then you get a sad look in your eyes when you look back. Do you understand?"

I nodded my head. I thought I did understand. Of course, I would only truly come to understand in the fullness of time.

"A lot of people faulted me for marrying your father. Even when I met him, he was a hellraiser. He cheated in classes, he drank too much beer, then whiskey, and he smoked. He looked at other women even when I was out with him. My friends all thought I was crazy.

"And you know something? I was crazy. I was crazy to stay with him all those years, and I was crazy to love him the way I did. But I did love him, you see. That was the important thing."

She took a few very long breaths as if the speech she had just given had exhausted her. Probably, it had. Her voice was soft and far away when she spoke again.

"Even after all those years. Even after he threw the lamps, and broke the windows, and yelled and hollered so that all the neighbors could hear him. I could have left anytime. I could have packed you and Rosy up and taken you to Florida, or anywhere else. But I stayed because I loved him."

"Why are you telling me all this?"

I wondered whether she was having a hallucination of sorts, brought on by the end of her life.

"Because I want you to know that love is powerful. The most powerful thing in the world. Don't you ever forget that, Elizabeth."

"I won't."

She nodded her head calmly and closed her eyes. My mother's breathing fell into a regular, soft pattern, and she fell asleep. She never woke up. By the time Charlie came home from work, she was dead.

I watched with cold detachment as the men from the funeral parlor took her body out of the house, loaded it in their hearse, and drove away. They had been expecting my call for some time, and they were compassionate and pleasant when I let them in to take her away.

And now they were gone, and she was gone from my life, and the most vivid thing I still had from her was her final advice, which I interpreted as one must always follow love and become its slave. I had promised her I would not forget, and I never did.

Twelve

The moment to hesitate is over. I must be strong and face whatever lies on the other side of Danny's door. I must face Danny. In that final moment before walking inside his room, I question my past decisions in a way I never have before: who let down whom?

Was I the one who let our hot, passionate love fizzle into cold dust? Or was it he, first distracted by caring for Jamie and then by finding another woman to take away his pain, who allowed me to flutter in the wind like the last brown leaf, clinging to a skeleton tree in autumn?

I decide that it does not matter anymore. I need to see him. I open the door.

The first thing that strikes me is how quiet it is inside his room. There is no beeping of medical machinery, no television, not even the sound of snoring. Just silence. I wonder briefly if there is anybody in the room apart from me; it feels as though I have walked into another dimension, one where perhaps Danny never existed at all.

But then I see the outline of his body, covered by the bed sheet. He is facing away from me, staring out the window. His hair is gray and, beneath the fabric, his shoulders appear somehow slumped, as if he is trying to occupy as little an amount of space in this world as is possible.

Still not ready to face him, I am scared to make a noise, for fear that he will turn and see me. But, that is what I have come for, and so I push away all the memories I have been dwelling on, and I say his name.

"Danny."

He groans as he turns in his bed to look at me. His eyes meet mine and he stops, frozen, as if his cheek has just been touched by the hand of God.

"My lord," he says, after staring at me for a moment. "It's you."

And then his face breaks open into his smile. That, more than anything, makes me feel at home in this cold, sterile place. Although his face has been ravaged by the passage of time, wrinkling the corners of his eyes, pulling his cheeks downward, yellowing his skin, his smile has remained the same open declaration of triumphant happiness I remember it being.

"You were expecting someone else?" I say, smiling.

I still have not stepped toward him.

"Just a nurse to give me a sponge bath."

"Sorry to disappoint you."

Now I step toward him, and I find myself at his bedside. I look him over, trying to be discreet about it. But the sheet is covering his body, and he could be missing all kinds of organs, limbs, and flesh, and I would not be able to tell the difference.

"I can forgive you that."

He reaches out and touches me. His hand is frail – he is frailer than I am, and that is the saddest moment of all, the instant I realize that he has aged so poorly and that his youthful, beautiful soul never deserved to be imprisoned in the grimy clutches of the hands of time.

As though reading my mind, he says, "I'm sorry you have to see me like this."

"Don't be sorry. I love you more now than ever before."

And that is true. Without thinking about it twice, because to hesitate would be the end of it, I slide myself carefully into his bed.

"Ooh," he says, moving over slightly to make room for me. "It's been awhile since I shared my bed with a woman."

I want to inquire about his health, but at the same time, I am afraid to ask. What if his time is short? I have seen so many people whom I love die, and he is the king of my heart. To lose him would mean my own death. So I do not say anything. I press myself closer to him.

Although some immature part of me misses the heat he used to incite in me, I find the kind of warmth he gives me now is just as pleasant, even better. I was meant to be by his side.

"Oh, Danny, why do we have to get old?"

He laughs. It is a choked sound, yet not entirely devoid of humor.

"I'll be sure to ask God about that when I see Him."

He stares up at the ceiling for a few moments.

"We had a good life," he says, contented.

"Not good enough. I missed you most of it."

He turns his head and I am shocked to see tears welling in his eyes.

"My dear," he says, "missing you was what kept me alive for so long."

The most selfish thing I ever did, the worst thing I ever did, was also the best thing I ever did.

Nicholas was six, Timothy three, when I ran away with Danny. I did not pack my bags. It was late one night. Danny had divorced Paula and he was in a period of unrest before finding another wife. I was tired of feeding kids and getting Nick ready for school every morning, cooking dinner for Charlie, who was increasingly reminding me of my father, before collapsing into exhausted sleep every evening.

It was the mid-sixties and the country was too worried about Vietnam to be concerned with what I was doing with Danny. So he picked me up in his Mercury.

The house was dark. I scribbled a note to Charlie.

I am going away for a little while. It's not because of you. It's because of me. I know it is the wrong thing to do, but hopefully, when I return, I will be able to be a better mother to our children and a better wife to you.

Don't hate me for this. I will see you soon.

Back then, it seemed a very rash decision, but in truth, it was nothing of the sort. I had been miserable for some time before I ran away, and I had been toying with the idea, either consciously or subconsciously, for many months. No, years.

We drove. I did not care where we were going. We did not seem to have a plan. Only to leave. It was my greatest fantasy, playing out in reality. We did not – we could not – speak much in those first few miles because the weight of what we were doing was so great, it stifled our words. Danny thought of it as a great betrayal of one of his best friends; I thought of it as about damn time.

West we went, through Michigan, headed nowhere and everywhere. Our quiet drive was sad and joyous; the best of times and the worst of times. Although filled with love for Danny, I could not help but dwell on the hate and pain I had left behind in Detroit.

We did not stop until we reached Lake Michigan. There it lay before us, big and blue and sparkling in the morning sunlight. There were no boats on the water, no sunbathers on the sand. It was autumn and too late for anybody to enjoy the weather anymore, and a cold breeze spiked off the waves and rushed through my hair.

Danny stood behind me and embraced me, his arms interlocking around my waist.

It was only the second day, and I said, "I miss my family."

"I know."

Danny kissed the nape of my neck. His lips were warm and I could tell by the shape of them that he was smiling.

"I don't want to go back yet."

"I know."

We stood that way for some time, staring out at the expanse of water and smelling the wet odor it brought in with its perpetual motion.

"We can't run forever," I said.

He placed his chin on the top of my head and rested it there for a few moments. Somehow, I could measure his breaths by feeling his jawbone with my cranium. This was the way I wanted things to be for the rest of time, this moment: I would always remember it clearly, every dipping seagull, every leafy weed blowing in the wind, clinging to the sand dunes.

"I don't want to run forever," he said. "I just wanted to

run for a little while. With you."

I nodded, and that seemed to put to rest the conversation. We stayed that way for an indeterminate time, which was exactly the way I wanted it. We clambered back into his car and drove to a diner and ate a big breakfast. He had pancakes, I had scrambled eggs. Nobody looked at us as if we were doing anything funny. The other diners enjoyed their own meals, sipped at their coffee, picked at their muffins, and smiled at us in a neighborly way.

That was the way our lives should have played out – Danny and me, going out, together, loving each other publicly, brightening up the rest of the world, if even just slightly, with our blend of passion for one another.

I wondered, of course, what my parents would say about what I was doing. I imagined my father's disdain: I had a family, and it was my duty to protect them and stay with them for the rest of my life. And he was right.

At the same time, I imagined my mother: I had finally pushed aside my fear and I had grabbed what I really wanted from life. And she was right. In the end, I did not care who was right and who was wrong. I cared about Danny.

We stayed at a little hotel by the lake. He parked his car in the lot outside, unconcerned that anybody would see it, recognize it, and come knocking at our door.

The room was small and liberally decorated in a maritime theme. The walls were lined with prints of paintings of ships, sitting placidly on the surface of the water, nets full of captured fish, all seemingly content to be left in the sun on the deck of a boat, happy to be someone's dinner.

I sat on a stool at the window, a shawl wrapped

around my shoulders, looking out at the dark trees, the falling leaves, the billowing clouds which, at a certain altitude, all seemed to melt together into a pastel gray soup. I heard Danny approach me from behind and my neck tingled slightly. I wanted him to touch the back of my head, to stroke my hair in easy petting.

He did exactly that. I listened to his fingers comb through my hair. My scalp felt fuzzy and warm. I closed my eyes and listened to his breathing, listened to my own breathing match his. I leaned back so the back of my head rested on his crotch; I felt the bulge there, throbbing beneath the fabric of his pants, contained by his zipper. He pressed himself against me and I sighed from some deep part of myself, from inside my soul.

I swiveled around to face him, my eyes aligned perfectly with his belt buckle. He kept his hand on the top of my head, and then he slowly caressed downward until it was resting on my cheek.

"I've needed you for so long," he said.

"We were fools to wait," I whispered.

"No." I thought he would say more, but he didn't. He unbuckled his pants and unzipped them and pulled them down in slow motion. His briefs came with them, and his cock sprung out, less sprightly than I remembered it, but still hard, still seeking, still magnificent. Bigger than I remembered it, although not as big as Charlie's.

I pressed my cheek against his thigh and rubbed my face there, never taking my eyes off his penis, which bobbed slightly up and down with my movements. I grabbed it at the base and pulled on it a few times, hard, like a train conductor blowing his horn. His balls slapped against my knuckles. They felt slightly colder than his shaft did. He breathed harder now, leaning back so that his manhood pointed up toward heaven.

And then I opened my mouth and took it in. It was hard but the flesh was soft. I twirled my tongue around the head and then bobbed, working my tongue to and fro, over every hot inch, acre, mile of his endowment, savoring the contours: the smoothness of this part, the elasticity of this skin here, the ridge of the head. I went deep and he poked into the soft inner part of my cheek. I felt my face bulge outward there.

It did not take long before I felt him bulge even more, grow even hotter. He guided me at a rhythm he enjoyed with his hands, and then he pulled me away, took himself out of me, and shot a load of semen up and over my face. Droplets and strands landed on my lips, my forehead, and then more cum spurted out of a geyser, pulsing out like white oil from a well. His cock, growing flaccid, still throbbed with his heartbeat, still half-hard and superheroic.

I looked over my shoulder and saw that his first jet had landed on the window, where it stuck like a strange, crushed bug.

"Wow," I said.

He laughed. His breathing returned to normal. He took me by the hand and then threw me on the bed.

"Take off your clothes."

"You can't possibly—"

"No. Now it's your turn."

And I took off my clothes in haste, and I spread my bare legs to him. He got on his knees at the foot of the bed and crawled up so that his smiling face was where my body met my lust. He kissed, and then his tongue popped out like a jack-in-the-box clown, and he started probing me.

At first I felt nothing, and then, quite suddenly, he touched a spot, and my guts were set afire. I arched my back and, encouraged by my reaction, he started flicking and licking faster, more deeply. It was too much: I put my hands above my shoulders and pushed against the bed. I screamed. I twisted the bed sheets as if I could tear them, as though I could cause them a pain that was equal to my pleasure. But I could not.

It was the most intense moment of my life and I nearly threw up, it felt so amazing. After, I relaxed every muscle in my body. I felt used and decadent and dirty and like a goddess. My belly trembled for a few minutes longer, as if haunted by the ghost of the pleasure it had been witness to.

Outside, the afternoon sank into evening. With time, it occurred to me to hope the neighbors had not been alarmed.

"We fit together," Danny said, his voice soft, tender.

I thought he was talking dirty to me, which I did not mind, but then I realized that he meant in a more profound way than simply sexually.

All I did was pat his head, kiss him on the eyelids, and fall asleep next to him.

We stayed for two weeks at the lake. Our mornings were late, unhurried affairs. Because our room looked out over the lake, there was no morning sun to wake us, just the casual, forgiving encroachment of another day coming to pass. Then we would eat, sometimes at a diner, sometimes just toast, fixed up in the cramped kitchen attached to our love grotto.

We swam, we lay in the sun, even if it was cold. I did not care if I fell ill. It was a pleasure to be judged by others, not because of the extra-marital adventure I was on, but simply because it was autumn and I was throwing myself into Lake Michigan.

Afternoons were dedicated to making love. These sessions often lasted late into evening, when, after we were finally satiated, we would lay in bed and watch bad television and my thoughts occasionally turned to the reality of what I was doing, and how Charlie would now know everything, and how even my neighbors would look at me, differently, scornfully.

I couldn't pretend those things did not bother me at least a bit. They did. I had brought a black mark on myself, which was fair enough, but my children would also suffer. Their teachers would whisper, in their secret teachers' room, about their mother, who ran away like a common whore with another man.

It was small consolation that those same teachers lived dull, cardboard-flavored lives, that they knew nothing about the true, burning love Danny and I shared, that their closest experience with true love was written in books or hidden in mathematical formulae.

Our last day was bittersweet. Danny only had two weeks of vacation time saved up from his factory. I wondered ironically if, at the same pay schedule, Charlie had also saved up two weeks' worth of time, and if he would want to spend them with me when he decided to take advantage of them.

"I'll stay with you if you want," he said.

He was sitting on the front steps to our room, low, concrete, squat, hard.

"I'll never go back to Flint again."

"Don't be crazy," I said, which was not saying no.

"That's what I want to do."

I nodded. That was what I wanted, too, and if I did not have two little boys waiting for their mother, I would not have hesitated to agree.

"You know I can't do that," I said softly.

I sat beside him and rested my cheek on his biceps. I curled my fingers around his forearm, interlaced my hands around his flesh, as if trying to capture him and keep him forever.

"I know," he said.

"How do you think Charlie is going to react?"

Danny should have been the one asking me; I was Charlie's wife, after all. But, Danny knew him as well as I did, and by asking, I could at least feign a kind of distance from the hurt I had certainly caused him.

"I think he's hurt," Danny said.

I didn't point out that his response did not actually answer my question.

"But I think it's me he'll be angry at. Not you."

"I think he'll hate both of us," I said.

"You're probably right."

"I can tell him I was somewhere else. With someone else."

My hopes suddenly soared: perhaps I could keep Danny clear of all this, after all. Who knew I was with him? Nobody.

But Danny quickly shattered those thoughts.

"No. I won't let you do it alone."

And then, after a long pause, he added, "Besides, he knows already. I'm sure the entire class we graduated with knows. There's no keeping a secret like this."

"I kept my love for you secret for so many years," I said.

If it was true that now it would be common knowledge, that everyone would know, I felt as if I had lost an important part of myself. That hidden, valuable part that you show so few people, only the ones you trust the most deeply, and even then with fear in your heart because you are afraid that person will use it to hurt you.

"That was when it was inside us," Danny said. "We've made it something bigger than us, now. It's not just ours anymore."

And that was the truest way of phrasing it; our secret belonged to everybody now. Perhaps that was what bothered me. Those two weeks of passion cost us more than Charlie's goodwill.

We packed our meager bags into his Mercury and I stared out at the lake while Danny went off to settle the bill. My mind was a blank calendar at that moment, with no thought to what I would say when I saw Charlie, what I would tell my children, how I would explain myself.

All I wanted was to stay there, waiting for my true love, until I was old and empty with years long past.

But it only took so long to pay a motel bill, and soon enough we were on the road, headed east again, Detroit-bound. We spoke very little during that drive, mostly because anything we ever had to say, we had said during those two weeks, when we left the world behind us and ran away together as we had always promised each other.

We spoke a secret language, more expressive than English. Besides that, with each mile closer to Detroit, my guilt grew, and I suspected that Danny's did as well.

It was late afternoon when we saw Detroit again. I mused that on any other day during the last respite from my life, we would have been making love right about then. We stayed on the expressway until our exit, and then we drove slowly down side streets until we were in front of my house.

"I don't want to go inside," I said.

"Why?"

"I want to stay with you."

"And you're scared," Danny replied.

"Yes, that too."

He patted my hand between his.

"I'll go with you."

"I can't let you do that," I said, trying to be courageous, but terrified.

Scared because I was wrong; I would never be afraid of Charlie just because he was big and possibly angry or vengeful or crazy. But because I was the offending party, I owed the universe at least my fear.

Danny opened his door and stepped out, which settled things. He joined me on my side of the car, and we walked together up the walkway. I did not know what we might say, how we would justify what we had done, how much we would explain, how detailed we would be in our description. All I knew was that Danny was beside me, like a man walking proudly to his execution.

Just before we climbed the front steps to the house, he said to me, "Remember ... we did something wrong, but it was right, too. Because love is always right."

I stared at him for a moment, unsure if he had actually said that or if my own mind had put those words in his mouth. They sounded like the poetry of my own denial.

Then the moment passed, and we climbed the stairs. I had the impulse to knock at the door, but I forced myself simply to swing it open and step inside.

It still smelled like my home: leather shoes, milk, coffee, shampooed carpet.

"Hello," I called out to the seemingly cavernous house.

The first to appear was Charlie's mother, Freda. A large woman, her hair in curlers, her face devoid of makeup and severe, her gait steady and sure.

"There you are," she stated. "Where in the hell have you been?"

Freda was a surprise, and she was a woman who usually meant business. She looked harried, I guessed from having taken care of her son and grandchildren in her daughter-in-law's absence. It made it somehow more difficult, to have to explain where I was, what I had been doing – how much easier it would have been simply to face a barrage of insults!

"I was with Danny," was the short explanation I settled on.

His presence encouraged and calmed me, and he took a step forward.

Freda turned her anger toward Danny.

"You son of a bitch," she said softly, but not gently. "Charlie's your best friend. Look what you did. Just look. Look at what you did!"

She screamed this last sentence so that it sounded like an age-long curse.

"I'm sorry," Danny said. "But I love her. And I love Charlie, too."

"So take Charlie away and fuck him, then!" she said.

Danny said nothing, but nor did he move, which I interpreted as an impressive show of strength. Most men would have hidden.

During the commotion, my children wandered into the kitchen, from where they could see us. I spotted them hiding by the refrigerator, and as soon as I made eye contact with them, they yelled out, "Mommy!" and ran to me.

I hugged them as tightly as I could muster.

"They've missed you," Freda said, unable to contain the note of spite which crept into her voice.

I ignored her.

"I love you guys so much," I told them. "And I missed you. I'm back now."

"Where were you?" Nicholas asked.

Because I was the type of person who always answered questions asked of me, as if it were a duty, I stared at him for a few long moments, deciding upon an answer. But I broke his gaze and I never answered his question. I suppose that he discovered the truth in the following years, but he never broached the subject.

Timothy did, when going through his divorce, in the process of moving to Washington, D.C., and that was the frankest, most human conversation I ever had with him. He sat with me on the front porch and asked me what it was like when I ran away from Dad, and I told him, mostly, the truth about it, and my motivations, and that I would have done it again, even if it were completely selfish.

After I ripped that truth out of myself and threw it on the ground between us, he told me how he had cheated on his wife, and how she would never forgive him, and how he did not do it out of love but because he was running away from stress.

I thought that was a poor reason to destroy a family, but I was in no position to tell him that, and so I just listened, and after that, I felt I knew my youngest son many levels deeper than ever before. And it scared me.

"Where's Charlie?" I asked Freda.

She stared at me vindictively for a few moments before answering: "He's gone out to look for you."

"Where?" Danny asked.

"I'm not going to tell you," Freda spat at him.

"Please," I said. "I need to find him. You want to let him stay out there, wondering, searching, when I'm right here?"

I hoped my children did not understand what was being discussed, but I suspected that Nicholas, at the very least, was well aware of current events.

"You don't deserve him," she said to me softly.

"I know," I said, and I believed it. "But help me find him, so that we can be a family again."

She nodded as if this were the correct answer to a particularly difficult riddle.

"He left for Hamilton," she said. "He called in sick to work, but they know what's going on. That was three days ago. He wanted to leave last week, but I told him to hold on, that you would come back. He kept trying to go – finally, I told him to go and find you."

"Do you mind staying with the kids for another night?"

She smiled the smile of the long-suffering.

"What's one more night?"

I hugged my kids and told them I'd be back very soon. They cried, and each tear tore a new hole in my heart. They were my doing; I deserved those tears.

We did not linger with goodbye. We left quickly and got back into the Mercury, which seemed a haunted shell of the car it was before. The engine sounded hollow and unforgiving as we rejoined the expressway and headed westward again. Neither Danny nor I spoke: I felt guilty, and I was certain that he felt even guiltier.

We exited the freeway and found ourselves on that same highway where we stopped so that I could pee behind a tree, and only then did we speak again, our voices sounding lost inside the car, which felt too much like a coffin.

"I was her favorite," Danny said.

Startled by his voice, and then scared, because it sounded small and hurt, I said, "What?"

"Freda. I was her favorite of all Charlie's friends."

He paused for a long time, frowning.

"And he was my best friend. All through high school, middle school. Even before that."

"He still is."

But even I did not believe my own words.

"No," Danny answered. "He's not. He was my only friend. And now he's gone."

A rabbit ran in front of the car and Danny swerved to miss it. I craned my head to watch it disappear into the foliage on the opposite side of the highway. Danny said nothing about the rabbit, and after a moment I wondered why I was even thinking about the animal. I supposed I had known a lot of boys and men who would swerve to hit the terrified rabbit; Danny was one who would do anything not to cause more pain in the world.

And yet, here he was, agonizing over what he had done to his friend Charlie.

And, if I was honest with myself, it was a bad thing Danny did. Equally as bad as what I had done to Jamie – perhaps worse because Charlie was so innocent, so naïve about my feelings for Danny, Danny's feelings for me.

We arrived in Hamilton. One moment we were in the country, and the next, new signs of civilization popped up at the side of the road. The town did not stretch out before us. It simply fizzled in, like turning the dial on the radio to find the strongest signal. We wasted no time. We drove directly to Charlie's childhood home. His truck was in the driveway.

"We're here," Danny said.

"Yes."

He inhaled deeply and let his breath out slowly.

"I'm not ready for this," he said, staring into my eyes. "It's not losing him that is going to hurt so much. It's losing you."

"What do you mean?"

"You know," Danny said. "After I confess to everything we did, I won't be able to see you again. It hurts to lose him as a friend, but I don't deserve him. What kills me is losing you."

"You'll never lose me."

"My whole life, I've been losing you."

The front door opened and Charlie's father stood on the porch, staring out at us.

"I suppose we should go," I said.

"Right."

We walked slowly through the front yard. Charlie's father, a burly man who often wore flannel shirts, and who wore one today, glared at us.

"Charlie," he called out behind him. His voice was loud and gruff. "There's someone here to see you."

He stared at us as he climbed down the porch steps and sat in Charlie's truck. He said not a word as he started the engine, backed the vehicle into the street, and sped away.

"I used to go fishing with him," Danny said, hanging his head.

"You used to go fishing with me," I whispered.

Danny did not have an opportunity to respond. Charlie came through the front door and looked down at us from the porch. His eyes were red and a few days' growth of beard darkened his features. His hair was uncombed and his t-shirt spotted with something yellow on the chest.

I suddenly wanted to be anywhere in the world besides here. I was conscious of a man playing catch with his daughter and son, a few houses down.

Charlie just stared at us. He looked how a child looks at the moment after hearing Santa Claus does not exist. I could have crumbled under his wide, questioning eyes. Danny was the first to speak.

"I'm so sorry, Charlie."

Charlie looked at me for a moment longer before turning his gaze to his best friend.

"So, what? What did you two do? Did you enjoy it? Did you have fun?"

Danny spread his hands: a gesture of concession, admission, frankness.

"I love her, too," he said.

Charlie stood, digesting that statement for a few moments.

Then he turned to me, "And you?" he said. "You love him, too? You want to leave me?"

What could I say? I could have told the truth, said, 'Yes, I want to leave you and run away with Danny. I want to spend the rest of my life with him. My life is complete only with him ... with you, I'll always be only partially whole.'

Instead, I said, "We made a mistake, Charlie. Can you forgive us?"

"No. I can't forgive you. And I can't forget it."

Danny nodded. "What can I say?" he said. "I don't blame you for hating me. I still love you like a brother, though."

"Go to hell, man," Charlie said.

He took a few stumbling steps toward the porch stairs and then, ungracefully, he staggered down them. He walked toward Danny, who still stood with his hands spread like Jesus on the mount. I thought he would come to me; I thought he would put his arms around me and say things like, "we'll figure this out," "We'll make things better," "Time will heal this. But he walked past me, approaching Danny.

"I'll kill you," he snarled and then threw a sweeping right hook.

I flinched when Charlie's fist connected with Danny's beautiful face. Danny lurched back a few steps, clutching at his eye, inspecting his fingers for blood. He did not fall; I could not have endured seeing him fall.

I ran up and grabbed Charlie around the waist. He was a big man, and even though he was drunk, I felt his power. It sickened me, in a strange way, that I should have to attempt to contain his gurgling rage this way.

"Stop it," I screamed.

But Charlie was not doing anything else. He only stared down at Danny, who squinted his swelling eye, already bruised. I wanted to wail.

"I will kill you, you sneaky bastard," Charlie slurred.

Danny nodded and straightened his shoulders.

"I deserve that. And you're right."

He turned to go. He walked a few steps toward his Mercury, not stumbling, not limping, not scared. I loved him with every particle of my soul. About halfway through the yard, he turned back.

"You have an angel," he said to Charlie. "Take care of her. Love her forever."

Charlie stepped between Danny and me, nodding his head in a cocky style.

"Just go," Charlie said. "I don't want to see you again."

Danny looked past him, at me, for a few moments before turning and stepping into his Mercury. He looked at me with love-struck eyes, one of them red and purple and pained. He had a small cut on his cheekbone. He started his engine and drove away.

I listened to the sound of his engine dying away in the fading afternoon. Softer it grew, until it disappeared, like a ship vanishing from view on the ocean's horizon.

Charlie, as if he were listening as well, waited until the car was completely gone before he spoke.

"I can't believe you did this to me."

He slurred his words but the pain was evident, and I felt a new rush of regret for what I had done.

"I am sorry."

"How could you?"

I turned to look at him. Obviously forcing back tears, his nostrils flared, but not from anger. His lower lip trembled.

"I have loved Danny for a long time," I told him softly.

I wanted to tell him something harder, something that would hurt him more, cut him deeper. I didn't know from where my thirst for his pain sprang; I only knew that I wanted it and that I had the power to inflict it on him.

"I loved him from the first moment I saw him."

But he had the power to hurt me more deeply.

"Maybe that's why Jamie killed herself."

We stood in silence for a time, neither of us even moving. Before me was the man I had married, and I could not fault him for his anger, but I could not find it within me to love him, either. After our accumulating silence became too much for him, he simply turned back to the house and climbed the steps and disappeared inside.

Caught in a limbo of sorts, I didn't want to follow him in and hide under his oppressive, hurt stare. But I had nowhere else to go: Danny was gone, my parents were dead and their old house had been sold.

I drifted in a barren desert, each grain of sand a mistake, a missed turn, a heat stroke and a heartbreak. So I turned in the opposite direction and walked down the street.

Dogs barked from backyards, and I heard a few voices carrying from inside houses, but besides that, I felt like the only person left in the world. It was a comforting feeling, at that moment. Each step carried me through a swirling, curdling river of self-hatred. I thought to pray to God, but I could not think of the words, and besides that, I had doubts as to whether God wanted to help me. My pain was self-inflicted, and I should accept my punishment without complaint or comment.

The afternoon died quickly, that day. Bright sunlight gave way to a haggard twilight, shades of gray and milky blue above. A few stars poked out of the universe, specks, tears, imperfections which created a perfection in the sky. I turned toward downtown, toward the ice cream shop where we used to meet as children. I saw Danny's car parked outside the shop.

I stopped there, while the earth spun on. Everything was cartoonish in its appearance; the Mercury was too white, the sidewalk too even. The night smelled both sweet and sour and I breathed deeply. I walked toward the car.

He sat in the driver's seat. I saw the back of his head, and then I saw his eyes in the rearview mirror. One of them was badly injured and swollen. He watched me. I stopped about ten feet behind the taillights. I wanted him to step out of the car, but he did not. I waited for him to do it and when he didn't, I thought he did not love me anymore.

So I walked to his window. It was rolled down, and when I bent down to better speak with him, he did not look at me. I told him to look at me. He only stared ahead.

"Don't be like this," I said to him.

"Why are you here?" he said, still staring ahead.

"I don't want to see Charlie right now," I said. "I don't want to be with him. I don't feel safe there."

"He won't hurt you," Danny said, glancing at me. His swollen eye was the color of the settling evening.

"I know," I confessed.

Charlie was too stupidly moral to ever hit a woman, even one who was killing him.

"You owe it to yourself and your family to go back to him," he said. "There's nothing more for us. Not today, anyway."

"I don't like that."

Perhaps I sounded like a petulant child.

"Neither do I. But it's the only fair thing. Think about your kids."

And I did think about them, small and innocent and wide-eyed, forming their opinions about the world and their mother already. "All right," I said. "I'll go back. For a while. But every second, I'll wonder where you are and what you are doing. I'll always think about you. Promise me we'll see each other again."

"I promise," he said, looking into my eyes, holding my gaze for a long few seconds.

Long, but too short.

He returned his stare to the road, started his engine, and put the gearshift into first. He said nothing more; nor did I. He drove away and again, I watched his taillights dim into nothing.

I walked back to Charlie after that, just as I'd told Danny I would. It was a difficult journey because it was hard not to be selfish. It was harder because we were not Romeo and Juliet, born into the wrong families and circumstances, but rather Danny and Liz, two fools who'd had every opportunity to make their love work but who never took the chance to try it.

Charlie was calmer when I arrived, and he sat me down and made me tell him everything Danny and I did together.

He stared at me with huge, bloodshot eyes, and he waited for me to recount the hours of passion we enjoyed.

Some evil part of my brain told me to lie to him: to tell him we robbed banks, or flew to China, or joined a traveling circus. But, instead, I told him everything in the most factual way I could; I told him about the sex we had, the room by the lake, the kisses we prolonged for hours, licking each other's lips and dotting eyelids with pecks of sweet tenderness.

And the whole time, Charlie only stared at me, silent and hurt.

I waited for him to be angry. I wanted him to be angry.

But, when I had told him the story of what we had done, he only said, "So, is it out of your system?"

"What?"

"I said, is it out of your system? Are you done doing this sort of thing? You aren't going to leave me again, are you? You love me, right? I am the one that you want to be with."

I did not allow myself to hesitate.

"Yes."

"Good," he said, nodding his head one final time. "Then we can work it out. We can work it out, babe."

I listened to the ticking of the old clock on the bookshelf. I could not count the seconds. I imagined a million of them passing this way, each more gut-wrenching than the last. How would the hundredth feel? The millionth?

We slept in the same bed that night, but to me it felt like trying to sleep on an asteroid, Earth just a speck in the cold, eternal, omniscient night.

Thirteen

I stare at his face for a long time.

His skin is wrinkled, a deeper shade than in his youth. His eyes are still squinty, and the crow's feet around their corners seem to pull them even more tightly shut. His lips are not full, his beard, just a shade of stubble, white and ghostly.

He often wore just that much facial hair in his adult years. Just enough to barely tickle.

His eyebrows are gray, streaked with the black of his earlier life, and his eyes are still dark and warm and they smile. His lips are not smiling, except when I look at him, and then, as if he has been caught doing something dirty, he stretches his mouth into a grin which looks a little like a lie.

We talk about the time we ran away. I tell most of the story because I like to tell it and, if I am truthful, because I am afraid he has forgotten some of the best parts.

But he smiles with the story, as if he recalls the caress of my lips against his, as if he remembers the taste, the way our breaths mixed when we held each other closer than close, forehead to forehead.

He apologizes again.

"You know how much that hurt me," he says. "The foolishness. Ha. We were fools."

"Yes," I say, "we were."

"I am still a fool," he says, raising his eyebrows and looking up at me.

I lean toward him and our lips meet, as casually as ever they did before, or perhaps as they never have before.

It is impossible to describe, how the physical contact can change, how the texture of his lips has changed over the decades, as I'm sure mine has, how we have grown old and yet how this simple thing, this kiss, is the same at its most fundamental level. It is like jumping into very cold water and loving the shock, and wanting to sink further and further until you are wrapped in dark, frozen solitude at the bottom of the lake, so cold that you can feel your blood, hot and coursing through your veins and arteries.

There were times when we kissed literally for hours, and neither of us has the endurance for that anymore. But though it is short, it is sweeter, and though we break it off, already my neck is a little sore from craning it at an angle, I am left with a tingling joy that I never want to let go.

This is what it must feel like to walk down that final tunnel, toward the famous big bright light. This is what approaching paradise must be.

The story of our youthful escapades completed, we turn to more serious conversation. This is something I have been dreading, but something I will not allow myself to avoid any longer. Ignorance is bliss, but ignorance of him is torture.

"So? What's going on with you?"

I look down at his body beneath the sheet to try to communicate to what I am referring.

He understands, of course.

"I'm in rough shape."

"Tell me about it."

He takes a deep breath and I hear how the air struggles through his airway.

"Pancreatic cancer," he says with finality.

The words are short and poisonous and I want to maim them, rip them apart and throw them out of the window like confetti.

"What?" I say. "How do you have cancer?"

He nods his head.

"Any day could be my last. The doctors said I can't expect more than a month."

"You have to be kidding."

Although I know that he is not, I love this body of his, I always have, and now I hate it, too. It has betrayed him, and it has betrayed me.

"I'm full of problems," he says, managing a simper. "Diabetes – I've had that for years. From the loss of something sweet from my life, I've been told."

He looks at me a moment too long, all my regrets reflected in his own eyes. He sighs and finishes the list.

"The cancer, you know about. Bad joints, bad eyes."

"We all have bad joints and bad eyes," I say.

But he does not respond to that.

"Already they tell me I have Alzheimer's, too, but I don't believe that one."

He pauses for a few long moments before adding, "Not that I would know the difference if it were true."

"A month," I say quietly.

"Just a month."

"Come live with me," I say abruptly.

"What?"

"Yes, come with me. We can live together. We can be together for as long as possible. Maybe I'll even save your life."

Smiling, trying for a joke, trying for anything.

But he shakes his head.

"You already saved my life. Besides that, I'll be dead before we can get the paperwork filled out. It was a nightmare when they put me in this place. The only way out is in a coffin."

"Don't say that."

He turns his head, looks out the window.

"I'm just trying to be realistic."

"We never were realistic. And that was the way I liked it."

"We were always *too* realistic. That was the problem."

He turns and looks at me now, and I see tears welling in his eyes. I hate to see him cry, but I do not wipe away his tears. My plan was to get him out of here, one way or the other, and I decide to tell him so.

"You're coming with me."

"If it were as easy as that, I would already be there."

I stare at him for a second longer, and I make what I know will be a decision equally as crazy as the one I made when I ran away with this man, all those years before. I take a deep breath.

"Where is your old car? The Mercury?"

He frowns for a moment, and I am unsure if it is because he cannot remember where his car is or because he is trying to figure out what my intentions are.

In time, he says, "In Christine's garage."

He looks quizzically at me for a few seconds longer.

"Why?"

"Where are the keys?"

Now a sly grin seeps across his face.

"I left them in the ignition."

I grin, too.

"Okay, you pack your bags, mister. I'm busting you out tomorrow. No problemo."

"I'll put you on a visitor list ... now that I know you want to see me."

And he winks.

But his words deflate me, take my breath from me for a moment. How could he ever assume otherwise?

"It will be all right," I say, standing from his bed. "I'm going to make this all okay, in the end."

I kiss him on the forehead before exiting.

The corridor is strangely silent and empty and I move with a little more confidence than before; no one will see me, no one will question me. I need to remind myself I am an old woman, and my intentions are not written upon my forehead for everyone to read. Still, the hallway creeps me out. It reminds me of too many lost days.

How strange to be my age and to be creeped out by anything!

I find the elevator and go down to the ground floor, hardly caring if the receptionist sees me, asks me what I am doing, who I am and what business I have here.

But the receptionist is not behind her desk. The lobby is empty except for a family, sitting on a couch, reading magazines. I give them a brief thought before pushing on my way; what could they be doing here? Waiting for someone to die, perhaps.

The front doors *whoosh* open and I am outside again. It is evening and I am surprised to see how much time has passed while I have been talking to my lover. I take a moment to collect my bearings. I do not know where I am, actually, and even if I knew, I would not be able to walk home from here.

I walk, anyway.

As I arrive at the road, a car stops to greet me. I do not know the make or the model; my automobile knowledge has not increased with my age. It is small and blue and the passenger seat is torn so that yellow stuffing protrudes like brains after a head is split open.

The window rolls down and I hear "So, how did it go?"

I wrinkle my forehead, then I realize it is Robbie, the pothead kid who snuck me into the building. I break into a smile, happy that he is willing to stop to talk to me even after the little matter of the blackmail I played on him and his friends.

"Can you give me a ride? I'll give you gas money."

He smirks and then nods.

"Hop in, ma'am."

So I get in his car. It is cramped and it smells of stale cigarette smoke mixed with cheap air fresheners. It is not entirely unpleasant. He turns down his stereo after I take my seat.

"Thank you."

"Don't mention it. You're a cool old lady."

I laugh at that, and after I am done, I tell him, "It went well, thanks. I love that man very much. I needed to see him today."

"Well, amen to that."

Robbie pulls a cigarette from his shirt pocket, sticks it in the corner of his mouth, flicks his lighter, and just before touching the flame to the smoke, he says, "Do you mind?"

"Not at all."

"How does this work?"

"What?"

"The gears. The car."

"Well," he explains, "you start in first. Then you go to second. Then third. Neutral means you don't go anywhere, the car just coasts. Reverse is back here."

"And the pedals?"

I know the stick and its positions already.

"Clutch, brake, gas," he says, pointing to each with his right foot. "You mean you don't know how to drive?"

"I've never driven a car in my life. But I want to learn. You know, it's on my bucket list."

"Ah, the things you want to do before you die."

"Something like that."

"You want to give it a try?"

I scoff. I consider telling him that I don't have a license, but I assume he must know this already.

Instead, I say, "I'll probably wreck your car, Robbie."

Now he scoffs. "Can't make it look any worse than it does already. Come on."

He stops the car at the curb and steps out of the driver's seat. I do not move, but he comes over to my side of the car and opens the door and I think maybe this is the kind of day when I can do anything. So I get out and take his seat behind the wheel.

Already I am a bit terrified. I have never seen the world from behind a steering wheel before. As I strap the seat belt around my shoulder, Robbie chuckles.

"Now," he says. "Press in the clutch."

I do as he instructs, which is to put the car into first and gently apply the accelerator while letting up on the clutch. My legs are not built for this: the bones and muscles are not accustomed to fine movements, controlled actions, planned maneuvers. The car lurches forward and stalls in a body-rattling stall.

"No problem!" he says, and for a jolting moment, I almost hear *no problemo*!

He tells me to do it again, and I stall it again. The street is empty. I crane my neck to look in the mirrors, which are not adjusted to suit me. On the third try, the car roars unhealthily and starts to roll forward.

"It's going!" I yell, my voice cracking. "It's moving!"

"Of course it is!" Robbie says, laughing.

We gain speed, and he says, "Now switch to second!"

I jam in the clutch, feeling like an old pro, and jerk the gearshift into second gear. The car protests, lurches again, but we keep moving after that.

"Yes!" I yell.

I take it up to a stop sign, where I shift it into neutral and let him apply the parking brake before we change seats again. I am trembling, but not just from fear; it's exciting and I feel as if I have just drunk a pot of strong coffee.

"Good work," he says, once we have taken our proper seats. "You learn fast."

I smile. "I never thought I'd learn to drive from a kid," I confess. "You're really all right, Robbie. Thanks."

I am envious of the way he massages the car into driving forward. We still have not seen any other traffic, and I am thankful for that.

"It was fun," he says. "I tried to teach my girlfriend to do it – she can't drive a stick. She can barely handle an automatic."

"Don't go too hard on her."

I smile secretly within myself.

"Eh," he says. "Things are hard, with her."

"Yeah? Want to tell me a little about it?"

He frowns for a moment before shrugging.

"Well, we've been at it for a year or so. Things are good. Good enough."

"But?"

"Well," he says, then trails off. "It's like that old song, you know, she's lost that loving feeling. And I think I have, too."

"Then why are you two still together?"

He shrugs.

"Good question. Convenience. We laugh sometimes. We have a good time, sometimes."

He shrugs again.

I do not know what I was expecting from him. He is too young to have felt the heartache I have, and I envy him while at the same time, I am overjoyed I do not have to go through the same mistakes again.

Fourteen

I lived with Charlie for the next several years without any additional specific mention of my running away, and without analyzing myself deeply enough to be angry with myself for living a tremendous lie, for each of my days being a mistake of sorts. We ate breakfast together, dinner together, and lunches alone.

Lunch was my favorite meal; I sat and stared out of the window and wondered about Danny, wondered where all those beautiful memories disappeared. If they still existed, if his were the same as mine, and, if they were different, if they were lies, too.

Our children grew to be happy, well-adjusted boys who neither bullied nor were bullied on the playground. Charlie taught them that, and there were moments when I loved him for the father that he was. Danny could not teach certain things, and how to fight was one of them; Danny was too well-loved to need to fight, except for extreme cases of wife-theft.

Danny married Paula in the autumn and I, of course, did not attend the ceremony. By that time, I had stopped viewing Charlie as a complete moron, and so especially careful to show no sign of the depression wracking me that day. Even so, he must have known. I was sure he knew my love still burned hot for Danny, that my heart still throbbed for him alone.

I never even sent them my congratulations. Charlie never even acknowledged that Danny had gotten married again. It was a normal day, in our household.

So often I wondered about him, about them, if this new girl understood the magic that was Danny, if anyone else ever would in the way I did. Who was I to make the assumption that she did not?

As for having lost that loving feeling, Charlie certainly had. It was almost better that way not to have to pretend the feeling was mutual while he kissed me, while he held me, while he whispered what passed for poetry in his brain.

We kept up appearances, not that we had many places to go and be seen; he draped his massive arm around my shoulders when we were in public. He kissed me sometimes on the cheek. But it lacked warmth and soul and it was a sweet emptiness to which I grew accustomed.

And you do grow accustomed to the cold. I had been cold for most of my life, and the few lovely nights I allowed myself to come in from it were the only truly happy times I'd lived. Those memories kept a special place in my heart where only I could access them.

The country went through a turbulent few years. I was alone in the kitchen when Kennedy was killed. I heard about it on the radio, and it affected me, as it did so many, on a personal level for some reason. Here was our leader, a man of contradictions, a cheater on his wife, a lover, and he was dead. It was impossible to think he deserved it.

That day, I cried harder than I cried in many years, and when Charlie came home, he held me, not understanding that I was not weeping for the president, but rather for Danny and how I had lost him. That simple fact made the tears sweeter for me.

Danny's first child came less than a year after he was married, a beautiful daughter. I received a phone call late one evening, and it was him. "I've got a baby girl," he whispered into the receiver.

"Danny," I uttered, stopping short for fear of waking Charlie, although I could hear him snoring from down the hallway.

"Her name is Christine," he said.

I did not know how to respond. I wanted to congratulate him because that was what normal people did in such circumstances, but I was overcome with grief, and I could not find the appropriate words.

"Danny," I said again, my voice no stronger than before.

"I know," he said.

I could imagine him nodding his head and smiling in a forlorn way.

"I can't pretend to know how you feel right now. I wish I were there with you."

"I do, too," I said.

We could not speak long – his wife, my husband.

"I think about you every day."

"And I think of you," he said. "We need to move on. I can't move on."

"I'll never move on."

My heart burned with longing. I wanted nothing more than to touch him, and just hearing his voice again reminded me how my life had turned out.

He said, "I never told Paula about us."

"She doesn't know anything?"

He did not respond to my question. "Is Charlie around?"

"Always."

"Hmm. Does he ever ... does he ever talk about me?"

I considered lying to him, but even to spare his feelings, I could not do it.

"He never says anything about you."

I listened to him breathe for a few moments. They were short, they were eternal.

"I need to run," he said. "We'll talk."

And, just like that, our conversation was over.

He had a little girl. I knew what that meant; his attention and his love would be further divided, and as a result, he would need me less. But, that was okay. It was okay because he was a father, and that was something that had been denied to him in the most awful way, just a few short years before.

Charlie gained weight and his eyes seemed to sink further into his face. He was still solidly built, but he carried himself something like a slothful animal which has spent too much time in a zoo. He drank more, ate less, smoked and cursed without seeming to consider who was around him or what impression he created.

I stopped caring.

He came home some evenings with sweat stains under his arms, bleary eyes, spots of food dribbled on the front of his work shirt. He collapsed into bed, oftentimes a lit cigarette dangling from his mouth.

He must have inhaled a lungful of ash doing that, and the only reason I plucked the cigarette from his lips and jammed it into the ashtray was so the house would not catch fire.

Danny had another child, but I heard about that one through an old friend. That, too, was by phone, and the person on the other end seemed to have no idea of our history together; the news came in joyous tones, and I did my best to keep calm.

Perhaps my friend did know about our escapades but did not understand the throbbing scar stretched across my heart for Danny.

The world had entered a time when extramarital affairs were more commonplace, even encouraged in some circles. I had mine long before it was cool, and I never agreed with it, simply forced into it by love.

The country really got involved in Vietnam and each day, sitting in the kitchen, listening to the newscasts, the rock and roll, the weather, I could not help but feel the world was nearing its end. And all I wanted was to see the end with Danny. If all this must be destroyed, I thought, I should be with the one I love while it happens. But I never went to him during those years.

My own kids did well at school and I liked to believe they didn't sense the distance between their father and me. In my heart, I knew that they knew something was amiss, and it did not reflect well on me that I did not particularly care. I was a bad mother, in that regard. I was selfish, and always had been. But I accepted that part of me, and instead of making me happier, I was still miserable.

The days seemed long, the nights too short. Both were full of dreams, for me, but while dreams are fun because there is always some small part of you that thinks they might come true, my dreams were torture, because I knew they were impossible.

I was not depressed on a daily basis, but a steel

framework of pure despair supported my life. The despair a man must feel, locked in prison for being an accomplice to a crime he never wanted committed; the sadness he must feel when he realizes he has destroyed not just his own life, but the lives of everyone he loves, also.

And so it went, for a time.

Listening to the news, I sat in the kitchen one afternoon, not paying much attention, and not doing anything else, either. Simply sitting there as my life ticked on. Anyone else might have been in despair to reach that point, but all I felt was emptiness to the point where the numbness was nearly pleasant. Then the phone rang.

I let it ring, confident that whoever was calling would give up after a few rounds. There was nobody I wanted to hear from; my parents were dead, I had no friends, and Danny was working. It might have been the school, and that was the thought that forced me to stand and answer its persistent ring.

"Yes," I said, perhaps too harshly, only because I felt my loneliness broken.

"Missus Toll?" came a voice.

"Yes. Who is this?" I heard hesitant breathing through the line. "If you don't identify yourself, I'll call the police."

Something hot and slimy shot up through my veins.

"Please, don't be upset, ma'am," the voice came back. "I have some terrible news. Sit down, all right?"

All right. What a strange thing to say.

"What is it?" I said.

Images flashed through my head, and the most ridiculous of all the thoughts I experienced was, is this about Vietnam?

"It's your husband, ma'am," the voice said. "I'm afraid ... there's been an accident at the factory today."

I listened to the silence between us, this unnamed, unknown voice and myself. Did this person exist? What was his status that he could call me and deliver this unbearable news? A tinny, plastic, barely-human rendition of a voice.

In my ear one moment, then disappeared like a melted snowflake the next, transformed into steady, shallow breaths.

"Ma'am?" the voice continued.

"Yes," I said, my voice hollow. "I hear you."

"Did you hear me?"

"Yes," I said, aware only later of how ridiculous this conversation was, how unmanageable, how inconsistent.

"He ... there was a forklift, and he was behind it. One of our drivers. Well, he feels like hell. Pardon me, ma'am. It was an accident. He turned and Charlie was there and it was an accident. I'm so terribly sorry."

"He's dead?"

No hesitation.

"Yes. He died here."

"Oh my God."

A fly crawled up the wall. I stared at the fly, I stared until it stopped moving. Some crazy part of me wondered if I'd killed it.

"Charlie ... everyone loved him here. I'm sorry."

"Thank you," I said and hung up the phone.

I stood there for a long time. News of the war was still being broadcast on the radio, but I heard none of it. There could have been an atomic bomb coming and I would not have been able to jump under the table and cover my head as I'd learned in middle school. I was not sad, not exactly, but I was devastated.

Just three minutes before, my day had been perfectly planned out, all the way to the moment when Charlie would walk through the door, at least slightly drunk, and kiss me sloppily on the lips as he walked past, waves of distrust parting behind him like the wake from a fast-moving boat. But now, he would never walk through the door again.

Not knowing what to do or where to go, I picked up the phone and dialed his number. I listened to the ring, and it rang and rang until finally a woman answered. I knew instantly it was Paula. I had never spoken to her, but I was too distraught to be angry at her voice just then.

"I'm calling for Danny," I said weakly into the phone. "Is he there? Please tell me he is."

"He's working," Paula said.

She sounded perturbed.

"I need to speak with him, please."

"He's at work," Paula repeated. "Who is this?"

"I'm—"

How could I tell this woman who I was? I didn't know how much she knew about me, if Danny had told her about our affair, if she had heard from someone else, if she had smelled me on him, even months after we last saw each other. Nor did I care enough to think long about it.

"I'm Liz. Do you know me?"

"Should I?" came her response.

"No. Not at all."

"What do you want with my husband?"

I didn't detect any particular jealousy or suspicion in Paula's voice, but I didn't trust her, either.

"Just tell him I called, please," I said, and then hung

up.

I knew it was one of the worst things I could do, that it would only open that dark part that exists in every woman, that part which is afraid and vulnerable and looking for reasons not to trust the man she is with; but I couldn't explain myself to her, not then, and probably not ever.

Sitting in the kitchen for a few hours, expecting the phone to ring at any moment, I did not read, I did not watch the television, and I did not listen to the radio, although it played for all those hours. I knew there were things I should do: call Charlie's parents, our friends, my sister, the hospital, the morgue, the police, a lawyer.

Somebody.

I needed to talk to somebody, to everybody, I needed someone to guide me through the moments that come after the sudden and inexplicable death of your husband. Where do you go and what do you say?

Danny called late that afternoon. I knew it was him as soon as the phone rang, and I jumped out of my chair and rushed to the telephone, but paused before answering. I wanted too badly to speak with him, and I was afraid. But the telephone insisted; it rang on until I succumbed and picked it up off the hook.

"Yes," I said.

"Liz, it's me."

"Danny, oh God."

"What's wrong? Paula told me you called. She was pretty upset about it."

"Sorry."

"What's wrong?" he repeated, as if he did not care in the slightest about his wife's mood.

"Charlie's dead."

"What?" he bellowed into the phone.

I pulled it away from my ear, momentarily hurt by the loud pain in his voice.

"What happened? Jesus Christ!"

"At work," I managed to say. "A forklift, or something. An accident. He got killed."

"No."

What to say to that simple response, that basic denial: no?

"Yes," I said. "They called me a couple hours ago and explained it ... said everyone loved Charlie at the factory."

"It can't be," Danny said.

Then I broke down and wept. My tears were hot and bitter; they did not gush, but rather leaked from my eyes, rolled slick and oily down my cheeks, dropped off my jawbone onto the kitchen floor, onto my feet. Danny's breathing changed and I could tell that he too was crying, on his end.

"What do I do?"

"I don't know," Danny said, and somehow that comforted me.

I thought I wanted to be told what to do, to be directed and helped, but what I really wanted was for someone to validate my own ignorance. Nobody knew what to do. There was nothing that could be done.

"I think I should go to the hospital."

"I'm coming with you," he said.

"No."

Although I wanted him to come. I wanted that more than anything else in the world at that moment, but something held me back, and it was perhaps the first time I ever felt held back in my relationship with Danny. That hurt me even more than I was already hurt.

But he said, "I'm leaving now. I'll be at your house in an hour."

We broke the connection and I waited while the sun sank further toward the horizon. The city outside my window seemed ghostlike, unreal, full of shadows and echoes.

My sons arrived home from school. Nicholas was in the seventh grade, and Timothy was in fourth. They stood at the door, staring at me, and I was afraid to tell them what had happened. So we only stared at each other until Timothy burst into tears for no apparent reason.

Nicholas came to me and stopped about a foot away.

"What?" he said.

He stared into my face.

How could I tell him what had happened? His boyhood was about to be shattered and I found it so difficult to do it to him. In that very moment, everything was still okay. Everything made sense. After I said the words, everything would be different and nothing would make sense.

Charlie's death would affect my boys far more deeply than it had me. And I had spent the afternoon swirling in despair and self-loathing.

"Sit down," I said to him. "You too, Tim."

I sat opposite them at the kitchen table. I took several deep breaths, but every moment I hesitated, it grew even more difficult for me to go on. So I plunged forward.

"Something bad happened to your father today."

They looked at each other, and I hated the way a certain understanding seemed to pass between them. What I didn't like about it, I wasn't sure, but the sentiment was there and it was real. Did they expect me to say something about Charlie and I having a fight? Were they waiting to hear that mommy had once left daddy for a few weeks, and now she was leaving for good? Their glance lasted only a split-second, and then they returned their attention to me.

"There was an accident," I said. "Daddy was hurt really badly."

"An accident?" one of them said.

Whoever it was, I assumed he spoke for both of them.

"Yes. He was killed."

There, it was done. Nobody moved, nobody breathed. As far as I knew, the earth stopped spinning in that moment. Then, Timothy wailed in a way I had never heard before, so animalistic, so primal, and so profoundly full with pain.

It broke my heart again.

So did Nicholas's reaction: he only sat there and stared through me. I grabbed them both by the backs of their necks and pulled them close to me; I tried to pull them into me, where I could protect them and they could protect me. But something separated us, something more than physical.

And my heart broke again.

"I want to see him," Nicholas said. "We need to go see him. Take me to him."

"Okay," I said without considering it.

Only later did it occur to me that their father was probably not in good shape, not after being mangled by a forklift.

"Someone is coming to help me. He'll take us to the hospital."

And we sat in the kitchen, the three of us, facing this new reality. They had been exposed to death before, of course; both their grandparents on my side were dead. But now they were old enough to understand death, at least as well as I understood it; I did not know whether that made the pain lesser or greater.

Danny arrived some indeterminate time later. I heard his Mercury coming from an age away, and a slow creep like dread curled around in my guts until he pulled up to the curb. I listened to the car door slam, his hurried steps come up the drive, and then his solid knock upon the door.

"It's Dad," Timothy said, and my heart broke into a million pieces.

I stood from the table and opened the front door. Danny's eyes were red and bleary, and we stared for a moment before embracing each other. He smelled like the factory, and so he smelled like Charlie, without the alcohol. I held him tight.

"Oh, Danny. Oh, God."

"I'm so, so sorry," he whispered.

Then he pulled away, looking over my shoulder, and when I turned, I saw that he was looking at my children, who stood at the threshold to the kitchen.

This was the first moment they'd seen the man who owned my heart. I wondered what they thought – did they think this was some old friend of Charlie's? They would have been right. Did they think this was simply a friend of mine, someone whom I had called for help? They would have been right about that, too.

But they never could have known how deep and passionate my love ran for this man. And I did not particularly want them to know.

"These are my kids," I said to Danny. "Nicholas and Timothy."

"Hi, guys." Danny gave them a small wave. My

children only stared back at him.

"Are you taking us to the hospital?" Nicholas asked.

Danny glanced at me, but I offered no assistance.

"Sure," he said, turning back to my children. "We're going to go to the hospital to see about your dad."

We readied ourselves to leave, and then we left, although we were not ready. How could we have been ready? How does one become ready to see a father, destroyed? A husband, tortured and forgotten, then killed while trying to provide for his family?

Nicholas and Timothy sat in the backseat, awestruck and quiet. I curled into myself in the passenger seat. This car had seen too much of my heartache, my soul, my outer skin as it sloughed off to reveal the fragile heart beneath.

Under my direction, Danny drove slowly and carefully toward the hospital. He parked in the expansive lot outside and cut the engine. We sat in silence for a moment, and for those bare few seconds, it was again just the two of us. I closed my eyes and imagined myself falling into his arms, letting him caress my trembling shoulders, letting him kiss my pain into oblivion. But then I heard my children sniffling in the back seat, and I opened my eyes.

We clambered out of the Mercury and followed Danny to the entrance of the hospital. It was a blur, for me; it was a huge place, all white and linoleum and sterile; all dark, mysterious glances, whispered questions, assumptions: What is wrong with these people? What tragedy has befallen them, what sickness plagues them? I could not have answered that last question. Was love a sickness? Was my need for Danny a fever, a curable illness? At times, it had felt that way. Now it felt like a warm blanket on a night in the Arctic.

Danny spoke to a receptionist, and I turned away when

she cast me a pitying glance from behind her desk. My children were hugging my legs, and I held them closer to me. All at once, I did not want them here, and not because Danny was with me.

Danny rejoined us and said softly, "He's downstairs."

We followed signs which read MORGUE, into the bowels of the hospital. Each corner we turned, the corridor seemed more silent, closer to abandoned. We were alive, walking among the dead in a mournful place.

After what seemed an age, we stood outside a big metal door and after a few minutes were greeted by an old man wearing an off-white lab coat.

"Can I help you?" he asked.

"Charlie Toll," Danny said.

"You are here to identify the body?" the old man asked, looking over his glasses at Danny and me.

"Yes," Danny said. "And to pick up his personal effects."

"You're family?" the old man said.

"Yes," Danny said without hesitation. "Now, let us see him."

The old man furrowed his brow.

"I don't think the children should enter," he said in an ominous tone. "This is no place for them."

Danny looked at me. I looked down at them. They were acting as if they were not paying attention.

"You guys stay outside," I said to them. "It's scary inside."

"I want to see him," Nicholas said.

I sighed. Why had I brought them, after all? I had no one to leave them with, that was one answer. But a better mother would have found another way, I supposed.

"I'll come get you in a second," I told him, not entirely

sure I was telling the truth.

But I had done enough lying in my life that this was no worse.

Danny and I followed the old man through the door. It was cool inside, with three beds, each occupied by a single corpse, a sheet draped over each one of them. One of the sheets was stained red with what I assumed was blood. We stopped in the middle of the room. It was well lit by a white light but there were too many shadows for me to feel comfortable. I moved closer to Danny and he took my hand in his.

For a ridiculous moment, I thought we had to guess which body was Charlie's. Like picking a door on a popular game show. But the old man studied a flipchart for a moment and then waved us over to the body farthest from the door. Danny and I approached slowly. The old man pulled the sheet down from Charlie's head.

His powerful face, silenced forever, the eyes open, stared at the ceiling, at heaven, at Danny and at me. There was no blood on his face, no scar, nothing indicating he was anything other than drunk and asleep with his eyes wide open.

I reached for him, touched his face, pulled my hand back; he was cold and the stubble on his chin felt unnatural because he was indeed dead. I wanted him to be clean-shaven. I wanted him to be alive.

"How did he die?" Danny asked.

The old man shrugged and pulled the sheet down further, exposing Charlie's chest and a gaping hole, and I saw inside him. I'd always thought I could see through Charlie; now I literally could. I could see his ribs, the unknowable mush of organs and fibers and sinews. Something that looked like a heart, a lung, intestines.

"Jesus," I gasped, turning away. "Cover him up. Please."

Only Charlie's face was exposed when I peeked again.

"I'm sorry," the mortician said. "I just wanted you to know."

"Go get my kids," I said to Danny. He turned and went after them obediently.

The mortician turned to me. "I think he'd been drinking."

"What?"

The old man nodded. He looked like a rat nuzzling a crumb of cheese.

"I said, I think he'd been drinking. Maybe not drunk. Maybe just a beer or two."

I believed it.

"Why do you think that?"

"I just get a feeling," the old man said, although I did not believe him.

There must have been some evidence.

"Anyway, I didn't look too hard for proof. Blood samples, things of that sort. Because I don't really think he was drunk, you know. I think he was just in the wrong place at the wrong time."

"Why are you telling me this?" I asked, suddenly furious that I was being put in this position, in this place, at this time.

"The factory where he worked might be interested to know if he was drunk or not," the old man mused.

His tone was one of a patient schoolteacher with a dunce.

"They might be less inclined to pay any kind of compensation to a grieving widow, if their employee was drunk while he was working. Drunk and getting killed like this. Such a shame."

I did not understand what was happening. It seemed the old man hinted at something, but what it was, I couldn't comprehend.

Danny joined us with Nicholas and Timothy, and he caught the last part of what the mortician was saying. I heard Danny grunt, and then he grabbed the old man by the elbow and led him toward the morgue door.

My children stared up at the gurney, up at their father. I lifted them each so that they could see his face. Neither of them touched him. I was glad they did not touch him. Neither of them cried. I was glad they did not cry.

There was a permeable silence in the room, interrupted by the sounds of lights, a scratching that might have been a small animal or an insect. I had never seen a dead body, never been to a morgue before, and it was nothing like I would have imagined. I was not scared. My emotions were nameless.

Danny and the old man returned quietly and the five of us stood around Charlie for a few moments. The old man was the first to speak.

"Well, I have his possessions if you wish to take them."

"Sure," I nodded.

"Come with me, please."

I followed him to a small office, leaving the kids with Danny. I saw, at the edges of my vision, Danny cover Charlie's face with the sheet and then put his hands on Nicholas's and Timothy's shoulders and lead them to the door and the hallway beyond.

The old man handed me a manila envelope.

"This is everything," the old man said. "And everything is taken care of."

I wasn't sure to what he was referring, and I didn't

especially care. I took the envelope from him. It weighed about as much as a glass of milk.

"Thank you," I said, for some odd reason.

"Take care," the old man said, and I left him.

Outside his office, I tore open the envelope. Charlie's wallet fell out and slapped against the hard, cold floor. A chain, with a silver cross, slithered out too, and last, the keys to his truck tumbled out in a jangling heap. I scooped all those things off the floor and put the keys and chain into my pocket. I opened his wallet.

All the years I spent with him, and I never looked through his wallet. He had about fifty dollars tucked away there, and a few cards. The wallet was worn a light shade of tan and I imagined I could feel his body heat still radiating off the leather. I opened the flap where he kept his photographs, and there was one of him with the kids, followed by one each of Nicholas, and then Timothy. One of all of us, taken when we were on a recent picnic, sitting on a bench; Charlie had asked a stranger to snap the photo and the stranger had obliged, smiling.

And the last photo, Charlie and Danny, on graduation day, arms around each other's shoulders, each of them grinning foolishly. I heard the Sam Cooke song in the background, for a fleeting moment, and I felt Danny's arms around me as we danced.

My thumb meandered over the protective plastic separating my flesh from the photo. It felt warmest of all, and somehow coldest, too.

"Goodbye, Charlie," I said as I passed his gurney. "And sorry."

Fifteen

The following years were spectacular in their dullness. I stayed at home with the children and lived off a large compensation package from the factory after Charlie's death. I did not realize until later that Danny had, in effect, set that up.

There was no question, in my mind at least, that Charlie had been drinking at least a little. And the factory rules stipulated that an employee must not drink at all while he is working. I never knew how Danny did it; if he simply spoke to the mortician, or if he slipped him a hundred dollars, or if they came to some other kind of arrangement. But as far as anybody official was concerned, the day Charlie died, he was sober for the first time in a long time.

Danny gave the eulogy at the funeral. Everybody in attendance knew about their relationship, our relationship, the sins and the sordidness. For some, that knowledge must have made his words seem hollow and fake; for others, like me, his words carried that much more weight because of the fire their brotherly love had endured.

Many wept. I wept, too, but not just for Charlie. For so

many more things, too.

I was a ship, lost at sea and operating with a skeleton crew. I was about to jump overboard and let the dark waters envelop me. Danny spoke of their high school days mostly, of how they helped each other with their cars; how they played football together, how they played with air guns together and how Charlie was always the better shot.

My children became quieter and more sullen in their day-to-day lives. Nicholas started a few fights at school, and I was called down to the office.

The principal, an old woman with mousey features, interlaced her fingers together and rested her hands on the top of her desk and told me about my son's worsening behavior and the things I might do to rectify the situation. I was unable to do much, because the biggest thing, according to her, was the lack of a central male figure in his life.

All he has now is Danny, I thought to myself but never said.

Danny and Paula separated not long after Charlie's death, but not before Paula became pregnant with another of his children.

He called me often on the telephone, but we did not manage to see each other. Why, I didn't know. He felt obligated to his unborn child, and to his firstborn, Christine. Paula had taken her and moved in with her parents somewhere in the southwest of the state.

At that time, I didn't want someone with whom to be romantic. I only wanted another human soul to share mine with, to stay with me, to comfort me and to tell me that, in the very end, things would turn out.

That was, once again, our opportunity. We could have grasped it, naysayers be damned, and been together for the rest of our lives, even if our history together was more thorn than rose.

But we did not do it. Every time we spoke, the question, veiled and mysterious, ran beneath our words like a shadow running underwater.

But neither of us asked. I never felt the necessary receptiveness from his end, and I could not handle rejection from him, even if I knew he would never reject me. I was afraid, again. Fear had dominated my life, and now, when I needed most to ignore it, to conquer it, the same fear controlled me again.

It wasn't only that, of course. Though it shames me to admit it now, the reputation of a woman whose husband had just died, marrying another, one for whom she had carried such an enduring flame, was a reputation I was not prepared to subject myself to.

He met a new woman, Tammy. She was pleasant and funny, and happy, and vivacious, and I hated her. She seemed a woman incapable of having a secret, and perhaps that was what Danny liked about her. She was simple and trustworthy. She was, essentially, a female Charlie.

My own love life withered and all but died. In the coming years, secretly and long enough after Charlie's death that it mattered less, I had men callers, and I slept with a few.

None of them brought me much pleasure. They were the type of men who had no place to go, who did not mind if I had two children because they had no plans to ever see my kids; all they wanted was to enjoy a night with someone and not to have any responsibility afterward.

They were as lost as I was, and there was something both disgusting and enlightening about being with those men, men who were my equals in that they were just blindly searching out the closest thing to pleasure they could find without putting in too much effort.

Neither Nicholas nor Timothy knew anything about any of them, except for one unfortunate incident when Timothy entered the kitchen late one evening to find a tall trucker kissing me, bending me backward with his hands around my waist.

"Momma?" he said, rubbing his eyes.

"Go back to bed," the trucker, whose name fails me, said.

Timothy looked hurt, turned around, dazed, and padded back to his bedroom.

"Don't talk to my kids that way," I said to the trucker.

"What way, baby?"

"Any way," I said, pushing him away. "I think you should go. Now."

He scoffed. "You can't bring me back here and then kick me out for saying a few words to your brat. I didn't even cuss at him or nothing."

"Leave."

He loomed over me. He smelled like Charlie used to smell, that familiar mix of aftershave and alcohol, the scent which accumulates with too many hours spent alone on the road.

"I ain't leaving," he said.

I felt behind me for the correct drawer, found it, opened it, all without turning. My hand crept like a spider until I found the knife, and once I did locate it, I yanked it out in a vicious motion.

"I'll cut you," I told him. "I will kill you."

"Hey, lady," he said, raising his hands before him and stepping back. "I don't want that. I really don't want that."

"Then go."

And he went. I listened for the sound of his engine as he pulled away, and even after he was long gone, I still stood in the kitchen, grasping the knife, afraid to move. I told myself I would have done it, I would have killed him; at the same time, I promised myself I would never have done such a thing. I was incapable of it.

As the minutes dragged on, I started to wonder if I could do it to myself. One slice across the wrist, a warm gush of blood. A quiet escape from the hell that had become my life. Charlie had been dead two or three years at this point, but it was not his loss I mourned.

Eventually I slid the knife back to its rightful place, trembling at how close I had been to the unthinkable. It was hard for me to fathom what I had become. I was the kind of woman my own mother would have warned me against when I was a child.

It was just past midnight, but I called my sister Rosalinda. I thought that, besides Danny, she was the only person to whom I could turn. A groggy voice answered from the other end:

"Hello? What time is it?"

"I'm sorry, Rosalinda."

"Liz? What's wrong?"

"I'm falling apart over here," I said with a sardonic chuckle. "I don't know what to do anymore."

I listened to her breathing on her end. She was living in Toledo still, but I knew very few particulars about her life. I assumed that was the way she liked it.

"Tell me about it," she said.

And I told her. I told her about Charlie, about the affair, about my children, about Danny and his new wife and his new child, about the trucker, about the loneliness, about the heartache, about the soul-wrenching emptiness that followed me wherever I went.

She listened to everything, even the parts she already knew, without interrupting.

And when it was all over, she said, "Why don't you and the kids come live with me for a while?"

"Do you mean that?"

"Of course."

And the next day, we packed our things and Rosalinda came for us in her pickup truck. I had not seen her since childhood. My first thought was that she was a rough-looking character. Wearing jeans and a t-shirt, her biceps showed, large and tanned; her brown hair tied in a ponytail, a cigarette hung on her lip.

"Sis!" she yelled after hopping out of her truck.

I smiled and she tossed her cigarette into the street. We embraced. She was a couple of inches taller than me.

"Look at those little boogers," she said into my ear, and it took me a moment to realize she meant my children.

I introduced them and Nicholas and Timothy hugged her from what I knew was a sense of obligation. Rosalinda did not seem to notice their hesitation and she breathed deeply as she held her nephews, then popped up in a lithe movement I doubted I could manage myself.

"So is everybody ready to go?"

She looked for what seemed the first time at the house behind us.

"We're all packed," I said, nodding.

"Good," she said, grabbing the nearest piece of baggage and throwing it into the bed of the pickup. "Let's hit the road, then."

We piled into her truck, Timothy on my lap, Nicholas sitting with one leg on either side of the gearshift in the middle. Rosalinda was a capable driver and, despite not having been to my Detroit neighborhood before, she never asked directions. We found ourselves on the expressway quickly, heedlessly passing semis and station wagons.

"So, what are you going to do with the house?" she asked me.

"What?"

"The house," she said. "What are your plans?"

I realized there was no reason to move back to Detroit; that had been a kind of default position in the back of my head. It made sense in a status-quo, illogical kind of way. But there was no reason to be there: Charlie was dead and I had no family there. Toledo made more sense. So did Flint.

Anywhere made more sense, when I considered the bad memories I had of the Motor City.

"I don't know," I said finally. "I guess I can sell it."

Rosalinda nodded and changed lanes. We accelerated past a sedan full of kids and their unimpressed parents in the front seats.

"There are other things we can do," she said. "Quicker things. We'll talk later."

The drive was uneventful besides that, and we crossed into Ohio and soon enough we were in Toledo, which seemed to me Detroit on a smaller scale. I did not ask where we were going specifically. I saved for tomorrow the business of signing my children up for a new school, getting to know the neighborhood, where the nearest grocery store was, changing my address so that my mail would arrive.

She lived in a duplex, her half of the house accessed through the backyard. The street she lived on was dirty and grass grew through various cracks in the asphalt. A group of small black children watched us as we took our bags from the back and shouldered them.

"Hey, boys," Rosalinda called to them. "Help me with some of these bags."

Two of the older boys, aged about the same as Nicholas, stepped forth and took the luggage from Rosalinda.

"I give them cookies," she winked at me.

I followed them around the house and inside. It smelled of cigarette smoke and coffee, but it wasn't entirely unpleasant. The small window above the sink let in little natural light to the cramped kitchen. We left our stuff in a guest bedroom; there were three bedrooms, a living room, a bathroom, and a large closet.

"We're really cramping you," I said, after dropping the bags.

The black boys stood near my own children and all of them watched us with something like zoological curiosity.

"Run along," my sister said to the strange boys, shooing at them. "Tell your momma to come around later for a game of dominoes."

The black boys ran away, laughing, and Rosalinda turned to me.

"I'm glad to have you here," she said. "It's been too many years since I saw you. I've never even seen your kids before. Can you believe that?"

"It's hard to believe," I agreed. "It's my fault."

"Honey, it's nobody's fault."

We stood there, breathing the same air for some time. I told my boys to go explore the yard. They did not argue. They went quietly outside and Rosalinda and I stepped into the kitchen for a cup of coffee and for her, a cigarette.

The afternoon faded quickly into a sickly evening,

colored orange and violet by this new city. We sat opposite each other at a tiny, wobbly table covered by a polka-dotted cloth which hung over the sides. Rosalinda stared at me, smoking, for so long that I started to feel uncomfortable.

"Sorry," she said. "It's just so good to finally see you again."

I took a deep breath.

"I expected to see you at the funerals."

Rosalinda nodded for a while.

"I thought about whether I should go. For a long time, Liz, I thought about it."

"So why didn't you come?"

She shook her head.

"I know they loved me. They always did. You know what it was like? How they found out I liked girls, I mean. I sat them down one evening. I was in college, I can't remember which year. Sophomore or junior, I suppose."

I did some quick math and figured I would have been in middle school, perhaps not too far removed from my first meeting with Danny. All of those times took on a hazy, fluid quality in my brain, and I remembered very few specifics in terms of years and months.

"Anyway, I sat them down and told them I had some news. They looked at each other like, oh man, what's this going to be? And at that moment, I guess it could have been anything. We didn't see much of each other, even then, but I was a bit of a hellraiser."

I knew only basic, nonspecific rumors about Rosalinda's partying and her wild inclinations. Too young to understand then, and now that I was old enough and had done enough wild things myself, I did not particularly want to know.

"So you told them. And then what?"

"I told them," she said, nodding. "I told them I liked girls. Dad was drunk already, and he sat there shaking his head for a long time. Mom was quiet too. And then they told me I was a liar and that I needed to leave the house. And I never went back."

"But you talked to them, right?"

She shrugged.

"Once or twice, I talked to mom. We talked about how my work was going, if I was thinking of coming up for Christmas, shit like that. She never asked if I had a husband or a girlfriend or anything like that."

"Do you?"

Never a forward person, something about her attitude made me believe it would be welcome.

"I have a few girls I see pretty regularly," she said, blowing a lungful of smoke toward the ceiling. "I wouldn't call them girlfriends, exactly."

"What do you do?" I asked, suddenly aware of how naive I sounded.

But she just laughed.

"What do you think we do? Play hopscotch?"

I wanted to ask several questions, but at the same time, I was unsure if I wanted to know the answers. So, instead, I just burst into laughter. My sister joined me after a few moments, and we laughed until we sounded like maniacs.

"Anyway, it's not important," she said eventually. "Something like this comes out, and everyone starts to look at you differently. It's just a little part of who I am. Same as you loving who you love ... it's not everything you are."

But she was wrong about that. I loved Danny so much that it was fundamental to the person I was. I didn't want to argue the point with her, however, and so I remained silent. I sipped my coffee and pretended the cigarette smoke didn't bother me.

"I asked about your house earlier," she said, her voice taking a brisk, businesslike tone. "I wondered what you were going to do with it."

"And I told you I didn't know."

"Houses can take a long time to sell," my sister continued. "And you rarely get what they are worth."

"How do you know all that?"

"One of my ... my friends, she is into real estate. She talks about it all the time. I don't really listen, but you pick things up just by being there, sometimes. Anyway, your house is insured."

"Of course," I said, laughing a little. "Charlie insisted on great insurance. He was always so careful about stuff like that."

Saying those words hurt. He was so very careful and yet his life was snuffed out in a wink. I'd never even said goodbye to his living self, never got to apologize one last time for all the pain I served him.

"Uh huh," Rosalinda said. "Now, what I'm suggesting isn't exactly – what's the word? – legal. I mean, I think there's nothing wrong with what I'm suggesting. But the law has a slightly different perspective on things."

"I don't understand."

"I know a guy," she told me. "He fixes problems that arise. Problems like the one you're having."

"I don't have any problems."

"Okay," she said. "Not a problem. Not exactly a problem, *per se.*"

"I'm not good at reading between the lines," I told her. "You might as well just come out with whatever you mean."

"Well, let's just say, one evening, your house is unoccupied, you are staying with me on a short visit. You and the kids. Someone comes along, strikes a match, lights his cigarette, flicks the butt somewhere dry. Starts a fire. Your house burns down. Problem solved."

I laughed. I knew nothing of insurance fraud and I was not the type of person who would handle prison well. But my chuckles soon died when I realized she was speaking sincerely.

"You can't be serious."

"I know a lady who has been trying to sell her house for the past year," she said. "Right up in Detroit. She's had one person come look at it, and when that person saw the negroes living down the street, she ran away."

I shook my head.

"There aren't many blacks where I live."

"It's Detroit," Rosalinda said. "And, mind you, I am not a racist. The problem is that the rest of the country is. So people will be less inclined to buy your house. It's not your fault. It's theirs. So what can you do, right?"

She had a way of shifting blame away from me which I rather liked, but I was still not convinced.

"I don't think so," I said. "We might move back, anyway. I don't even know what we're going to do."

But, in my heart, I knew we would not go back there. The house was too full of ghosts. It was the house where Charlie lived, the house where my ailing mother came to live in her final months after my father's death; it was where I'd raised my children, and the house from which Danny picked me up so that we could run away. An unexpected yearning to watch it burn raced through me. I stared at my sister as she slid another cigarette out of the pack, jabbed it into her mouth, and lit it. I watched the smoke rise, the tobacco burn bright orange, dull, angry red.

"Who is this person who fixes problems?"

More as a hesitant plea than a question.

"He's a solid guy," she said, her tone indicating that I would get no closer to his identity than that. "He's done one or two things for me, actually."

"Do I want to know details?"

I sounded prudish to my own ears.

"You might," she said, smiling around her cigarette, "but I'm not going to tell you. Anyway, it doesn't matter."

"How much does it cost?"

"Cost?" she said, sounding positively shocked. "You let me worry about that end of things. I just need you to say okay."

I wanted to ask exactly how these things worked. Would the police know how to find me? Would they mail me a check? Would they interrogate me, my children, my neighbors? Danny? Would he know the truth? Would I be able to tell him? I thought of the incident with the train from our childhoods.

Then I pictured myself, standing on the opposite curb, a mysterious smile drawn across my pursed lips, the hot flames reflected in my watering eyes.

"Do it," I said with a finality that thrilled me. "Just do it. Destroy the place. Turn it into ashes."

My sister smiled devilishly.

"Consider it done."

After a long pause, during which she jammed her cigarette into a nearly full ashtray, she asked, "So what do you guys want to eat?"

Sixteen

But I do not tell Robbie all of this; I am in his debt, but I think that his love problems are, compared with mine, no problemo. Thus, I give him the ordinary advice he might expect from someone my age: relationships take work and time and trust, and, if he is unwilling to commit, he should think about moving on. That the world is a big place, surprisingly devoid of love; that if he ever finds real love, he should never let it go, and he will know it if he does indeed find it.

He drops me at my house.

"Thanks again," I tell him.

"Don't worry about it," he says.

For a moment I again thought he might say *no problemo.*

"Thanks for the talk."

I bid him goodnight and then I walk up my walkway and enter through my front door. No messages on the answering machine; my bird is quiet. The only sound, besides my movement and my breathing, is the steady ticking of the clock I keep near the toaster in the kitchen.

It is dark but I do not bother turning on any lights. This is probably a foolish idea, for somebody my age, somebody who can break a hip if the wind blows hard enough. But I know this house, and today I can do anything I want to do.

Sometimes it is important to sit in the dark, alone with your thoughts. I began believing this after my house burned to the ground.

I received a phone call about a week after telling my sister to go ahead with the arson. I had not forgotten about the discussion, but I had reached the point where I no longer believed Rosalinda's friend would go through with it.

The phone rang as I read the newspaper; Rosalinda was at work, so I was alone with my kids, whom I still had not enrolled in any school.

"Let it ring," I called out.

But it rang and it rang, much like the call to tell me that Charlie was dead. So I gave in and answered.

"Yes," I said.

"I am calling for Elizabeth Toll," came a man's voice. "I haven't been able to contact her. And you, Rosalinda Beamer, are listed as an emergency contact."

For some reason, I almost lied and told the voice that I knew no Elizabeth Toll, that he had dialed the wrong number. But the voice sounded like an authoritative figure, and I crumbled and said, "I am Elizabeth."

"I'm afraid I have some rather bad news for you, Ms. Toll," he said.

I kept silent. All I could think was that something bad had happened to Danny. The logical part of my brain insisted they would not even call me if something had happened to him; he had a wife, and he had parents. I was but a distant memory, already fading into the mist.

"Go on," I said at last, detecting the trembling in my own voice.

"Last evening, your house caught fire," the man said. "I'm afraid it's a total loss."

"A total loss," I repeated.

"Yes, I'm afraid so," the man said. "It took three fire engines to put it out. The fire started somewhere in the back. The neighbor's house caught fire too."

"What?"

"Nobody was hurt," the man continued, almost sighing in relief himself. "It was lucky you're at your sister's with your children, ma'am."

My mind did cartwheels.

I said, "Yes, we're visiting."

I thought that was the right thing to say.

"The Harrisons lost their dog," the voice went on. "Smoke inhalation. Poor mutt."

I was on friendly terms with the Harrison family, a young couple with a daughter and their Labrador, Henry.

"I'm sorry."

"Did you have any problems with anybody?" the man said. "I mean, I'm sure you didn't. People like you don't generally have enemies."

I thought for a moment. I supposed I did have enemies, or at least people who disliked me. Danny's wife. Danny's first wife, too, perhaps. The ghost of Jamie, stalking the streets, searching for me. Myself.

"I have no enemies, I get along with everybody."

"Yes, I thought so," the man said. "Well, it should be a pretty straightforward investigation, but I'm not sure we'll ever find who did this."

"Good," I blurted. "I mean, that the investigation is

straightforward."

I did not even know what that phrase meant.

"We'll pass the information on to the insurance company," the man continued.

I realized I did not even know to whom I was speaking. The police? A fireman?

"They've already had one of theirs out to look at the place."

"Okay," I said, imagining what my old house looked like, and the Harrison family's, singed beside that smoking rubble, overcome with regret for having done this evil thing. We broke our connection cordially after he thanked me for my help. I expected a police cruiser to pull up outside my sister's house and for a uniformed man to come to the door and pound on it, cuffs swinging from his fist.

Calling Nicholas and Timothy into the kitchen and telling them to sit down, I relayed the news that our house had burned down as if I was surprised myself, as if I too were a victim. They cried. I said nothing about the Harrisons' dog.

My sister arrived home from work and I watched her closely for some indication that she knew what had happened, but she simply walked through the front door, kicked off her boots, and then collapsed into the recliner.

My boys were in the backyard, throwing a baseball. I stood a few feet in front of Rosalinda and she stared up at me, her hands on her knees.

"You're starting to make me uncomfortable," she said, grinning up at me. "What's up, sis?"

"You mean you don't know?"

She shrugged and I believed her.

"I got a call today," I said, only half-believing what I

was saying, myself. "It seems somebody set fire to my house in Detroit."

Rosalinda clucked her tongue and shook her head in feigned disappointment. "It's a dangerous world," she said.

"The neighbor's dog was killed," I said.

"Oh," she said, sitting up a little straighter. "Sorry. I didn't think that would happen."

I nodded patiently.

"But that's the risk we took, right? I mean, we knew it was dangerous."

She stared back at me for a long time before speaking.

"Look, Liz. I'm sorry about the dog. Fires get out of control, sometimes. You can't exactly stand there and direct the flames."

"I know," I muttered.

"And look at the bright side," she said. "Now you're free. You have a big check coming in the mail. The house is going to pay off, and you got money in the bank from the factory. Think about it. You can start over. This time without a man."

For some reason, I wanted to say something hurtful. I felt she was pushing her own agenda onto me – this time, no man. But I said nothing. Rosalinda was not the kind of person to push agendas, anyway.

"I'm going to leave," I said.

"Where?" she asked, not defensively, but with what sounded like pure curiosity.

"I don't know. I'll take the kids and the money and we'll hop on a bus."

She nodded, raising her eyebrows slightly.

"Sounds like a plan," she said. "Doesn't sound like much of one, but at least it's a plan. You know you can always come back here if the road doesn't suit you."

I told her I knew that and I thanked her. A month later, as soon as I had the insurance money, we were on the road.

Chicago, St. Louis, Kansas City, Wichita. The sky in Kansas was as wide as memory, as deep and pale as the eyes of a drowned man. We stayed there for a few months, because it was far away, because nobody knew us and we knew nobody, just because ... I learned the vastness of America, looking up at those Kansas clouds.

I had a bank account very full in Michigan and a roll of cash that could have lasted us for many months. I hit times of great despair while we traveled, my children sleeping on bus station chairs, slumped into the most comfortable positions they could muster.

So many nameless men accosted me in those bus stations, and I became practiced at hugging my children close to me while they slept, in such a way that I would not wake them. I practiced my dirty vocabulary, too: words like fuck, as in off, and hell, as in go to.

Wichita never felt like home. It was a big city and it was clean and it was boring. The neighbors were kind, and when we left a few months after moving into our little apartment, I imagined they thought I was a fugitive. And, in a way, I was, running away from my past, but my past was too quick, and I could not lose it, no matter where I went. So I returned to Michigan.

I bought a little house in the same town in which I grew up, Hamilton. My sister drove us there and waved us goodbye. I never saw her again in the flesh, although I often spoke to her on the phone.

She became involved with scores of women, but gave her heart away to none of them; she remained happy until struck down by a heart attack at eighty years old. I could not make the funeral because by that time my own health had deteriorated. But that is a story for another day, perhaps.

Hamilton was the answer; the place where my children belonged. Where they could fish in the creek, eat ice cream downtown, and flip trains off the tracks if they so desired.

They felt none of the lingering, bittersweet heartbreak that accompanied me when I walked those streets, picking out places where Danny and I used to talk, where Charlie and I stole kisses at dusk, hiding behind a lamppost. Where Jamie and I made foolish plans about our futures, how we would always remain friends, no matter what, what our children's names would be.

Those places seemed haunted, now. So it was, with happiness turned sour and dull, I enrolled my children at the same school I attended as a child, and some of the teachers remained. They spent the rest of their childhoods happy, and if they remembered the heartache I put them through when they were younger, they showed no signs of it.

Danny remarried again, this time to a woman named Henrietta. I heard about this long after the fact, and that made the pain both greater and easier to accept. Easier because it was done, and I could do nothing to affect the course of his life; hard because it had been long years, it seemed, since I last heard from, or of, Danny.

The first news of him came through a casual acquaintance in town, asking about his newest wife, smirking about his inability to hold onto a woman, asking prying details about my situation.

Henrietta would be his last wife, and they had a son together, but that too is a story for another day. She turned to drugs in the early seventies, and their marriage fell apart.

I saw him only one more time, in 1973, after his last divorce. I was in town, picking up a gallon of milk, feeling very haggard that evening.

Nicholas and Timothy, my oldest now at an age where he could ask me questions about sex and drugs, had refused to do their homework and were generally being unmanageable brats. I loved them, but I left them alone in the house under the pretense that we were out of 2%. And I took the long way when I walked to the store.

I recognized the Mercury, parked against the curb, but I refused to believe my eyes. Better to be a mirage, or hallucination, or joke. But my heart still thudded. I scanned the storefronts, seeking out his smile, watching for his sliding gait, his sloped, squinting eyes. But I did not see him.

A moment later, I heard his voice from behind me.

"Oh, my," he said. "It's you."

I froze, afraid to turn around and face him.

"Say my name," I said, feeling foolish. "I won't think this is real unless you say my name."

I heard him breathing and I imagined his smile around those breaths.

"Oh, Liz," he said softly. "Oh, how I've missed you."

I spun around and ran to him. They were only a few steps, but they were steps on the moon, and I jumped into him and embraced him, pressed my face against his chest and inhaled the scent of him, sweet and old as stardust. Too many years often enduring sour relationships changes in at least subtle ways the manner in which we stand, speak, or look at each other.

Not with Danny. He kissed me on the forehead.

"What are you doing here?" I asked breathlessly.

He hung his head.

"I'm hurting," he said.

I caressed his cheek and he tilted his face into my touch. The stubble there scratched against my flesh but it felt good.

"Do you want to tell me about it?"

"No," he said. He looked at me, the pain in his eyes deep. I saw the hurt of lost years, bad decisions, the regret of having learned a lesson long after the test.

"I'm going away for a while," he said.

"What do you mean, you're going away?"

I pulled my hand away from his cheek.

"Henrietta ... she's gone. I kicked her out."

"Henrietta," I repeated.

"She was shooting up. We have a kid. Well, she has the kid."

I did not speak. I only stared at him, trying to comprehend his agony.

"We both have scars," I told him, although I could not explain why.

"I know," he said. "I need to get away for a while. I took some vacation time from work. Told them I was ill."

"Ill?" I said.

"Sick. That I needed to see doctors. They told me to take all the time I need."

"What's your plan?" I asked, experiencing a sudden flash of déjà vu, except the last time it was my sister asking me what my plan was for running away from my own problems.

"To drive," he said, looking into the unknowable distance. "Do you want to come?"

God, yes. Every part of me burned for him, even the tips of my hair.

I wanted to jump into his arms, have him carry me to his Mercury, and then I wanted to set off for nowhere and everywhere. The idea was too sweet and I nearly crumpled there on the pavement.

"You know I can't do that," I said, hoping that he would tell me of course I could do that, that all I needed to do was to drop my kids off at my sister's in Toledo, and that after we would be free to live the life we were meant to have lived from the first time I saw him, in a dingy classroom an age before.

"I suppose not," he said, grabbing my hand. "I suppose it's a stupid idea. You have children. You have responsibilities."

Damn my responsibilities! I wanted to forget all of them. The world was not a bad place, not in the end, and things like children would be taken care of, even if the mother was a two-bit whore who ran away with a mysterious man, to live a mysterious life.

"I owe it to them," I whispered, and I knew that to be true, although I wanted so badly to say something, anything else.

He nodded and squeezed my hand. I saw him, in my mind, as an old man, stooped and beaten, regretful and hopeful still. But hope had been our greatest friend and our most solemn enemy. As Francis Bacon once remarked, hope makes a good breakfast, but a bad supper.

He walked with me in those streets that were ours, once upon a dream. The same corners that looked haunted not too long before now glimmered with some distant relative of hope, now that Danny held my hand. But it was nearly time for supper, and he was leaving.

"You don't have to go," I offered weakly. "You can move here with us. Stay for a little while."

He ran his thumb over my knuckles and his touch was too sweet to bear. My breath caught in my throat.

"I took you once, and look what happened."

"Nothing bad happened because of that," I told him.

"Everything happened because of that," he said, although he did not offer any specifics. "Anyway, I wouldn't take it back."

"Exactly," I said. "So move in. Come here, with us."

I glanced at him, afraid to look for too long, afraid of what I would see written on his face.

I lowered my voice and said in conspiratorial tones, "We've had so many chances, Danny. So many chances to make things right. Here is another one. Will it be the last one?"

He sighed.

"I just can't do it," he said, finally. "I want to do it. More than you'll ever know. And it's not just because I have kids I have to take care of, and it's not just because I don't want to ruin your reputation even more, and it's not just because I'm getting older and there are a thousand things standing in the way. It's something else, too. Something stopping me from doing this. Even if I want to more than anything else in the world."

I had no answer for his speech. There was no answer, as far as I could tell, because he did not have any reason for what he was saying. In a moment of fury, I yawped. I'd never made a sound like it before. It was like the sound of an injured wild animal.

"I don't get you," I said. "Here it all is, right at your

fingertips. True happiness. Now or never."

"Not now," he said. "But not never, either. Someday."

He took a deep breath, leaving me with the impression that he was warding off tears. He opened his mouth as if to say something else, then he closed it again and remained silent. We continued walking, our footfalls rapping against the sidewalk concrete. We rarely saw another soul outside, and that made our walk more pleasant.

Soon enough, we found ourselves in the park. It was dark, illuminated only along one edge, near the entrance. A sign warned that the park closed at dusk.

We jumped the low fence. Danny boosted me over and held my hand the entire time until my feet were safely on earth again. It felt like a secret world, this side of the iron, populated by shadows and the spirits of yesterday. In our culmination of years, we'd sat at every table in that park, every bench, too, and slid down every slide, swung on every swing.

We picked our way through the children's toys, and each seemed like an accusation leveled at me: you once were innocent, and look what you've done with your life.

We found a bench in the darkest corner of the park and we sat close together. His thigh touched mine; he wrapped his arm around my shoulders and instantly I ceased trembling. I let myself yield to him. He breathed through his nose and every time he exhaled, his sweet life force washed over the top of my head.

"We'll see each other again," I said.

"We have said that so many times," he countered.

"And each time, it's been true," I said.

We sat in silence for a few more moments – I lost track of time. Then I craned my neck and kissed his throat. I heard him swallow and I kissed along his jawbone, to the soft spot just under his earlobe. I kissed him softly, delicately, my lips parted just enough so that it did not feel innocent.

I wondered how many times I had made love to this man. There was the first time, and then there were many times when we ran away, and that was all. But did dreams count? If so, the number was unknowable. Even so, he was better and sweeter now, for his age, and for my age, than he had ever been before.

His hands sought out the parts of me that needed seeking; the soft parts of me, my shoulder, my lips, the backs of my knees. His fingertips danced across these secrets, played me like a harp, the strings of which are old but still quiver in harmony.

My own fingers unbuttoned his shirt, then his pants, and we sat that way, kissed that way, while he was half-undone and hidden in the darkness. Things were heating up to hot when we heard voices, indistinct and far away, and we paused our separate explorations as they walked along the edge of the park, down the sidewalk, out of our lives. Danny laughed and wiggled out of his pants and shirt.

He stayed my hands with his own as I slipped off my dress and said, "Keep your clothes on. You're too beautiful. It's hotter this way."

So, I slipped off my underwear, kicked it away, and let the cool breeze float under my skirt and caress my inner thighs, let it both cool and stoke the fire there.

Danny stood and stepped out of his own underwear. His pants lay in a bunch at his ankles. By the amber streetlights, whose light was almost dead here, I made out his penis, hanging long and soft in the night. He sat beside me and I ran my hand down his chest, his stomach. It tickled him and he convulsed and grunted with happiness. Then I grabbed his dick and started squeezing it.

I felt it grow hard in my hand, and I played with it gently, running the pads of my fingers up and down and all around until he emitted little hisses of pleasure from his nearly pursed lips.

"Oh, I love you so much," I said.

I leaned in and kissed his left nipple. He kissed the top of my head and then he changed his posture on the bench so that he was slumped further.

"Come on," he said.

I sat on his lap like a little girl with Santa, except this little girl was not little anymore, and she was not wearing underwear, and this Santa was not good, and his only gift was love and sex. I lifted my skirt and sat on his pubic bone, and then I helped him help me.

It was difficult but we managed. He did not have enough leverage to thrust very hard, so it was down to me to ride him in the way I deemed most enjoyable. I planted my feet upon the ground and used gravity and my leg muscles to force his manhood to pleasure me.

It was what sex was always meant to be; the physical rapture of it was almost secondary to the feelings it stirred, or confirmed, in my heart: the dedication, the passion, the need, the compulsion.

I came quickly. I shuddered and my abdominal muscles tensed into a hot coil and I felt I might shoot off his lap in the way a rocket would. All this without making too much noise, for fear of passersby hearing.

Danny had his orgasm a few moments later, as I, in increasingly lazy increments, rubbed myself up and down on him. He moaned long and loud, the escape of a bottled-up need to which I could certainly relate.

I dismounted and found our clothes strewn across the grass. I stepped as delicately as I could into my drawers and hitched them up, feeling the dirty way I always felt immediately after sex. I watched Danny dress, plaintive, morose, deliberate. He kissed me on the cheek and again, I breathed him in.

"This life isn't fair," I said to him.

"No life is," he responded.

We hopped the fence just as a young couple passed by. For a long moment, the young girl and I shared a look. It burgeoned within me to tell her to search out her true love and never let him go, whether that was the boy on her arm or not. To impress upon her the most important thing, which was that it was not too late for her and her lonely, searching heart. That there would come a time when it would indeed be too late, if she did not capture the fleeing love she sought. But she only giggled and the boy did the same and they continued on their way.

The walk back to the Mercury was too short, or perhaps it was only my perception of time and distance that was ruined. He paused at his driver's side door, hand on the doorjamb, foot already inside the vehicle.

"I know we'll see each other again," he said.

Shadows cast by the streetlights, all lined up like ancient soldiers marching toward a battle they were sure to lose, clouded his face

"I know. I just don't know when."

"That's what keeps life interesting," he said, smiling. "You can't know all the secrets too early."

"It's just not fair," I echoed, and I did not care that I was basically repeating myself.

It was too true for me to care.

He inhaled as though about to respond, but he said nothing. Instead, he let his breath out slowly into the evening, and then he leaned forward drastically and kissed me.

One moment, he was a man on the edge of a precipice; the next, he had flung himself into the air and was falling, falling into the truest kind of bliss, lips on lips, fingertips like swooping birds through my hair.

It was the finest kiss I had ever had. Stars opened and exploded into dust in the time our kiss lingered; lifecycles were completed, great paintings painted, horrific scenes of death and famine played out across the surface of our world, the souls of men were admitted to heaven and condemned to hell, and God let fall a tear He had been saving especially for us, in His infinite wisdom and sorrow.

Then he sat behind the wheel, started the engine, and drove away. I saw all the guilt and shame I imagined he felt in those departing taillights. I realized that I, too, had felt those things, once upon a time, before I stopped caring about them.

I did not see him again for almost forty years.

Seventeen

The next day is bright and crisp, the kind of day which has always inspired love and warmth inside my heart, even in dark times, even when I was bored out of my head. My bird, Spit, is active and chirping in his cage, as if he too knows how important today is. Perhaps he does. Perhaps it shows in the way I move around the house, preparing, faster than usual, giddy in an almost schoolgirlish way.

What a fool I am! To be doing something like this at my age, after an age of avoiding problems but making countless mistakes.

Spit has a pile of seeds and his water dispenser is full to the brim. I tell him, "Well, buddy, this might be goodbye. You take care of yourself."

He, little and yellow, stares back at me in incomprehension, but part of me believes he understands.

"Goodbye," I tell him then, hoping it is not the last time I will see him.

I have the things I need: a good pair of walking shoes, my purse, a few hundred dollars and change, a mirror, a bit of lipstick, a bottle of water, my cell phone, nothing more. I breathe deeply before I step outside into the day.

It is mid-morning, a workday, and there are few people to be seen. No cars, only one elderly neighbor walking his dog. He raises his hand in salutation and I return the gesture, friendly enough. Nothing about me must seem out of the ordinary, except that I am rarely seen walking anymore. My joints have simply protested too loudly these past few years.

I turn left to begin my trek. I know the address, and I know the shortest route: almost one mile to Christine's house. She has children, but they should be in school. Both she and her husband should be working.

These are things I am taking for granted because I have no other option. If anybody is home when I arrive there, everything will be destroyed, and all my effort will be for naught.

As I walk, I consider this; but I spent last night considering it, too, and it stopped me from sleeping very well. I know that if I fail today, I will probably not have it inside me to go through this yet again. Not only the physical trial but also the mental anguish, the mystery of the future.

A prisoner must feel like this when he takes his first steps toward escape, when he breaks the wall with his pickaxe for the first time; or a soul, freshly released from Earth by death, waiting to see whether it will rise toward heaven or descend toward hell.

I am lucky the weather is fine, and the temperature is comfortable. At the first intersection I reach, I take special care to verify no cars are coming – how foolish would it be if my story ended that way! After I cross the street, I take a sip of my water, recap it, replace it in my purse, and continue.

I have time to reflect on those forty years.

Danny left for far-flung places, and I did not hear from him often. Sometimes, the phone would ring, and when I answered, I'd hear his voice, breathless, on the other end, calling just to check in, to tell me where he was. Sometimes it was Louisville, Kentucky. Other times, he was in Maine. Once, he was back in Detroit, just clearing up some business, as he put it.

He checked in on his children more often, but even they missed his presence. This I felt and knew but could not prove, for we had no communication. They did not know how much their father meant to me, not until the recent past, when Christine told me she thought Danny would like to see me.

One day, in the early eighties, the postman delivered a yellowed envelope to my mailbox. In the same way I always knew, I knew even then that it was from him. It is a letter I still have with me, tucked away with my birth certificate, my social security card, and the other few precious documents that prove that I am indeed a human being.

And as far as criteria go, perhaps that makes this letter the most important document of all of them.

Dear Liz,

Tonight I'm in a little berg in Nebraska, Stone Eye. Strange name for a town, but it reminds me so much of Hamilton, and so it reminds me so much of you, too. But everything reminds me of you. I'm holed up in a tiny motel. The next room over is playing the loudest TV I've ever heard. And I'm here in bed alone. And you are on my mind.

It's possible to imagine that the years which have passed

without us seeing each other have dampened the hot flames burning for you in my heart. Perhaps, for any normal love, that would be the case. Distance and time, I think, either destroy your love or they make it something supernaturally divine. It's like a test, to see how real your love is. I have learned that mine is painfully real.

And I was a goddamn fool. Tonight I write you so that I can tell you that I was an asshole to ever leave you — all the times I left you, from the first time in the church basement, when it felt so innocent, to that last time in the park in our little hometown, when I saw your face for the last time, when I tasted your lips for the last time.

We had so many chances. Too many chances. Always, we had an excuse. Always, something stood in the way of the purest feelings we had for each other. Until, that is, the very last time, when you were unmarried and I was unmarried and we were just two lonely people looking for love. But we didn't even need to look for it, because we held it in our hands, we held onto it together and even while you made a fist to try to hold onto it, I opened my fingers like a fool and let it drift away.

You must hate me for that. At least a small part of you must. I wish I had a good explanation for running away, but the reasons I can give you are weak and pitiful.

I was hurt. I had been through so many heartbreaks, even though none of those women could break my heart, not truly. Failed marriages, kids growing distant. My own biological father failed me, and I promised I would never repeat the same mistake. But I did. And then I made another mistake, with you.

Those women hurt me. First Jamie, then Paula, then Henrietta. But the hurt was only a scratch compared with the torture you could inflict upon me, by doing anything, or nothing. Of course you could only hurt me so hard because I loved you so deeply, and I know the same is true for the pain I caused you — it is too deep to measure with words or numbers, isn't it?

I think I decided to break my own heart, and yours too, before God or the Universe or just the ugly old world could do it for us. Too many things got in our way. Too many times had we failed for me to ever hope against hope that we could find happiness together. That sounds pitiful now, and I know I made a mistake. But I was a weak bastard, and weak bastards run away. They find themselves in Stone Eye, Nebraska, writing letters they are not sure they will ever send. This is not the first I've written. America has been littered with my many attempts at writing you, all letters torn into tiny pieces and scattered to the wind. Maybe there is no point in telling you any of this. Maybe you have gotten married again. I hope you are happy.

One thing riding around this old country of ours has taught me is that people are pretty much the same, all over. People here love and they hate, people there love and hate, they take jobs and they chase after happiness or some illusion of it — it's sad, and yet, in some dark, tiny, still beating part of my heart, it fills me with a bit of hope.

A bit of hope that one day, we will see each other again.

A bit of hope that even after all these goddamn fool mistakes we made, we might be able to set things right.

Remember I'll always be thinking of you, no matter where I am or where you are. Believe it or not, the memory of sweet, sweet you is the one thing that keeps me alive out here.

And that was it. Signed with love from Danny. I wept when I read it, and the tears were bitter. I had an impulse to tear it up and scatter it to the wind, but that was as impossible for me as biting off my own finger would have been. I never showed the letter to anybody.

My own children grew through middle school, high school, left for college. I was alone but not entirely unhappy after they were gone. As much as I loved them, they also represented Charlie, and he was a memory I could not try hard enough to forget. And that it was not his fault was the worst condemnation of all. It was mine.

I had other men in my life, of course, but they were smoke and Danny was fire. They were open hands, Danny a fist; they were ashes and Danny was a match, about to be struck. Those men kept me sane in a feminine way; the way I imagine any woman needs to feel desired and beautiful, regardless of her age and her physique. I was never proud after spending time with any of those men, and I wanted to forget them as badly as I wanted to forget any of my mistakes. With those men, I have been mostly successful.

Danny was as elusive as a shooting star during those forty years. It was my drought, my self-inflicted punishment for my own foolishness, that even after my own children left the house and I was left without excuses, I still never searched for him, I still never called out for him.

Sometimes I imagined that was all he was waiting for: for me to contact him, somehow, and tell him that I was coming. Other times, I was sure he had forgotten me, and his life was taking him farther and farther away.

My thoughts turned often to the last evening we spent together, when the idea was on the edge of his lips and mine, that then was our chance and that we should take it. But during those years, that evening might as well never have existed. It was too long ago, it had taken on a sepia tone in my mind, and it had turned from something beautiful and full of hope into something that smelled like stale cigar smoke.

How he spent the entirety of those years is, for me, an eternal mystery. I can formulate a million stories to encompass all that time; all manner of odd jobs, odd country, wayward trail. Working as a fisherman somewhere off the coast of Washington State. Selling magazines and newspapers from a stand at the side of the street in San Francisco. Riding the rails, sleeping wherever he could, picking bugs off his body during the evening, sharing cans of beans with other hobos. I tell myself that perhaps I will ask him when I see him again.

But I know this is unlikely. I prefer the mystery that ignorance allows me. I do not want to have built up these beautiful castles of sand for him, only for the tide of his words to come in and wash them away when he tells me he was just a paperclip salesman in Cleveland.

Of course, I knew that his daughter, Christine, had moved to Hamilton some ten years ago. It sent a sudden pang through my nerves when I heard that through the same shifting network of small-town tongues I heard all my local news. I realized then that the pain had never gone away, but that it had merely hibernated until some tangible evidence of Danny came back into my life, something more than the often folded, many-times-read letter from him that I saved.

But when Danny came back, I knew not; probably he had grown too old to care for himself and finally Christine made the executive decision to move him to the only old folks' home in Hamilton. The more recently that might have happened, the better; I cannot stand the thought that he was so near and that I never went to see him.

Do you know what forty years are? There were moments in my life when I could not imagine four seconds without thinking of him, without being able to touch him, for to do so would render me insane. Forty years is a sentence handed down by a cruel judge to a cold-blooded criminal. I was Moses and punished for something so much simpler than wickedness. Punished for my weakness, and even after I had the chance to grow strong, I remained a weakling.

I have walked a few blocks now. The sun has changed position above me. I do not dare look at it. I keep my gaze trained on the sidewalk. I am an exile, wandering the desert. I am adrift on the ocean, with only a bit of water and my bittersweet memories to keep me alive. I am going happily to be crucified, but the cross I bear is love. I am, I am.

I want to dance with him again, but he is unable to dance. All his steps have been taken in life. I want to make love to him but we are both too frail, too tired, and too old. What once was supple, fresh, and pliant, is now as useless as a single sock.

A few more blocks. My knees are the first to revolt. I feel a twinge, and then a pop, and then a sharp pain in the left one with each step. But I do not care about the pain, I do not listen to that part of my body any longer, and I press on.

My right hip is next, probably thrown for a loop because I am in some way compensating for the left knee. And then my head starts to throb, and I take a short break beneath an oak tree. But I do not rest long, because forward progress is the only thing that matters today, and to stop means death, somehow.

So I stand and catch my balance, and a middle-aged man passing by asks me if I am all right, and I tell him yes, I certainly am, and he continues on his way. And I continue on mine.

A few more blocks. I am approaching the house now; I can feel it in my blood and in my bones. Especially in my bones, each of which feels like it is ready to snap. I am reminded of an Internet video I saw of an old woman jumping rope, and a sudden envy leaps up in my heart. But I quash it quickly, because today has no place for a feeling like envy. And I walk on.

America is huge. I learned that when I took my children to Wichita, watching the countryside roll away as we rolled away from our previous lives and into a worse one. But even this America, this miniature, microscopic slice of it, even here it is huge – huge being a matter of perspective and a means of transportation, I suppose.

And a matter of age, which is not to my advantage.

A few more blocks and I am there. Number 1908, a modern, two-story house, with a big garage and a spacious front lawn, short and manicured. I stop at the foot of the driveway, staring up at the house, catching my breath. I take some more of my water and sip at it, and then I pool a handful in my palm and splash the back of my neck with it. It is cold and the cold shocks me, but immediately thereafter it feels good.

Do not stop for long. Keep moving.

I walk up the driveway as if I belong there. I do not, and I am afraid someone will see me and call the police. Then I refuse to be afraid anymore. If the police come, there are a million lies I can tell which will save me from getting in trouble: I was sick and needed help, or simply, I'm lost, can you take me home?

I approach the garage. It is monolithic and the sliding door is white and massive. I spend little time in front of the garage, opting instead to move to the side to investigate.

There is another door here, the same size as my front door, and it has a glass window in it. I peer through. There is Danny's car, and just the sight of it makes my tired knees buckle. Instinctively, because that car is mine, too, I try the knob. The door is locked.

"Huh," I mutter. There is no doormat under which there may be a key. I try the knob again, but it does not move but for a minuscule amount of play in the internal mechanism.

"Fine," I say, and cast my eyes about.

I locate a rock, about the size of a softball, and I stoop to pick it up. My joints scream at me, and for one terrifying instant, I almost freeze there, half-bent. But I force my body into a standing position again, and then I hurl the rock at the window.

The sound is deafening, and I take a cautious look at the neighbor's house nearest to where I am. There is a tall fence there, and I thank God for that small favor. I reach through the broken window, careful not to slice myself on any of the glass, and somehow I manage this little trick, too. My old fingers are still nimble, and they find the lock and turn it. The door swings inward, and I step neatly inside, where it is cool and dark.

It smells like oil rags and old baseball mitts in here. The car sits dormant and dark, a dinosaur, a fossil; but there is power there, too, and I feel giddy thinking of the sound it will make when I turn the ignition. I wonder if it will echo inside this small place, if it will be like a premonition of Armageddon. The floor is concrete and I shuffle across to the Mercury. The door is unlocked and I open it.

The car sits low enough to the ground that it is difficult for me to slide behind the wheel, and so I am careful to be sure I am prepared to steal it. I have thought this part of my plan through most of all. I must check to make sure the keys are in the ignition first. Then I must open the big door, using the button on the far wall. The button is cleverly illuminated by a small red light, like a piercing eyeball in the dank darkness.

Then comes the hardest part: backing it out of the garage, righting it on the street, and driving it off to Bliss.

I feel for the dangling keys but they are not there. My breath stops in my throat. No – not this way. Not all this way, and with this inane ending. I straighten my back and walk over to the passenger window, through which I peer at the ignition to verify there are no keys. And there are none.

"Oh, Lord, no," I say aloud, and my voice startles me. It is someone else's voice, cutting through the solitude. Someone younger, someone abler than I am.

I look around at the walls and I see nothing. No key pegs, no workbench where an old heap of junk might hide the means to our salvation. "Where can they be?" I implore the darkness.

And the darkness answers – rather, a barking dog answers from the other side of the door leading into the house from the garage. It seems a plausible option: some quaint rack by the back door, a place where a young couple can keep things like keys so they are not easily lost. I hesitate only for a moment, then I steel myself and climb the two wooden stairs that lead to the door.

This one is unlocked. Surely Christine and her husband never thought anyone would break into their little abode: to steal what? This neighborhood is too friendly, and the world too bright a place for intruders to encroach upon the sanctity of their seclusion. I open the door an inch and see the snout of a big dog sniffing me out. Its teeth look as though they could tear leather without much difficulty.

"Good boy," I say, my voice lost in the animal's whines for attention and affection. At least it is not growling, I tell myself.

I imagine the newspaper: Old Woman Mauled in Attempted Break-In!

But the woman who stopped because of thoughts like that is dead. I swing the door open and pat the dog atop the head. Its tail wags violently. It lets me pass after sniffing me, and as I enter the kitchen, it follows close enough that it almost guides me.

I do not bother shutting the door behind me. I tell myself that I will stay only two minutes, and if I am not successful in finding the keys in that time, I will run away. But even this is a lie to myself because I will be caught here before I leave without that car. This is something I know in my heart as surely as others know God.

"Hey, boy, let me be," I say, and the dog does not listen.

It has been an age since I have been in another person's

home. I cannot remember the last time, in fact. The place is cozy, unkempt in a charming way, not to the degree of being messy, but simply utilized. I am in the kitchen and the sink is free of dirty dishes, the floor is clean. The refrigerator is overfull of tacky calendars, advertisements from a car dealership, kids' drawings, coupons for local grocery stores. In this home, lives life; it looks so different from my own empty husk of a home, in which only I and Spit stay.

I am drawn to the kitchen table, strewn as it is with magazines and newspapers, a note from one spouse to the other: *Don't forget the dog food.* I place my hand atop these lived-with things, and I try to decide if I can feel any sense of energy emanating from them. But there is nothing.

My eye catches the top of the refrigerator: there is a bundle of keys there. I know the Mercury's key is there, too, and I shamble over. The dog follows me. I cannot reach. My fingertips brush the top of the freezer door, but that is as far as I can get. "Lord," I mutter.

Then I swing my purse like a lasso, and an avalanche of junk comes flying from the refrigerator. Oven mitts, a pepper shaker, a knife which mercifully lands on its handle on the floor, the keys, and all the other miscellanea I have so impudently set to crashing down like a space capsule returning to the surface of this world. I bend down and pick the keys off the floor.

A momentary regret for having caused this mess passes as I exit the kitchen and enter the cool sanctuary of the garage again.

I close the kitchen door. Now the garage door: I press the button and it opens with a grating growl, alien, letting in too much sunlight, searing my eyes and scarring my sense of solitude. I hesitate no longer.

Grimacing and wincing at the pops and creaks my old joints and muscles emit, I sit behind the wheel of the Mercury. I have never been on this side of this car before. Transported back all those years, to the time we ran, to the time we were free, I am happy again.

Maybe this is all I needed; to sit here, to breathe this air that Danny and I breathed together, to touch the steering wheel, the gearshift, where his hand once directed things.

I jam the key in the ignition, press in the clutch. It is easy for my left leg to do, and this is either because of my adrenaline or because of some mechanical defect with the vehicle. I will shortly know. I take a deep breath and then I turn the key.

The engine rolls over a few times and then coughs, sputters, dies. "No, no, not like that," I say to nobody in particular. I try again, and the same thing occurs.

I let the engine rest for a moment, and I tell the car, "You've taken me many miles. Take me just a few more."

I glance in the rearview mirror and see someone walking up the driveway. My heart shatters. I know the jig is up, I am busted, and I have failed the love of my life. It is a man, wearing blue, carrying a bag. He raises his hand in greeting, but I am frozen to my spot behind the wheel. The man disappears from my view in front of the house for a moment, and then he walks away.

The mailman. Okay, my nerves need a moment to settle again. Calm, I push the clutch in carefully, sure this is my last chance. I turn the ignition, praying, pumping the accelerator with my right foot, ignoring the pain. The engine sputters again, spits, and then roars. It is alive.

I want to weep for joy, but I cannot spare the time. The gearshift is unmarked, or the marks have faded, and so I carefully yank it into reverse. It makes a horrid grinding noise, and I yank once more, and then it falls into its rightful place. Grimly, my jaw set, I ease the car out of the garage. The front of the hood taps the garage as I go, but I ignore this. I am more concerned with what is behind the car than what is in front of it, at this point.

The driveway is straight and I am veering off it. I turn the wheel the wrong way and then sharply correct. To anybody else, I must look at least a few drinks past drunk. I go sideways into the street, and I can imagine phone calls already being placed to the local police. I right the wheel and jam the stick into first. I ease off the clutch and ease on the gas. Then I am moving forward, and soon I am well enough on my own side of the street, moving toward Danny.

I try to slow my breathing, which is coming at the rate of a furious dragon's. Second gear comes smoothly, and then I coast up to a stop sign and stall the car, having forgotten to put it in neutral or depress the clutch. Such a complicated exercise is driving! Three pedals and a gearshift, not to mention the steering wheel, watching for pedestrians, and remembering which direction to go, which street to take. I do not know how so many do it so effortlessly.

I go left and then at the following intersection I make a right and then I am on the street where Tricia picked me up with her kids in her massive SUV. Here, I turn left, keeping a watchful eye out for cars, dogs, and potholes.

At a red light I stop expertly. A vehicle has appeared behind me, and to my horror, it is a police cruiser. I stare at the light bar atop the car, red and blue, not flashing, sitting like a coiled snake preparing to strike. I see the light turn green only in my peripheral vision, and I realize that if I stall the Mercury, or do anything remotely erratic, he will pull me over, demand to see my license and haul me off to jail.

"Please, Jesus," I whisper as I give the car some gas. It rolls forward as smoothly as a butterfly taking off from a flower petal, and I shift carefully and logically as I drive down the street. The police cruiser keeps a distance behind me, but I dare not look too long in the rearview mirror to try to read the expression on the officer's face.

After a few moments, I decide simply to ignore the police car, and this seems the best strategy to avoid prison. He turns off after a couple more blocks, and I breathe a deep sigh of unearned freedom. Except, damn it, it has been earned. I feel blood is about to pour from my ears.

The retirement home is another uneventful mile away. I park the Mercury in the big visitor's lot to the side of the brick building, slide the gearshift into first, and then begin to weep.

The tears come salty and uninvited, but I have learned in my years here to not fight them when they do come. I let them roll down my cheeks, warm in the warmth of the car, and only when they subside do I wipe them away with my wrist.

It is my belief there is nothing strange about an old woman crying, be it in the bathroom, in the lobby of a hotel, in a hospital, or in a parking lot. Anybody who sees me must carry on with his business, and if one should decide to further investigate my situation, to hell with him.

I pull the keys from the ignition and slam the door behind me. My muscles are sore and my knees pop. I lean for a moment against the doorframe, catching my breath, thanking God, telling myself that the hardest part of the day is over and I have been successful. I find it hard to believe that I am here, that I have driven. But I do not linger.

I sidle my way toward the front door of Bliss. I will not be stopped by the receptionist. If she tells me that Danny is not accepting visitors, I will simply walk past her and get on the elevator. She will do nothing to me. She cannot.

The door slides open and inside is the manufactured coolness of air conditioning. There is nobody at the receptionist's desk, so I simply walk past, breathing another deep well of thanks toward God or whatever deity is allowing this to go so smoothly.

I remember his room number and I punch the button 3 in the lift. The doors slide shut and I am alone again. I feel an unwarranted sense of peace, as if I cannot be touched in this place. A very minor sense of vertigo sweeps over me as the elevator lifts me, but it stops with a too-abrupt hum and the doors open on floor number three.

I tell myself I belong here, as much to convince myself as anybody who might stop me. But again, nobody does. Room 302 is on the right, and I do not bother knocking on the closed door. I simply open it and slide inside and shut it quietly behind me.

He is sitting at the window. Thank God again, he is here, he is alive, he is waiting for me, he is Danny.

"Hi," I say.

Although he is peering outside, I can see a smile draw across his face by the way his right cheek distorts. He hangs his head before turning around to face me.

"Liz," he says. "I thought you might not make it."

Here the tears want to come again, but this time I fight them back.

"Of course I came," I said. "Of course I did. I would have come through fire."

I walk over to him and put my hands on top of his thinning crown of hair. His hair is so white and soft. I am relieved not to see any medical apparatus attached to him anywhere; I was expecting something, some way of keeping his dwindling life afloat just a little longer than natural. A catheter bag, an artificial limb, an IV hookup. Or perhaps he needs these things and has ripped them out of himself, eschewing them as the aliens they are. I do not want to ask.

"I've been waiting for you," he says. "I've been waiting a long time."

"The wait is over," I tell him.

The enormity of the moment nearly overcomes me: this is staring through a barred prison window at the sweet, free world beyond, and finally hearing the scrape of the jail cell door opening just for you.

"Let's get you out of here."

He looks up at me and his face is open and hurt, almost embarrassed.

"Liz," he says, "I can hardly walk."

Automatically I look down at his legs.

"I mean, I can do it. Physically, I can do it. But not far. And not for long."

"Me, either," I tell him. "But your legs work, don't they?"

He shrugs and gives me his old grin.

"If I really make them do it, they do it."

"That's good," I say.

I produce his keys from my purse.

"Because I'm not driving that damn thing anymore."

He takes the keys from my hand and now he begins to cry. Even his tears are beautiful things, each a poem and a heartbreak in itself. They stumble out of his eyes like wounded soldiers, and I run my hands through his white hair. I love him more now than I ever have.

"Oh, Liz," he says. "Thank you so much."

"Come on," I say. "I want to run away."

So he stands. Rickety, like an old corncrib on a desolate farm, surrounded by high winds, dark skies, tornado warnings.

He takes my arm and I help him to a wheelchair parked in the corner of his room. He settles into the wheelchair and I move behind it. It is easy to push him; in fact, easier than walking by myself, because I can use the handles to help bear my own weight.

In this way, we support each other as I take him into the corridor to wheel him out of this place they call Bliss.

I get the impression that everybody is watching us stroll down the corridor; old men and women, sitting on vinyl chairs, peering over newspapers; young women in flowery shirts, nurses and aides; a visiting couple, walking a foot away from each other. I wonder about them. Are they here to see his or her parent? Are they happy together and do they feel the same love now as they did when they were young? Answers I'll never know.

The elevator is already on our floor and when I push the button, the doors *swoosh* open for us. Nobody has said a word as we are making our break. I could be his wife, taking him for a daily stroll; it is as though nobody knows him, and I am at once thankful and hurt that this is the case, that he has sunk into this level of anonymity where it no longer matters whether he is present or absent, alive or dead.

We say nothing as the elevator descends. Danny dries his tears with his sleeve and I listen to him sniffle. The sobs of an old man, in his moment of redemption.

The doors open for us on the ground floor and there are a mere thirty steps between us and the merciful freedom of outside. The receptionist is back at her desk, talking into the phone receiver.

"We're just going for a walk," I say to him softly.

"I know," he says. "I love walks."

The receptionist calls out as I pass her desk, and I turn and see her still talking on the phone but holding up her index finger for me to please wait. I do – why? Because it is in my nature, yes, but I am at the point where my nature will not stop me getting him out of this place. I stop because I know she will let us carry on, and so there is no reason to risk raising any red flags for her.

She replaces the phone on the hook. "Where are you going?"

Danny speaks, and his voice is loud and clear. If I close my eyes, I can imagine him in high school again.

"We're going for a walk."

The receptionist counters, "We have a place for that in the back. On the grounds."

"I like the flowers out front," Danny says.

The receptionist looks at me, almost as though she sympathizes with my plight, I being the long-suffering wife of an Alzheimer's patient whose demands are fickle and prudish.

"Well, all right," the receptionist concedes. "But stay on the sidewalk."

She looks to me in a conspiratorial way and adds, "We've had a few wheelchairs stuck in the grass out there. It gets wet."

"I'll remember that," I say, and then I turn and push him toward the door.

Each step is a monument, a milestone, a miracle. My

heart is beating so fast I think it will not bear this work; I wonder if Danny's is thumping the same as mine. I know it is. It must be.

The doors open for us and we move through the foyer and then we are outside. Danny breathes in deeply and we let the sun wash over us for a moment. The air is crisp and fresh and the grass is plump and green and the sky is blue and open. "We made it," I say.

But we do not wait here long. There are other people: families, nurses, coming up the sidewalk, soon to enter Bliss, and any of them could ask a question which derails our train. I will not give them the opportunity. I push him farther along, and at the front sidewalk, without casting a glance backward for fear of turning to salt, I turn with Danny left, toward the parking lot.

It is a short walk to his car. I glance down at him as we ride over the cracks in the sidewalk, and he stares at his Mercury. He clutches the keys in his right hand so hard I am afraid he will draw blood. I take a deep breath and help him up and out of his wheelchair and, in one swiveling movement, which any other day would have broken my legs, I place him in the driver's seat of his Mercury. He pulls his legs inside and I slam the door.

I all but hop and skip to the passenger door and then I am sitting in the car with Danny. This is a cloud which will take us to heaven. I am his angel.

"Are you ready to go for a ride?" he says, popping the key home.

"Let's roll," I say, and he starts the car.

Its roar is more vibrant than ever it was before, its animal juice runs hotter than I remember. I am instantly warm again, in a way I have not been warm in what seems like a generation. Can it be? I am excited, and an old, recognizable ghost visits my loins as they tingle, like a limb I have slept on, coming awake.

Danny is forty years younger, I am his lady. He backs the car out of the parking space and the tires give a little peal as we roar out of the lot, leaving the wheelchair sitting on the pavement like a lost dog. We make a left out of Bliss, continue on through two or three intersections, make a right, another right, a left.

At some point, I realize that we do not know where we are going, but I do not say anything, not yet. It is enough to let the window down and to invite the cool breeze through my hair; to watch his hand as he shifts through the familiar gears, and to listen to the engine as it revs through them.

They seem to know each other intimately, Danny and this vehicle, and I am not jealous.

"Where do you want to go?"

I know we cannot go far. The car must have been reported stolen already: I imagine Christine coming home to find her garage door open, her father's car missing, her kitchen a mess. The first few terrible moments of cold fear, wondering if someone is in the house. Then the chilly feeling of violation, knowing that someone else has been through here, followed by the call to the police, the description of the car, the license plate.

"I know a place," Danny says, seemingly unaware of all these hitches I am pondering. "A nice, private place."

I think I know where he is talking about, but I am not sure until we take a few more roads out of town.

Hamilton has changed so much in these past forty years that it is almost unrecognizable, though I have spent that time here, myself. Somehow my world has shrunk as I have grown older, and Hamilton has ballooned at the same time, sucking some integral part of myself dry all these years.

How Danny knows the way, I cannot tell. Perhaps it is ingrained in his memory like a sweet, childhood dream. Perhaps it is in our collective memories; perhaps all roads lead to Hamilton and are Hamilton roads, somehow and someway, and they are by default, ours.

We leave our city behind and join up with a disused country highway. There are no other cars. Only birds, rabbits, and some flash of dark red I imagine is a fox, darting into its hole away from the metallic monster eating up the asphalt. The air is fresher out this way, crisper, cleaner, and freer. Trees give way to vistas of cornfields, now reaped and dark.

We meander for half an hour and I do not bother Danny with words. I love to watch him. This is his natural habitat, driving this car, liberated and young again.

He pulls the Mercury off the side of the road and down a narrow dirt track. He parks behind a clump of lilac bushes past blooming; the road is just visible if I look through their branches.

"This should be safe enough," he says.

"Oh, Danny," I say.

I step out of the car and go over to assist him. But he does not need much of my strength. It seems that being here has rejuvenated him, and he is able to stand on his own feet without swaying, without shielding his eyes from the battering sun above.

We pick our way through branches and weeds until we find a suitable pathway. The dirt is soft beneath our shoes, and, I imagine, cold. Shaded from the sun and from the world, we walk downhill.

Bugs make their chattering, snickering symphony all

around us as we go. But none of them bothers us beyond their noise. We walk beside one another, perhaps so that we can help one another if the other should stumble; or perhaps because it is the way we were just meant to walk together.

We reach an opening in the path and laid out before us is the gravel pit. The water is as blue as the sky and the sand as yellow as honey. Our souls are the only ones here, and I breathe slowly and deeply as I watch the water.

"It's beautiful," Danny whispers beside me. "But not as beautiful as you."

I kiss him on his neck. His flesh feels so different from what it once was, but my lips do not contemplate the difference. My lips belong there. They linger there but all things must pass, and I pull away from him and content myself with holding his hand.

"You are my life," I say to him.

"And you, mine," he tells me. "Let's go down to the water."

The hill is steep and I glance at him doubtfully.

"We'll never make it back up here."

"Maybe that's okay," he says.

And before I can press him for details, he wades down the sand dune which leads to the water's edge. I carefully pick my way behind him. The sand gives way beneath me, but generally I feel on solid footing, and if I turn myself like a skier, I am stable as I descend. I have no idea how Danny moves so well, given his poor health.

The sun is hot and we sizzle at the shoreline. This is the place we made love before, I in my dress, we conjoining in three feet of empty, chilly water. We created a little warmth here, once.

Now we create it again.

Danny unbuttons his shirt and peels it off. The hair, sparse on his chest, is white, like some delicate grass, frosted over.

"You can't be thinking of swimming," I say to him.

He steps out of his loafers, and he is not wearing socks. His feet are the whitest part of him, and I can see the delicate blue veins wrapped around his ankle bone. I want to kiss him there.

"No, not swimming," he says, unbuckling his belt and pushing his pants and underwear down.

I have a jolting thought: is he mad? But no, he is not. He looks at me, naked, his grin wide and innocent. He is my Danny. His penis is a soft protuberance of flesh, dangling between his bony thighs. His pubic hair is thin and gray.

"What, then?" I say to him.

I am a few feet away but I close that distance with a couple of breathless steps. I want to make him work again.

I am a horny old woman.

I press myself against him and I listen to his breath as he smells my hair. I grab his butt and squeeze. His flesh is living and warm and, by God, I feel his manhood swell. But I do not look, for fear it is an illusion, a dream. I squeeze his buttocks harder and press myself into him again.

There can be no doubt. He is erect. He moans.

"I don't have long," he says.

"You're not going back to that place."

"No," he says. "I don't mean that. I mean, I don't have long to live."

"Oh, Danny."

"It's true."

He pulls away from me for a moment and I can tell by

the unmistakable sadness in his eyes that he is telling the truth.

A week or two? A month or a year? But I do not want to know. If he has said this much, he has said enough. He will die soon.

"I don't want to die alone," he says.

"You won't."

"And I don't want to dissolve into some worthless thing, just pain and disease."

It dawns on me slowly what Danny is driving at.

"No," I say.

His penis is fully erect. There is enough room between us for him to glance down and smile.

"Why, hello," he says, grinning. "It's been a while, hasn't it?"

I slip out of my underwear, toss them onto the sand, and hitch up my skirt far enough for him to rub against me. I wrap my old body around his old body and neither of us has enough strength to do anything except dance carefully on the sand, under the blue sky, with his penis seeking me out.

But the angles of our bodies are wrong, and we are too old and useless to change them enough to make this work, in the traditional way. Something, on one or both of us, would break. So he rubs that way, his heat bubbles up inside me, ignites a chain reaction, a domino effect, and it has been so long anyway, and it is Danny, my Danny.

I breathe harder and harder, and I moan, my voice raspy and ages old; it has moaned before, but that was with the explosive pleasure of youth. This pleasure, though it is less, is greater.

My climax comes by surprise, and I feel my mouth form a little 'O' with shock. My lips pucker. I feel like a light bulb which has just burned out.

Danny gyrates against me a few more times and then he begins to settle. I do not feel any splash of semen, but he spasms in my arms, and I think that counts as a climax. We break our embrace and he stands before me naked, his penis falling to a half-salute.

"Thank you," he says.

"You don't have to thank me," I tell him.

I am standing with my back to the water, and I see his gaze settle over my shoulder. He sighs and hangs his head.

"Wait a few minutes," he tells me, "and then call the police. It will take them a while to get down here."

"How do I explain everything? The car? I stole it from your daughter's house, you know."

"I know you did. You did so many things for me. This was the best thing."

He sighs again.

"Give me your phone for a minute."

I pluck it out of my purse, which is lying haphazardly in the sand by my underwear. I give it to him and he talks with his daughter. He tells her to calm down. He tells her he took the car and is going for a swim. He tells her no, he is not crazy, and that he picked me up from my house. He tells her where we are. He hangs up the phone.

The whole ordeal is almost funny, but I see the regret in his eyes after their conversation is over.

"That is the last time I'll talk with my daughter," he tells me. "God, that was harder than I thought it would be."

"I don't want you to do this."

"I know," he says. "You know, I would have just rotted away in that stinking home. I would have just sat there, staring out the window, dreaming of seeing you one last time. And now you gave that to me. Now I can go happy. There's nothing greater."

"I did it for me, too."

"I know. And that makes it even better."

He puts his face in his hand for a moment, as though he is hiding his tears from me. But when he raises his face, I see no tear tracks.

"The only thing tying you to this is the receptionist. Don't go back to that prison they were keeping me in."

"I never will," I say.

He steps toward the water until his tiptoes are wet. I watch them sink into the coffee-colored sand and wiggle.

"If there are lives after this one," he says, staring into the lake, "let's be smarter the next time around."

I wail, rush to him, wrap my arms around his chest and kiss his naked back. He holds my hands close to his heart for a few beats, and then he pulls them away.

"I'll love you forever," he says, turning toward me one last time, grinning.

I say nothing; I have said everything. He turns toward his fate and slowly walks into the water.

Epilogue

Reading page two of the local newspaper through dry eyes:

Daniel "Danny" Cummings, born September 14, 1941, went to be with his Lord and Savior on August 17. His life was long and full and he was beloved by all whom he met. He was courageously battling cancer, but his smile always remained. He graduated Hamilton High School in 1958 and worked at an automobile assembly line directly after marrying his childhood sweetheart.

He is survived by three children: Christine, Jennifer, and Roy; seven grandchildren: Matthew, Harry, Carrie, Thomas, Lucas, Lucinda, and Ashley, and numerous cousins. The funeral will be held on Thursday at Finn's Funeral Home.

His beloved daughter, Christine, mentioned his favorite lines of poetry, from Robert Frost:

Love at the lips was touch
As sweet as I could bear;
And once that seemed too much;
I lived on air

We are placed on this earth for one worthy purpose, and that is to love. Life is love. To live without love is sleeping a dead dream, something you have tucked away in some shady corner of your numb heart, some cold, meaningless stretch of minutes here. I know whereof I speak.

The police have not yet asked me about the car, about breaking Danny out. It has been only a few days, though; I find I do not much care, one way or the other. I sit in my kitchen, as I have most of my life, and I coo to my bird, but even Spit knows something is wrong. He cocks his head at an inquisitive angle and looks at me ponderously. And I sit and drum my arthritic fingers over the tabletop, and I wait.

I know he is waiting for me. I know there are many souls waiting for me: Jamie, Charlie, my parents, Rosalinda. I do not know why I am hanging around, anymore.

So my days stretch on, and sometimes, I wake from my fitful slumber with an icy fear clutching my heart: perhaps I am immortal and I will never see them again.

But in my brain, I know this to be untrue. Danny and I ruined our lives on earth, except for the few moments when we allowed ourselves to be lost in each other's arms, eyes, the oceans of our souls. But we will not ruin it, this next time.

That time is coming soon. I feel it in my bones and in my blood. And we will live on air.

Acknowledgements

Jayne and EJ. Jayne for all her hard work and insight. EJ too, and also for kicking my ass literary-style nearly two decades ago.

For your grandmother. You should listen to that woman.

For you, reader, for coming here and sitting with me for a moment to enjoy a story.

About the Author

Jacob Lucas Luciano prefers slow dancing to fast moves, sunsets to sunrises, straight razors to safety. He spent years of his life running with the gypsies in Eastern Europe and playing rhythm guitar in an unsuccessful band. He is a self-appointed drifter who has narrowly avoided jail time on several occasions and on various continents, but despite this, he remains unwanted.